SMILING CHARLIE

Also available in Large Print
by Max Brand:

Hunted Riders
The Bandit of the Black Hills
Silvertip's Roundup
Nighthawk Trail
The Fastest Draw
One Man Posse
Mighty Lobo
Big Game
Stolen Stallion
Riders of the Silences
Singing Guns
Black Signal
Mountain Guns

SMILING CHARLIE

Max Brand

G.K.HALL &CO.
Boston, Massachusetts
1992

Published in Large Print by arrangement with
G. P. Putnam's Sons.

G.K. Hall Large Print Book Series.

Set in 18 pt. Plantin.

Library of Congress Cataloging-in-Publication Data

Brand, Max, 1892–1944.
   Smiling Charlie / Max Brand. —Large print ed.
     p. cm—(G.K. Hall large print book series)
   ISBN 0-8161-5086-9
   1. Large type books. I. Title.
  [PS3511.A87S544 1992]
  813'.52—dc20   91-37944

CHAPTER 1

I REMEMBER THAT A stranger once said to some of us:

"How did Colonel Stockton get his title?"

And somebody answered:

"From the devil, because he's going to command a regiment in hell. D'you doubt it?"

No, the stranger didn't doubt it, and I don't suppose that most people would have doubted it, because the moment that you looked at Colonel Stockton you got an idea that he would never have to waste time weaving wreaths or strumming on a harp up yonder.

But I suppose that he was called the Colonel chiefly because there was no other title that would exactly fit. Something he had to be called, because he was the next man to God Almighty over a territory about two hundred miles square, and you wouldn't call him Governor because that was rather familiar, and you couldn't call him judge because

1

that was too semi-official. And there was nothing official about the Colonel. He was just himself.

He was a cracking big man, a couple of inches over six feet, and in the days of his youth they say that he could break the neck of a steer with his bare hands. At fifty, he still looked like a chained-up tornado—not chained up by any authority, you understand, but controlled a little by his own pride and sense of dignity.

He looked exactly the way that a Colonel of the South ought to look. That is to say, he had long, flowing hair, and a short gray beard trimmed to a point, and a pair of neat moustaches. He wore his clothes so that he looked like a million dollars and a diplomat, and you would suspect him of being the second cousin of the last king of England—which he probably was, because his family history didn't stop with a bump on the shores of Virginia or Massachusetts, but jumped the ocean and ran back into the good old whacking, armor-smashing days of the Plantagenets. His people had been barons, and lived in castles, and had troops of armed retainers, with whole towns under their control, and ships in port with their monogram stamped on the sails. But things had not changed much with the line. The name had passed through a few variations, but the blood was the same, the manner was the same, and the rule was the same. When he was angry you half expected him to draw a sword and cleave you through the mizzen, and when he stamped on the floor, a hundred men were ready to ride to the gates of hell and back again, not armed with shield and spear, but with Winchester and Colt—which is a better and deadlier combination any day of the year.

I should like to have you see, at a glance, the tens of thousands of the Colonel's cattle filling the fat valleys of the range, and his great house on the hill, and his river thundering around the foot of that hill, and his mountains standing up in the distance, all around, pawing at the sky. And I should like you to see the men who called the Colonel chief, with their guns at their hips, and their rifles at the sides of their saddles, and their mustangs ready to go. And I should like to show you the Colonel's two towns, where he owned every street, and every back yard and front yard, too, and the houses which stood on the ground, and the people who lived in the houses. Because everything and everyone belonged to the Colonel.

Because, after you've seen all of these things, then you can turn around and take a look at the power that was to fight the Colonel to a standstill and prove worthy of his metal. I introduce him to you at once, just as he was when he reached us.

I was working in the sheriff's office, just then. Oh, yes, we had a sheriff. We had elections, too, and everything was run off regular, and according to the law, except that the only political party in the inside of the Sierra Blanca mountains was the Colonel; and there was always only one nomination for any office, and that was the nomination that the Colonel made. At any rate, I was working as a deputy under Sheriff Steve Ross. Our job was to run down the crooks that tried to run off the Colonel's cattle through the mountain passes; and after we finished with the rustlers, we always had plenty of odd jobs on our hands in the shape of the yeggs and the thugs and the general, all-around crooks who would drift up into our valley not knowing what sort of a place it was.

One afternoon, there was a long telegram handed in. It was me that opened it, and I read:

4

"CHARLES LAMB ALIAS SMILING CHARLIE LAST SEEN HEADED FOR SIERRA BLANCA BADLY WANTED HEIGHT SIX FEET ONE BROWN HAIR AND EYES MANNER MILD VERY HANDSOME REWARD OFFERED TWO THOUSAND."

It was signed by the sheriff two counties north and as I read it over I wondered a little, because I have never yet seen a legal description, as you might say, that used such words as "very handsome."

"Some pretty baby," I said to myself.

But six feet one didn't sound like a baby, at that. So I put on my hat and my best Colt and went out to see what I could see.

I didn't find anything worth reporting, at first. But after two days I happened down to the hotel, and there I chanced around in back to see if the apples were ripe in the orchard and saw the prettiest waitress in the hotel sitting on a bank under the biggest tree with a young fellow sort of reclining at her feet and looking up into her eyes and playing a guitar and singing words that I couldn't quite hear.

Well, I didn't have to hear them, because, as I watched his brown eyes reading her face while he sang, I knew that he was probably making up the words as he went along. And they were good enough to please that girl. She was in a trance. And every now and then she breathed a sigh and rolled her eyes as if she would have said: "How can there be so much happiness and sweet sadness in the world?"

I laughed a little as I watched, because that girl Betty had broken half the hearts of the cowpunchers inside of Sierra Blanca. She wasn't a gold-digger. She was just a natural destroyer.

I looked a little closer and I saw a whacking big tray all covered with the empty dishes of a bang-up meal, and I knew that that loafer had been sponging on her good nature.

You could tell that it wouldn't be hard for him to have his way with a woman. Take him, all in all, I never laid eyes on such a handsome man. Outdoors handsomeness, all brown, you understand. After a moment, he finished the piece and she leaned over and said something, and he smiled at her. A most amazing smile. It lit up his face more than you would believe; and it simply made Betty tremble.

Then something jumped through my head like chain-lightning:

"Brown hair and eyes—very handsome!"

Yes, there was a reason why that "very handsome" had been put in the telegram. And I walked up from behind the tree and drew down on him with a Colt.

Betty screamed and he twisted around to his feet quicker than a wink, with a gun already in his hand—as neat and fast a draw as I ever saw in my life.

"Bill Jacks!" screamed Betty. "Don't you dare to hurt him!"

This fellow, when he saw the gun in my hand trained on him, let the muzzle of his own gat droop a little, and a smile came on his face. You see, he didn't smile very often, but when he did, you could understand how he had gained the name of Smiling Charlie.

"I think you've made a little mistake," says he.

"Perhaps I have," says I. "You're not Smiling Charlie Lamb, are you?"

"I've never heard the name before," says he.

I looked him over for a moment, almost inclined to believe. Because he had the biggest, steadiest pair of brown eyes that you ever saw in your life. As a liar, God gave him talents that it would have been a shame to throw away. I said:

"Well, I suppose that you haven't, but

you come along to jail with me, will you? There you'll have a chance to get used to the new name!"

"Jail!" sobs Betty. "Jail! Oh, dear Billy, you've made an awful mistake!"

"Have I?" says I.

"Oh, what could he have done that was wrong?" says Betty.

"There's a two thousand dollar reward hung on him, honey," says I.

How do you think that she would take that? You never would guess, because she clasped her hands together and smiled at him, and says:

"Oh, I just knew that you were someone important!"

That was the woman of it. You never can guess them. No sense. None at all! Why, I've known a woman to—but I'll leave that for later.

At any rate, I said:

"Drop that gun, Lamb. And put up your hands!"

"My friend," says Charlie Lamb as smooth as silk, "I want to oblige you, but in the case of a great mistake, like this—"

"Betty," says I, "you'd better tell him that I mean what I say and that I hate to waste time!"

"Charlie!" she gasped at him. "It's true—he's killed men!"

"Killed men!" says Charlie. "How terrible!"

I looked hard at him. His face was as serious as you please, but somehow I guessed that he was laughing at me.

"That gun!" I yapped at him.

"Don't shoot!" says he, and dropped the gun.

But still, I couldn't help feeling that he was laughing at me. Though it hardly matters how a man laughs, or when, so long as he hasn't a gun in his hand.

"Now, turn around and stick up your hands and march!" said I. "And watch yourself, because my eyes aren't shut."

They were not shut, either, and I give you my word, that I never used more care in my life, so that I'm absolutely unable to explain what happened.

I remember that he seemed to be turning when all at once a hand shot out and knocked my gun aside, so that the bullet I fired hit the ground not far away, and then a fist like a club of iron lodged against my chin. A lightning flash ripped across my eyes, and several buckets of thickest darkness were dumped over my brain.

CHAPTER 2

WHEN I WOKE up, Betty was pouring water over me. And when I opened my eyes she said:

"Isn't he wonderful!!!!!"

That was the woman of it!

I sat up and watched the trees and the houses spin around, very sickening. When they quieted down, a little, I dragged myself to my feet by pulling against the trunk of that apple tree.

"Wh-where did he go?" said I.

"Who?" said Betty.

"Are you feeble-minded?" I asked her. "Him—Smiling Charlie Lamb, I mean?"

"What a duck of a name!" says Betty.

"Damn it, girl," says I, "tell me where that fellow went."

"Somewhere over there, I think," says Betty, and she waved to the northern half of the skyline.

That was illuminating, but of course I guessed, as I staggered for a horse, that the direction he'd really gone in was just the opposite of the one which she had pointed out. He'd gone somewhere south.

Well, that was eliminating half of the difficulties. If he'd started south, we could look in that direction. I got to the sheriff's office as fast as I could and, as I broke in, Steve Ross looked at me and the lump on my jaw, unable to speak. At last he said:

"Who sandbagged you?"

"It was a fist, Stevie," says I. "And the gent that was behind it is a hundred per cent worth catching; maybe you could guess for yourself. I want him. I want him bad. I want him served up on toast. You understand? It's that Charlie Lamb that has two thousand dollars on his head. Here's where we collect!"

Because, right away, we knew that we had the game in our hands. I've said that the valley were filled with the Colonel's men and no other men except accidental ones that didn't count. I've said, too, that rustlers often tried to run cows through the mountain passes, but I should explain the lay of the land, a little.

You see, the Sierra Blanca ran in a big, loose circle around a great bowl into the midst of which they dumped their creeks and small streams to join the Blanca River, so that the whole place was like a great amphitheater, with about ten thousand square miles inside, and the only real comfortable exit was through the Blanca gorge, where the river ripped its way out to the plains beyond.

The territory of the Colonel was like a trap. There were several doors to that trap, but they could all be closed. That was before the days when telephones cluttered up the countryside and put a period to real freedom, but there were other ways of sending messages that acted almost as fast. We had fire and smoke signals for night and day, and the first thing that the sheriff did was to send up smoke signals which were repeated at once from the tops of the nearest hills, and which would be repeated, we knew, clear on to the tops of the mountains.

Those signals told the guards that blocked the mouth of every pass that they were to stop every man that went through, except known men from the valley. It was inconvenient, and it meant a good deal of trouble to a lot of honest men, but it was the system that worked in those mountains, and we always stuck by it. It made the Sierra Blanca the big black spot on every crook's map of the United States. The very air was poison to them, down there.

After the doors to the trap were closed, we started our man-hunt in leisurely style, but we never dreamed what it would lead to. We organized our men. I knew that this fellow was handy with a gun. I'd proved that he had the strength of a mule. And I'd proved, too, that he was a little quicker than the snapper on the end of a whiplash, so we warned all the boys that, if it came to a matter of guns, they had better shoot from cover, or else shoot first! That meant, to take Smiling Charlie Lamb dead or alive—which is another way of saying: Dead!

Then we waited. Or rather, we rode and waited. It wasn't long before we had news. He had tried the big Southern Pass and rode right into a hornet's nest—and out again.

Not that he broke through. No, he was turned back, but in the process of being turned, he had his horse shot under him. He borrowed another from one of the guards in the pass by means of first tapping the poor fellow along the head with a forty-five caliber slug of lead, and so scooted back into the valley again.

The man he'd shot didn't die. He lived and wasn't badly hurt, but now we knew that we had a real man-hunt on our hands, and we prepared to make the most of it.

We split the valley up into sections, and we appointed a commander of each section to work the ground carefully and turn up the man we wanted. But that was a slow job, because ten thousand square miles, split up with hills big and small, and running into mountain canyons, are not a parlor floor to sweep.

But we worked, and in the meantime, we had more news about Smiling Charlie. A man came into the valley riding hard and fast on top of a fine buckboard with a span of neat blood horses pulling it. He had come down from New Jerico and he was the fellow who had put out the reward for Charlie Lamb.

It wasn't murder; it was worse. What Charlie had done, they said, was to steal a farmer's horse while making his getaway, but the thing he was getting away from was the daughter of this same fellow who had pushed out the reward.

He entertained us with a little account of the affair—how Charlie had rambled up to his place, and seen his pretty daughter, and how, after that, he was the only man in the world for her. She couldn't see that there was anything else in the world except the handsome face of that rascal.

The father tried to fight against it. Then he surrendered. He decided that it would about kill his girl to lose this man, and so he offered to give Charlie a chance to work on the ranch and, at the end of a few months, if he seemed to be carrying on fairly well, there would be a marriage, and everything would be hunky-dory.

Charlie allowed that that would be fine, and settled down to work. For two weeks he worked like a trump. He had the men swearing by him and eating out of his hand. He was a wonder with a horse, a good man with a rope, and a devil with a gun. And then one day he was missing!

There was a little note that arrived the next day for the girl, saying that Charlie regretted that he had to go, but that he felt that it would be unmanly for him to be dependent upon the money of the father of his wife to be, and that some day, if he could make a respectable fortune, he would come back to marry her—and that in the meantime, he would always love her, and carry her with him wherever he went——

Well, the girl collapsed. She came to and went to bed with a raging fever, with the letter pressed like poison against her heart. She cried all the time she was in her senses, and she raved all the time she was delirious with the fever. Her father, half mad, had

15

turned loose a hot pursuit on the trail of Mr. Lamb, and when they caught up with him, he slipped through the hands of the hunters, and borrowed a fast horse without asking permission from the owner. Thereby he became a full, registered horse thief, which made the business serious and gave the father a right to use the law, which he did.

In the meantime, he had looked up the past record of Mr. Lamb. It was hard to trace. He had worn a good many names, it seemed, but he could be spotted here and there across the continent by stories of pretty girls who had seen a tall brown-faced, handsome fellow, and fallen madly in love with him—and then he'd vanished.

In fact, this Charlie Lamb seemed to be a hundred per cent philanderer—a real heart-wrecker. But what made his case puzzling was the fact that he was also a hundred per cent man, as my purple jaw still bore witness.

You can see that it was a complicated affair, from every angle.

But worst of all, our reputation up there in the valley was being blasted to pieces, because one man was running a hundred of us ragged.

We tried everything that we knew, but he

was like a jack in the box, always popping out at the place where he was not expected. The cool devil once rode right into the town and got a hand-out from Betty at the hotel. He went over to the porch of the Sheriff's office in the evening and ate his dinner, and he wrote a little message on the wall of the building:

Dear Steve Ross,
I enjoyed the comfortable chair and the view of the street, but I wish you would improve your garden. Otherwise, it will hardly be worthwhile for me to call again.
Thanking you for all your past courtesies and attentions, I beg to remain
Respectfully yours,
Charles Lamb.

When the Sheriff came down to his office the next morning, he found a crowd gathered reading that message, and poor Steve Ross was a wild man.

However, it was that visit of Lamb to the town that called the Colonel into the picture. I was not supposed to be present at the interview, but I got the facts of it later on. And as a matter of fact, when the Colonel came down, I was tightening my horse's cinch in

17

front of the office, and as the chief went by I had a look at his face and could guess that there was something important in the air. He had a way of smiling when his mind was fully occupied. And just when you thought that he was growing benevolent, you could guess that he was about to be most dangerous.

And when the Colonel was bent on making trouble—!

I wondered what it was that brought him to the office, and I half guessed that it must have something to do with young Lamb, but I wasn't prepared for what actually happened. No one would have been, because there was no one in the world that could possibly follow the mind of the Colonel, or guess the ways his thoughts would travel.

CHAPTER 3

IT HAPPENED LIKE this:

The Colonel came walking into the office of Steve and sat down in the big chair beside the window.

"Can we be alone for a while, Ross?" says he.

Of course Ross closed the two doors, and then locked them. He said, by way of making conversation:

18

"I hope the Baron is liking things in the valley, sir?"

"He seems pleased, I'm glad to say," said the Colonel, with his best smile.

By this, Ross guessed that the pleasure of the Baron didn't matter a great deal to the Colonel. But, of course, there was no doubt that the Colonel's daughter had arranged a good match for herself, from the social viewpoint.

This Baron Wakeness belonged to a tolerably old family, and they said that he was a clean, decent fellow, as well, and by no means a beggar. The Wakeness barons had always been bankers, and big bankers. However, an ordinary fortune looked like small potatoes, compared with the millions of the Colonel, so that it would ordinarily have been far from certain that young Baron Wakeness was not making this marriage for the sake of the Yankee capital that it would bring into his hands.

But when one had seen Olivia Stockton, one stopped wondering. She was made to make a man love her at the first glance. And we all took it as a matter of course that the young Baron was just like a thousand others. He had seen Olivia and felt that she was manifest destiny for him.

19

"Now the matter that has brought me here," said the Colonel.

"Yes?" said the Sheriff, taking notice, you can be sure, and running his eye over all the black spots in his record, to see which one might have caught the eye of the chief.

"You have been having a good deal of trouble with young Lamb, it seems."

"Sir," says Steve, "the fact is that youngster is the very devil."

"So it seems."

"I've had out every man that I could lay my hands on. And still I haven't been able to land him."

The Colonel frowned.

"Are you sure," says he, "that you've made every possible effort?"

"Absolutely sure, sir."

"H-m-m!" says the Colonel. "We've had some rough characters in the valley before this time, but we've never had any that we couldn't handle, I believe?"

"Never any before this time, sir!"

"And you've told your men to use their very best endeavors—of course?"

"Strict orders, sir!"

"You've told them not to spare powder and lead?"

"He's a will-o'-the-wisp, sir. Moves like a streak of lightning."

"However," said the Colonel, "he must soon be run to ground."

The Sheriff sighed.

"As a matter of fact," said the Sheriff, "I'm not at all sure that we're going to have this game in our own hands!"

"Ha?" growled the Colonel.

"The men are willing, but the women are against us."

"What the devil do you mean by that?"

"I mean that the women are wild about this fellow."

"Ha?" murmured the Colonel again.

"Wherever they may be, they have their heads out the window, hoping and praying that they can have a sight of this here Lamb coming galloping over the hill. They got their hearts out, ready to drop into his pocket to take along with him!"

"Ha! Ridiculous!" says the Colonel.

"It is, sir."

"And horrible, eh?" says the Colonel.

"Disgusting," says the Sheriff.

"How can it be explained, Ross?"

"God can explain women, but I can't attempt it, sir!"

"Extraordinary!"

"You see, sir, the things we have against him, don't bother the women."

"The fact that he's a lawbreaker and a horse thief, you mean?"

"That doesn't bother the women."

"I suppose not. Nor the fact that he's fairly well known as a philanderer, here and there?"

"That's the crowning touch, for them. That finishes them. Let a man get a reputation as a heart breaker, and the girls are all ready to have their hearts snapped right in two! That's a fact, sir!"

The Colonel lighted a cigar and stared up at the ceiling.

"To him that hath," said he, "it shall be given."

He made another pause and puffed again.

"To him that hath not," he said, and made another halt.

"By the way, Ross," says he.

"Yes, sir."

"You've done your level best, with this man?"

"Exactly."

"He still escapes from you?"

"I think, perhaps, that he could work his way out of the valley, if he cared to. He's the sort of a fellow who could get across the mountains, if ever a man could."

"Then you mean that this is not a tight trap against him?"

"I mean just that."

"Explain, then, why it is that he doesn't break away, if you can?"

"I can explain it easily enough. But you might find it hard to believe."

"Try me, Ross."

"I think that he stays with us here in the valley because he likes the game."

"Ha!" says the Colonel, and frowns again.

"I mean just that."

"Likes the game of being hunted by a hundred men, like a dog?"

"Yes, likes it."

"Likes the danger of being shot down on sight?"

"He does like it, sir."

"Likes to live in the wilderness, with rocks for a bed?"

"Yes, sir."

"And enjoys all of that?"

"Colonel Stockton, I'm convinced that he looks on it all as a great game."

"But what the devil has put that into your head?"

"Why else would he stay here?"

"Stay in danger of starving to death?"

"No danger of that—not while the women of the valley do the cooking."

"Just so! Just so!" He added:

"By the way, this man has killed no one here, as yet?"

"He's too intelligent for that," said the sheriff.

"Intelligent?"

"Yes. Only a fool takes a life if he can avoid it. And this fellow Lamb is not a fool, by any means. He knows that if he shoots to kill, there's apt to be a rope noosed for him in the end."

"Come, come, Ross, this reckless devil has shot down seven men since the man hunt started for him here!"

"I understand that, sir. But he shot *not* to kill!"

"You mean that he placed his bullets?"

"Always for the legs. Always shot for the legs. He knows that a forty-five caliber bullet through the leg will stop the bravest man in the world and make him get off his horse and curl up on the ground. But a bullet through the leg never sends the shooter to the electric chair or the hangman's rope."

"True, true!" said the Colonel, and frowned again. "Very true, Ross."

24

He frowned so much, in fact, that the Sheriff began to suspect that the Colonel was secretly rather pleased by something which this discussion had brought to his mind.

Suddenly he said, "Ross!" snapping the word out.

"Yes, sir."

"I think that I had better take a hand in this."

"Of course—as you please."

"And in the first place, I'll have you put up a notice."

"A higher reward, perhaps?"

"Not a penny. Put up a notice—offer Charles Lamb immunity for his crimes if he'll come in and have a talk with me."

The Sheriff turned frightfully red.

"Sir," says he hoarsely, "I'd find it sort of hard to bait a trap for any man—even for a horse thief and a heart breaker—by——"

"Come, come, Ross," says the Colonel. "Do you think that I could do a thing like that? Sell my honor for the sake of capturing a horse thief who has broken the hearts of a few little country girls? No, do as I say, and let the notices be posted at once."

With that, he got up and left the office.

He found me outside.

"Jacks," said he, "that horse of yours looks like a speedster."

"He's a fast one," I admitted.

"But not quite good enough for you, Jacks. Come up to my corral and look over a set of horses there. Perhaps you can find one to your liking."

And he walked on down the street, leaving me giddy twice over, with the thought of having one of his thoroughbreds for my own, and with the knowledge that the Colonel had noticed me. But that was his way. He walked past you like a stone wall, till one day he suddenly saw you. And after that he would never forget you to the end of your life.

I knew that I was a made man, that day!

CHAPTER 4

I MIGHT HAVE EXPECTED that strange things would happen the minute that the Colonel noticed me, but I hardly expected that I would be called right into his close service. However, once he had set his eye on you, he didn't lose time. Some people said that he never noticed a man until he needed a man.

At any rate, a message came down to the Sheriff's office the next day that I was wanted at Stockton House as soon as I could get there. I had just come in from putting up big signs with the ink still wet on them, announcing to Smiling Charlie Lamb that there would be protection for him if he would answer the call of the Colonel at once and come to see him. I dragged the saddle off my horse, cinched it up on a pinto that had the endurance of brass, and then I headed up the valley road along the river.

That was a tired horse that carried me through the big gate into the private grounds of the Colonel, and the big dark trees on either side of the drive went whishing past me as I galloped. I felt that I was coming hand over hand upon my destiny, though what it was to be, I couldn't begin to guess.

I was told, when I asked, to wait outside the house for a moment. The Colonel was coming out. And so I gave the pinto a breather, walking him up and down, and after a while out came the Colonel, with Olivia and her baron. This Baron Wakeness I gave a hard look, I can tell you. I feel the way most good Americans do about the girls of money who are snagged by foreign titles worn by saps who never did a stroke for the honors that they carry. So I was all prepared to look at this young Wakeness as though he were a snake. But I couldn't carry that thought for long.

You could see that he was a pretty good fellow, even in the distance. He had a rather slouching walk, and his head thrust forward a little, so that he had a rather snoopy air when you first laid eyes on him, but when he came close, you saw that the length and the thinness of his face was more than made up for by the strength of his jaw and the width of it at the base. And though you couldn't call him a heavyweight, still he was an athlete. He had a pale face, but there was a healthy look about it. You could tell that he had had to put in his time indoors, a lot, working over books, and that had probably brought his head sticking out, that way. But his eyes were as sharp as a hawk's and they looked at you as steadily as a hawk's, too. And his hands had a rumpled look that comes along when a man has used the strength of his arms a lot at something or other. Rowing in a crew at Oxford had done it for Wakeness. That and polo, and what not, polo being honest to God work, I guess. And there was a crease between his shoulders that meant strength, too. And he had a light step, rolling up on the tips of his toes, so that you could see that he would be a hell-bender when it come to running, short or long.

Altogether, I was surprised. I hadn't figured that Olivia would have the wits to catch anything as fine as this, in the shape of a foreign man. Because it takes a pretty long-headed girl to see the facts about a man even in her own country, but when she gets abroad, she passes into a fog, you know.

Because, most usually, all that she can see behind one of these foreign gents is the moldy old turrets of his doggone ivy-grown castle, and she gets the features of his lordship mixed up with the features of his ancestors, done in oil paintings, and showing 'em all in a bordering of lace and iron.

And Olivia was not the sort of a girl that you would expect to see very deep into things. I mean, what her father was, she wasn't. He was as deep as the sea. She had her depths, too, but they were depths of goodness, crystal clear all the way down. Just to see her was to know her, and to see her twice was to love her. She was no more grander with all her money than Betty, say, slinging ham at the hotel in town. And now as she come sashaying out of the house beside her pet Baron, she was no more set up than any girl would be over a beau. And every once in a while she would turn and look up into his face, as much as to say:

"Does this man really belong to me? All of him?"

It made you laugh, to see Olivia. It made you feel plumb good.

The Colonel, he says to me:

"How are you, Jacks. Wakeness, this is Bill Jacks, one of the best men in the mountains."

"Hello, Bill!" says Olivia, without no Europe about her at all, and she shakes hands with me, and gives me a smile right from the hip, as you might say, and makes me a little dizzy. But then, I'd been known in those parts for some time.

This Wakeness, he shook hands with a good, steady grip, looking into me. I liked him better than ever. He was a man.

The Colonel says:

"Wakeness is a sportsman. He's quite a rifle shot. I've been telling him about the long-distance eyes that some of you fellows have, and he finds it rather hard to let the thing go down."

"You misquote me a little, Colonel Stockton," says Wakeness. "I haven't doubted you."

"Not at all," says the Colonel, smiling

30

very polite. "But I want to give you a demonstration to show that I haven't stretched things. You have your rifle and your Colt with you?"

He looked hard at me, and it nearly gave me a chill. I could see that if I'd happened to forget them, I would have been finished with him, but I'd sooner forget my head than my guns.

I told him that I had them; and he says:

"Take your Winchester and see if it's loaded. Bring that rifle here to Baron Wakeness, my man!"

This last was to one of the servants, who come out with a couple of rifles over his arm.

"You might want to try your own hand at some of this work," says the Colonel, "and if you do, pick out a target."

"I'm a fair shot," says Wakeness, "but not a great expert. I'll be glad to shoot at something. And this rifle is a beauty. Suppose I say—well, the bird in the top of that tree."

It was a mean target to hit. On a top twig of that big tree there was a little what-not of a bird bouncing up and down in the wind and looking smaller than a glint of dust in the sunshine.

"Very well," says the Colonel.

Wakeness dropped on one knee, gave his gun a steady rest of his left hand, and then took a fairly quick aim and fired. The bird hopped off into the air with a whirr of wings that seemed to almost make it disappear.

"Jacks!" snapped out the Colonel.

Good God, says I to myself, he wants me to hit that nothing!

It made me sort of despair, but the Colonel had a way of making you try anything. That snappy voice of his turned me steady as a stone and gave me telescope eyes, so I jabbed the butt of my rifle into my shoulder, followed the twisting trail of that bird through the air for half a heart beat, and let go. The bird dissolved into a fluff of feathers and floated slowly downward.

"Oh!" cries Olivia, and gives a look at the Baron to see if he's displeased. Not a bit. His face lighted up.

"Absolutely cracking, Mr. Jacks," says he. "I've never seen a finer shot."

The Colonel didn't relent. He didn't so much as notice me, and he was frowning a good deal, by which I knew that he was more terrible pleased than if you had handed him a million dollars on a diamond platter. Some way, he was trying to put the Baron in his place. I couldn't guess why. I didn't even want to guess. The Colonel was something like God in those parts of the country, as I may of said before, and to please him was far enough ahead for any of us to look.

"They do things like that with a gun around here," says the Colonel, drawling a little. "But when they shoot a rifle, of course they're working with their left hands!"

At this, the Baron blinked a little, and no wonder. I'm a right bang-up hand with a rifle, and no mistake. I've got the eyes and the nerves and the liking for the game, and I've lived all my years with guns in my hands, but I never made a prettier shot than that one.

"I suppose that means," says the Baron, very cold, "they are even better with revolvers?"

"I'm about to show you," says the Colonel. "Just jump on your horse, Jacks, if you please, and loosen your revolvers in the holsters."

I did that, feeling a little shaky, and wondering what the deuce I'd be asked to hit with those guns. I give them both a grip and prayed to them to be good to me; or I'd lose all of the ground that I'd gained with the Colonel up to that time.

Says the Colonel:

33

"Can you pick out a target for him—something to hit while the horse is standing still, say?"

There was a black stone on the gravel of the drive. The Baron pointed to that.

"Shoot when you're ready, Jacks," said the Colonel.

I knew by his look that he wanted something good. And I swore to myself that I'd win again or bust trying. So I whipped out my right hand Colt and fanned a bullet a quarter of an inch behind that stone and started it rolling, and then I trotted the pinto forwards, and with every step it trotted I fanned another bullet just behind that rolling stone and made it spin and hop like a good one. It was a pretty fair exhibition, take it all in all.

When I'd finished, the Baron couldn't get over it. He ran and picked up the stone, and his face was like the face of a happy boy as he turned back to us.

"I'll have to send this home, with all the bullet nicks in it," says he, "otherwise they'll hardly believe this one!"

I was fairly happy myself.

"Thank you Jacks," says the Colonel and gives me a steady look, that meant something, as he takes his pair off into the garden.

34

I wondered what that look meant, and I judged it to be a signal for me to wait behind. So I went on out to the stable and put up my pinto, to wait and see what would happen.

CHAPTER 5

OUT AT THE stables, the head stableman come up to me. He was a pretty important man in the valley, because he handled all the breeding of the Colonel's fine horses. He says:

"You're Bill Jacks?"

"I am," says I. "What about it?"

"Don't be nasty," says he, sort of disgusted. "I understand that you are to have a claim on one of the colts, here?"

"Horse was the word that the Colonel used," says I. "He didn't happen to mention 'colt' when he was talking to me. But maybe you've changed his mind for him?"

He looked me in the eye, real mean. I could see that he didn't fancy handing over one of his beauties to any common cowpuncher like me.

"Very well, very well!" says he through his teeth. "Suppose that you step out here and take a look at them for yourself!"

35

We went up to a paddock where there was a dozen fine ones sunning themselves.

"They look fit," I couldn't help saying, but he took no notice.

"The gray is the Colonel's favorite saddle horse," says he, very dry. "Maybe you'd take a fancy to it. And over yonder in the next field there is a chestnut with the white off forefoot. That's Miss Olivia's best mare. Maybe you'd rather have her?"

You can see that he was handing me a kind and glowing reception, but I didn't mind much. When you win, you can always afford to take a piece of lip from the loser. I says:

"Will you catch up that tall bay and the brown mare, yonder?"

He turned about quick and stared at me. He actually turned a little gray, and so I knew that I'd happened to hit on a good horse. Maybe both of them was fine, and maybe only the one of them; I couldn't just tell, for though I can read a cowpony as well as the next man, I have to admit that those long-legged thoroughbreds are just a bit towards the end of my book. I ain't so familiar, and the one of them looks about like the other.

He calls for an assistant who catches up the two that I'd selected and they're both

36

paraded before me. I started to go over them inch by inch, but then I seen that I could never tell the difference between them, really. They both looked almighty fine, but the bay was bigger, and I figured that he was the best, there being more of him.

The poor stableman, he couldn't stand the terrible strain of it, and he turned away with his back to me, and his hands knotted together behind him.

"All right," says I. "I'll take the bay."

His hands unknotted. He turned around with the look of a man that's just had his pardon from the governor.

"Well," says he, "thank God for that!"

"Is the bay a hound?" says I.

"My lad," says he, "you'll never own as good a one again. I hope to God that you ain't intending to feed him barley in the place of oats?"

"I'll give him a try-out," says I.

"Meaning that you'll put your armchair on his back, then?"

And he pointed to my big saddle.

However, I was never anything but scared when I looked at a man sitting on one of those leather postage stamps that they call an English saddle. I strapped the big range saddle on the bay, and when he was bridled up I stood back and looked him up, and when I thought of the sensation that I'd make riding that nag into the town, it made my mouth water. It would be a considerable girl that would be too proud for me, now that I'd got the eye of the Colonel, and one of his horses.

I should say that that was his way. Everything in the valley was his, of course, and all the men as well as the land. Once in his service, somehow, you never could get out, or want to get out, unless you were kicked. But there was a special few that he picked out to be his chosen men, his hard workers, his "knights" as he called them. And whenever he'd picked out one to add to the list, he always made a present to the new man of one of his fine thoroughbreds, and he always let the man pick his own horse from the bunch, including all the best. There was one fellow long ago that had picked out the Colonel's own stallion. But the Colonel let him have it, and they say that he was apt to value a man, in a way, according to the brains that you showed in making your selection.

I knew all of this, and I hoped that I had picked high enough up the string to please the Colonel. But I doubted that a good deal. That stableman was too relieved when he seen my choice.

I got on the bay and walked and trotted and cantered and galloped him. He was silk underfoot, and silk in the hand. Then I loosed him on a straight stretch of soft road, and he blinded me with speed.

So I came back and got down and I says to the stable master:

"He'll do me proud. Now that I've been on him, I wouldn't give a damn for all the rest of them. He's my horse!"

The stable master looked at me with a new eye. He looked me right up and down.

"You seem to know something about horses, Jacks, after all," says he.

That was a sort of a sassy speech, but he had gray hairs. And I was too tickled with everything that had been happening to me lately to make trouble.

"Thanks," says I, "and if I have a chance to hang around here, perhaps you can teach me more."

He didn't see that I was stringing him a little, and he says perfectly sober:

"You're too old to do real learning. But consult your heart, Jacks. Consult your heart and it'll often tell you things about a horse that your eye can't see and your wits can't judge!"

I didn't laugh. I sort of respected this fellow Albemarle and his school-teacher ways about his horses. He lived by them and for them. And he goes on:

"There are some that I could speak of and won't that don't know all they might about horses, and I'm free to tell you, Jacks, that you're not the first one to miss the best of the lot. And the two best in all the fields that the Colonel owns have never been claimed by any man or woman! They're just let run!"

I stared at him.

"You mean," says I, "that some of these here fine horses that cost so much blood and money ain't ever used?"

"I mean just that," says he, very sad. "There's more horses here than the Colonel can use and his household and his 'knights.' " He give me an ugly sneer as he said that word, and then he went on: "But the cream of the lot has never been claimed, because it took a man with horse-genius to recognize their points! They run out there to waste, and perhaps they'll never have a strap on them again, except when they're gentled every spring by the stable boys!"

He looked real sad about it, like a father, say, that sorrows over the talents that his son has, and don't show to the world. And he went on, soft and slow:

40

"Back on some of the tracks, they could do their work. They could show what they're made of. But they never have their chance. They won't be sold. He's too proud for that. Dog in the manger, I call it. Damn dog in the manger!"

And then he looked up with a jerk, startled, and stared at me, because he knew that he'd said enough in my hearing to cost him his place, and he was really frightened almost to death.

But I didn't bear no malice against him. I rather liked the way that he'd been carrying on, because it's always pretty fine when you find a man all wrapped up in his work, that way. It eases your heart a lot. You say that there's something more than money in the world. You say that God ain't so far away, when men can be like children.

Well, I'm getting off the track. I mean to say that I only smiled at Albemarle and I said to him:

"It's all right, partner. I'm kind of deaf on that side of my head!"

That soothed him a good deal and all at once he busted out:

"Jacks, I'll let you change your mind about the bay. The mare is worth two of him, and I give you my word for it!"

41

"Thanks," says I. "But she ain't my horse, and the bay is."

"I understand," says he, with a grin.

And just then word came out that the Colonel was coming. And he walked out, then, and looked at me and at my horse.

"You've taken the bay?" says he.

"I have, sir," says I.

"You must always remember, Jacks," says he, "that quality in this singular world of ours matters a great deal more than quantity. However, that's a very serviceable animal. Am I right, Albemarle?"

"It will never let him down," said Albemarle. "But I suppose that it would find the distances a bit short on the track!"

And he gave the Colonel and me a lopsided smile. He could say mean things, that Albemarle, as you may have been observing for yourself.

"Jacks!" says the Colonel.

I stepped aside with him.

"I have made arrangements for a room for you in my house," says he. "I hope that you will be able to get your things moved out here by night?"

He didn't wait for his answer. He turned around to Albemarle.

"Jacks' horse will be cared for with the rest of mine," says he.

And that was that!

But it nearly beat me! Because the Colonel never kept more than a half dozen extra choice picked men around his house. He had that half dozen already, like a sort of a guard of honor. Every man had a servant. Every man had his string of horses with one of the thoroughbreds at the top of the line. Every man had everything that his heart could wish and a fat salary besides.

It wasn't a job. It was a position.

"Betty," says I to myself, "will you look at me now?"

CHAPTER 6

GOING THROUGH TOWN, I just dropped in to see the Sheriff.

"I got to resign quick," says I.

"Hey—wait!" yells the Sheriff. "I ain't given you leave to resign. I need you to——"

"You tell that to the Colonel," says I. "He needs me out at his house, now!"

You better believe that that made all of the difference to old Steve Ross.

He run right out behind me from the office

and he stood hanging on to the bridle and keeping me from running away. And he says:

"You don't mean it! D'you really mean it, kid?"

"Don't I?" says I. "I would of rode the thoroughbred in, but I thought that I didn't want to waste him burning up the road to this rube town."

"All right, you're fixed," says the Sheriff with a sigh. "Remember me, Billy!"

I shook hands with him.

"I never forget a pal," says I, and went right on to see Betty.

She didn't have much time for me when I sashayed into the hotel, because God, he never wasted much time over the making of my face. He finished off the rest of me good and careful, but when it come to the head, he just roughed it in and called it a day. And you know how the women are. They pay a whole lot of attention to the little things, don't they?

I just lighted up a cigarette.

"I'm in a hurry!" says Betty.

"Just fetch me a cup of coffee," says I, "and then you stand over there by the window and hold onto yourself. I might be needing something more, after a while."

44

She give me a good long look.

"You impudent good-for-nothing-pie-face!" says Betty.

"I'll have you disciplined!" says I, right back at her, quick and mean.

She had been so mad that she had got all white. But now she got all red again. She leaned over and put both her hands on the table and stared at me close.

"You're shutting out the sun, kid," says I to her.

She didn't pay no attention, but kept on looking into me until finally she busted loose with:

"William Jacks!"

"Did you speak?" says I.

"William Jacks!" says she.

"Pass the sugar," says I, "and stand back from the table or I'll have to report you to the boss."

"William Jacks," says she, "you don't mean to tell me that you've got it!"

"Got what?" says I.

"You've got a right to lord it over folks in the Sierra Blanca now! That's why you have your chin in the air. And it's happened! I always sort of guessed that it *would* happen. Because you're so——. And now you've got it!"

"Got what?" says I.

"I heard a whisper about it," says she, "but I hardly didn't dare to believe it! But it was true, and the Colonel has picked you for one of his men!"

"Oh, that," says I. "Sure. That's a fact."

I lighted up a cigarette. I hardly dared to look at her, I was feeling so lit up inside.

"That? Ain't that enough?" says Betty. "What more could there be?"

"I dunno what makes you curious," says I. "I didn't come in here to talk over my private affairs! I come in here for coffee!"

"Billy, you darlin'," says Betty, and sits down on the table and looks down at me. "Tell me all about it!"

"Humph!" says I. "Humph!"

I mean, as I sat there and looked up at her, I says to myself that she had ought to be ashamed of herself. Because she knew that I knew that I'd been hounding her for years, ever since she tied up her pigtail and called herself a woman, and trying to get her to go to dances with me, and trying to get her to dance with me after she got there, and trying to get between her and a smile that she might have intended for somebody else. But all she'd ever been able to see of me was the careless way that my face was made.

46

You would really of thought that some of those things would of come into her head and slowed her up a little and made her ashamed of herself, but a woman, she's beyond shame, in some directions.

There was Betty looking past my face for the first time in her life, and beginning to see that maybe I amounted to something. After all, it ain't right to blame a woman for the nature that God has put into her. It ain't right. They got not much sense of right and wrong. But what they need they take. And the man that they didn't know yesterday, they up and marry him today.

Besides, I didn't want to be too curious. I knew that I wanted Betty, that I'd worked years for her, and that I would work years more, if need be, to get her.

"All right, Betty," says I. "I won't tell you about the times when you gave me the cold shoulder. I ain't going to dwell on that!"

"Billy!" says she.

"Well?" says I.

"Don't be so silly. Talk!"

"About what?"

"You'll drive me mad!"

"Will I? Sorry to hear that!"

"You're just stupid! Tell me what's happened. What could have happened more than that!"

"You guess for yourself," says I.

"How high may I go?"

"The sky's the limit, kid," says I.

Her eyes fairly popped.

"Billy Jacks!" she whispered. "You don't half mean to tell me that you've been taken in to the Stockton House—that you're one of the Colonel's right hand men!"

I just leaned back and eased my shoulders comfortable into the back of the chair.

"That's what I mean, Betty," says I. "And I hope that you bear up, under it!"

"Oh, Billy Jacks, you darling!" says Betty, and she leaned right forwards and kissed me between the eyes.

That's a fact, though it's kind of hard to ask you to believe it. But you see, women, they're that way. They don't mean to be gold diggers, but they can't help it. And they have to look up to a man. If he's standing on a professorship or something, that makes him high enough for them. Or if he's standing on a heavyweight championship, say, that's tall enough, too. Or maybe he's a deep, a secret gent, like one of these fellows that looks at the stars at night. Or maybe he's elevated by the pile of coin that he's got. But between you and me, almost anything that gets a man into the newspapers also gets a girl to fall in love with him.

I mean by that even divorces. Or perhaps I should say chiefly that. By which I wouldn't be wrote down as running down women none. There is one of them that I like a lot. But there is none of them that a man can really understand. Even the crystal clear kind like Olivia Stockton, they blind you the most of all. Because they dazzle you, y'understand?

Betty, she didn't dazzle. But she blinded you with her womanliness; there was so much sweetness in her that you couldn't help overlooking what a little gold-digger she was.

But there I had my fine place at the Colonel's house, and how could she very well help being swept right off of her feet? But she didn't waste any time. She says:

"Now you'll be able to do something for poor me!"

"What do you mean?" says I.

"You can get me a place in the big house, too!"

"Why, Betty, you want me to talk to the Colonel and ask him favors this soon, before I've done nothing?"

She smiled down at me and nodded:

"You'll find a way, Billy dear," says she.

And she slips down off of the table and goes away to the kitchen.

You see, she knew that I loved her, and so when the time come along when she was ready to waste a thought on me, she just took me for granted. That's the way with a girl. They don't waste no motions. They're labor saving devices, as you might call 'em.

I looked after Betty for a while, sort of enjoying the taste of her, and tasting the future, too, and half closing my eyes, and wondering how it had happened that God could of suddenly jerked open the doors of the world and showed me so much happiness so crowded close together.

And then I got up and sashayed out of the hotel and idled on the veranda for a while.

Pretty soon, after closing up time, a lot of folks come by, and they all seemed to of heard something. Gents that had slapped me on the back that morning, they went by me now and they says to me:

"Good evening, Mr. Jacks! Hot weather we're having, isn't it!"

They talked like that! But I didn't laugh. Holding down a position like I had then, you got to be careful about yourself. Because just a look from you can let a man down very hard.

So I was kind and spoke right back to everybody, no matter how foolish they was. And I was like a bird on a golden cloud, I thought.

But oh God, how could I guess how far I was from any real happiness just then?

CHAPTER 7

WHEN I TOOK on with the main drag and got to be one of the Knights of Sierra Blanca, as somebody had called 'em, there was six of them, altogether. There was Chet Murphy, and Jeff Hudson, and Hal Doolittle, and Roger Bartholomew, and Joe Laurens, and Dick Wace. I put Dick Wace last because, of course, he was really first. Dick was so important that when he fell out with the general boss and foreman of the whole valley, the foreman was fired, and Dick was kept on. I mean to say that Dick was important. You could tell it by the look of him. But for that matter, so was all the rest of them. There wasn't a man of the six that mightn't be put at the head of ten thousand cattle to be drove to a distant market, and that man had everything left in his hands. He could hire and fire drivers, and he could make up his expense accounts, and turn them in, and they was paid, and no real questions asked.

There was a story told about Jeff Hudson taking three thousand head clear overland to San Antonio. When he come back and turned in his accounts, he had everything exact.

"And how much for foolishness?" says the Colonel to Jeff.

"Sir?" says Jeff, his eyes getting big.

"And how much for foolishness?" says the Colonel, frowning. "Because I'd rather have that drawn down in cash than in credit!"

And he wrote off a check for twenty-five hundred dollars and handed it to Jeff, along with a month's vacation for blowing in the loot. There was some that said it was because Jeff had done a monstrous fine job in that drive to San Antonio and had caught the market just right and had made thousands and thousands of dollars for the Colonel. But those with more sense pointed out that the Colonel was always handing big things to his "knights."

There was several of them that had growed pretty old and retired, rich. They was spotted around through the outer edge of the mountains, each one with a fine herd of cows in the mountain valleys, and each one getting richer every year, with the Colonel helping them no end to help themselves. All of those retired men, they was a great strength to the Colonel, because they held the outer lands, and when the cattle rustlers came along, they had to pass through those outside limits, and that was just where the old fighting forces counted the most. Because it was a good rustler that could slide cattle away from such hands as Champ McGinnis, and Lord Marvin, and a lot of others.

However, it wasn't all roses for the select inside circle of the gents that worked for the Colonel. There was somebody that figured it out that only one man in four ever lived long enough to retire. Most generally, they got bumped off by thugs while they was handling a big cash shipment, or when they was managing some round-up of cattle thieves, or when they was doing any one of a dozen hard jobs such as generally come along pretty frequent up in the Sierra Blanca. But when one of them died, the Colonel, he always give them a right bang up funeral in the town, and then there was a great big procession, and everybody went out to the burying grounds near the church, and the Colonel himself was there and made a fine speech and told what a great man the dead fellow was, because after a man was dead, there was nothing too good for the Colonel to say about him.

Yes, sir, it was an amazing thing how the Colonel, he would hand out fortunes to the few men that was on the inside working for him and his interests. You take Champ McGinnis, he could write you a check for a cold half million, and there was Lord Marvin that was worth a cool million, and no mistake, and there was others that had done just as well. You take Roger Bartholomew, just to show you how the Colonel worked. He called Roger in to see him one day. He says:

"Mr. Bartholomew, I understand that you spend nearly everything that you make, and that you are often in debt!"

Roger was rather stumped. Because he was a great spender.

"I understand, Mr. Bartholomew," barks the Colonel, "that there has been a money-lender out here trying to collect a ridiculous sum of money that he claims is owing to him from you. I told the man that I would have him lynched if he dared to show his head in Sierra Blanca again. But is it true that you owed him the money?"

"Sir," says Roger, down headed, because he felt that he was about to get the sack. "Sir, I'm afraid that I owe it to him!"

"Humph," says the Colonel. "Ridiculous. Never let me hear of such a thing again! And if you pay the man, that moment our connections cease! In the meantime, here is ten thousand to start your bank account!"

And he gives him a check for that amount.

Well, I been telling you these things, just so that you would understand why it was that a man got rather excited when the Colonel asked him to work for him and live at Stockton House. But just the same, though I have to tell you how set up I was, I never want you to lose sight of the fact that the main thing of interest, all of this while, is the case of Charlie Lamb. He's sort of dropped out of sight, for a while. But that's because I don't know how to keep your eye on him. The way things piles into my brain, that's the way that they piles out again, y'understand?

However, I'm asking you to follow me still, for a while, and the way that I rode out to Stockton House, feeling that most of the world was using my name in vain behind me.

When I got out there, I looked around and was showed to my quarters, which was up on the third floor, where a Negro opened the door and he says:

"Good evening, Mr. Jacks, sir."

By which I gathered that that was my servant.

I settled down in a fine big room about twenty by twenty and looked out the windows south towards the rim of the mountains, where they was butting their heads against the sky. I felt pretty good and reached for cigarette makings, when along comes the valet and hands me a humidor filled with tailor-mades. And then I reached for a match, but he had me beat and holds a light. I stared at him.

"Have one yourself," says I.

"Thank you, sir," says he. "I can't smoke now."

I seen that I was out of order and got a little red.

"What's your name?" says I.

"Vincent," says he.

That's a queer name for a black man, as you'll agree. But this was a queer Negro.

"Vincent," says I, "you and me is going to get on fine."

"Thank you, sir," says he, and sort of fades out into the general background, while I sat there and takes a new look at myself and sees that Bill Jacks has rose to be somebody in this world, and no mistake about it.

I took another look around my quarters. There was that big room, with an alcove off of it with a bed, and then there was a bathroom, and a room for Vincent, and another room with a fine bed in it, and all fixed up.

"Who stays here?" says I to Vincent.

"Any friend that you care to ask to the house, sir," says Vincent.

That staggered me again. Here was I fixed up with three rooms and a bath, and I could understand why it was that Stockton House was all spread out over creation.

Just then there come up a gent to the door that looked like a butler.

"The chef wishes to know what is your particular fancy in menus, sir," says this gent.

I stared at him until I'd gathered his drift.

"Bacon and eggs is my main line," says I, "with flapjacks and maple syrup second," says I. "I'll think up the extras later."

And he backed away saying:

"Very good, sir!"

Of course, that sort of put the tin hat on everything, made it more like a dream than ever, so that I made up my mind that I would have to talk to somebody real, right quick.

I asked Vincent where I could find Dick Wace.

"I shall go hunt for Mr. Richard Wace, sir," says Vincent, and he disappeared.

Pretty soon, he come back, just before I got delirious thinking about everything. And he says that Mr. Wace would be happy to see me in his rooms.

So I went down, and I was showed into a layout like mine, but a good deal better. And by the lay of the land, I could see that I was important, but that there was no doubt about Wace being a lot more importanter than me.

Dick, he met me at the door and shook hands.

"You know me, Wace?" I asked him.

"Not exactly," says he, "but I passed up Sugar Cañon one day just behind you, so I know something about you!"

Which was by way of a compliment, Sugar Cañon being the place where I once met up with three thugs. And modesty sure forbids me saying what happened when we met. Anyway, in a minute, I was having a drink poured for me by Dick's servant, and after that, I just busted out and said:

"Wace, why am I here?"

"Because the Colonel needs you," says he.

"But he's never kept more than six fellows like us before," says I.

"It may be," says Wace, "that he expects that there will be vacancies, before long!"

I let that idea shiver down my spine and get assimilated.

"Between you and me," says I, "I understand that the rest of you are all boss cattle men, or else you know farming, and you got other business qualities. But I got none."

Wace, he fiddled with his pipe for a minute and then he looks up sudden.

"You shoot very straight, old fellow," says he.

"Hello!" says I. "What are you driving at?"

"Jacks," says he, "I may be saying more than I should. Frankly, I don't know what he wants with you, and if I did, I'd let my tongue be cut out before it would tell you anything out of school. However, I don't mind guessing that the Colonel always has all sorts of business on his hands, and if he hired you, he needed you, and if he needed you, it was probably because of the greatest talent that you possess!"

That was certainly to the point, and it was true that I knew guns.

So I broke in on another tack, seeing that

I would have to do my own guessing about the case.

"Look here," says I, "they employ girls out here a good deal, don't they?"

"In the house? Yes. Servants, and secretaries, and what not."

"I dunno what they do," says I, "but I know a girl that wants to be here."

"How well do you know her?" says he.

"Not half so well as I'd like to," says I. "And not half so well as I hope to."

"I understand," says Wace, who was extreme decent in every way. "I suppose that something can be done about it. Only, partner, you have to bear one thing in mind: The Colonel will do almost anything in the world for us. He doesn't care hardly what we ask. But each of us has his limit. And before you ask a favor, you want to decide for yourself that it's a thing that you really want a lot! You follow me?"

"I follow you," says I. "But I want the girl here, if it can be arranged."

"Certainly," says he. "I'll see to it at once."

"And how the hell can you do that?" says I.

He looked at me for a minute, sort of surprised.

"Of course," says he, "I'll simply speak to the housekeeper in your name."

"And she'll do it—in my name?"

"Why, man," says Dick Wace, "you don't understand the position that you have in this house, now. And you don't understand the position that you have in the valley!"

Which I shut up and said no more. I could see that I'd been handed a lot bigger diamond than I could lay a value on.

CHAPTER 8

WELL, I WOULD like to tell of a lot of things that happened along about this time, and about chiefly the things that tickled me most after I settled down in Stockton House, and how when I was late for breakfast, it was brung to my room on a tray, and about how everything that I asked for was mine as soon as I asked, and about a lot of other things that made a man comfortable, but there was nothing as important to me as the coming of Betty.

The very next day after I asked about her, which was the second day for me at the House, she was brought out in a buckboard and she was showed into the room of the housekeeper, who says to her:

"Mr. Jacks has suggested that Stockton House employ you, and since Mr. Jacks is a person of much consideration here, of course it is my duty to find a place for you. You can enter the laundry department."

"I cannot," says Betty. "You've missed me entire, ma'am."

The housekeeper got red and stabbed her pen at the paper that was before her, and she says:

"Ah-hem! Some other arrangement is perhaps possible. The care of the rooms——"

So Betty was let in on that job, and there being that many rooms in Stockton House, you can see that they had a whole flock of maids, there.

She come up and tapped at my door, and when I opened it and asked her in, all grins, she made a bow to me and said that it wasn't for her to talk to her betters or enter their rooms, but that she had come to thank me, and then she told me about everything that had happened, and how the whole staff had to be nice to her because it was known that she was my friend.

"And are you the Colonel's uncle, or something?" says she.

Well, I almost felt like it, I was so dizzy with the things that was taking place, but now I got to get back to the things that was taking place about that Smiling Charlie Lamb.

I was given nothing at all to do about the place for three days, except to drift around, and ride my bay gelding, and such. And then the Colonel, he sent for me. He says:

"I have word from Charles Lamb," says he. "And now I wish you to ride to Los Gatos and meet him at once. You are to find him there sometime after dark, at the hotel. And when you meet him, you're to tell him that I have a position waiting for him, and that I shall arrange to have all of his crimes forgiven by the state."

That was all that the Colonel said, and so I went out and first oiled up all of my guns—because I sure felt that I'd need them, perhaps—and then I saddled the bay, and away we went for little Los Gatos, off in the mountains.

I passed Olivia Stockton and the Baron, as I started off. They was out riding, and they swung in beside me for a ways, and the Baron was very keen to have me use a gat. And when I pulled down on a jackrabbit that we scared up, and knocked it over with the third shot that I fanned out of my Colt, he was as pleased as a kid with his first pair of long pants.

Well, I said good-by to them and sashayed along through the country, thinking about Betty most of the while, and wondering what sort of a bang-up wedding the Baron would have with Olivia. And so I went on until night found me forty miles away, with the lights of Los Gatos winking ahead of me on the hillside.

I rode right up to the hotel, down the one winding street, and put up my horse in the stable and booked a room in the hotel. Then I went out on the veranda and sat there for a while, digesting the dinner that I had ate.

But there was no sign of Smiling Charlie.

I remembered, then, what sort of a reputation he had, and what I knew about him, and so I circulated around in back of the hotel and snooped around until I got to the kitchen window, and there I looked through and seen Smiling Charlie as big as life seated at the kitchen table with about five girls all sailing around and getting things for him, and one of them pouring coffee for him, and another loading more ham and eggs onto his plate, and another offering him something else on a platter, and another leaning on the back of his chair.

64

He was sure comfortable, and don't you make no mistake.

I stepped through the back door with both guns ready. They screamed and scattered like a flock of hens, and Smiling Charlie, he turned around slow in his chair.

"Charlie," says I, "will you please put up your hands?"

He didn't ask no questions at all. He just put them above his head. I went and jammed a Colt into his stomach, while the girls all screamed again and said it was murder, and I frisked Smiling Charlie for his guns and got three Colts and a derringer slung around his neck, from that lamb, not to say nothing about a whacking big bowie knife, good for a sword or a javelin, as you might say. And him able to use it both ways, as I could guess.

"All right," says he, "now I suppose that you're ready to talk business?"

"What sort of business do you expect?" says I, curious and mean.

"Something very attractive," says Lamb, "if I'm to give up this life."

"You like it, eh?" says I, remembering what the Sheriff had often said to me, and what he had said to the Colonel, also.

"Of course I do," says he, and he throws an eye towards all the girls, where they was huddled with pale faces in a corner of the room. "Did you ever have that many ladies frightened for your sake, Billy?"

I couldn't help admiring the cast iron nerve of him. He was all together, that fellow was, and you couldn't take him by surprise.

And all the time, he seemed to be laughing up his sleeves at me, and at the girls, too. I could see why he was called Smiling Charlie, because his eyes was always smiling, even when his lips was still.

He looked a little browner and leaner than before, but a shade more fine and handsome, if anything. Nobody ever seen such a man as him. I says:

"All right, and now I'll talk turkey to you. You're so damn lucky that I never heard of anything like it. But I got to follow orders. You're offered a job by the Colonel. And I suppose that it'll be something fat. And besides, he'll see that your slate is rubbed clean!"

But he didn't seem a bit excited. He just got a little thoughtful, and he said:

"And if not?"

"If not," says I, "you trek back to town with me, and the Sheriff will find something to start talking about where I leave off."

"You fellows are very rough," says Charlie, with a sigh, and he looked across the room at the girls. Yes, sir, I give you my word that he didn't seem tempted a bit.

"You got ten seconds to think it over," says I, "because I'm a little rushed."

"All right," says Charlie. "If I don't like it, of course I can always quit."

"Quit the Colonel?" says I. And then I laughed. I had to. The idea of anybody ever leaving off work for the Colonel sort of amused me. Because when you started in for the Colonel, he didn't rent your body and hands only. He rented your soul, too.

"However," says I, "it looks as though you just decided in time. I might ask you if you've made up your mind firm?"

"I have," says he.

And just then six men busted into that kitchen by three doors. They had got onto his trail, somehow, and they had arrived just too late. They was all over guns, and they looked at me like gold diggers when somebody else has just found the pay dirt.

"We'll help you guard him!" says one of them.

"He don't need guarding," says I. "Here's your guns, Charlie."

"Hello!" sings out one of them. "What the hell is this? Hold off with those guns.

Lamb, if you touch one of 'em, you're a dead man!"

And he jumps a double-barreled shotgun to his shoulder, all ready to let her fly.

That made me a little irritated. The last few days I'd been enjoying a good deal of authority, and I hated to be crossed.

"Drop that shotgun, you fool!" says I.

"Keep your pet names for yourself," says this man with the cannon. "Seems like I got a better right to Smiling Charlie than you have, and I intend to have him!"

"You intend to have hell," says I, extreme polite. "Drop the butt of that gun and drop it quick."

He meant fight. There was a tight look around the corners of his mouth. But just the same, he wasn't going to press the scrap unless he had to. And just then, a fat man come busting through the side door, and he sings out:

"Chris! Chris! Are you crazy?"

"What's the matter?" says him of the shotgun.

"This is Bill Jacks!" says the fat man.

"Hello!" says Chris. "You mean the Colonel's new man?"

"I mean just that."

Well, it worked like a charm. It was plain

that it didn't take the valley long to learn the names of the new gents that was taken into Stockton House. He let down on his shotgun and he gives me a good, long look.

"All right," he mumbles at last. "I'm beat."

And he turns on his heel and strides out of the room.

Well, it made me feel pretty good, take it all in all. So I passed the guns back to Lamb, and we walked out of the room together. But he paused at the door and kissed his hand to the girls.

"Wait for me, dear," says he, "because some day I'm coming back."

Says I, when we got to the yard below:

"Which one of them is the dear?"

"I can't guess," says he. "Can you?"

CHAPTER 9

WE HEADED RIGHT back for the home place. I never even thought of stopping for the night in Los Gatos, because somehow when you were on the road for the Colonel, the shortest and fastest way of doing his work always seemed the only possible way. We cut through the night, riding side by side. It was a queer journey, too. I laid my cards on the table right at the beginning.

"Some day, old timer," says I, "I'm going to have the chance to shoot the heart out of you. Or else you'll have to shoot the heart out of me. But just now we're both going on the Colonel's pay roll. So I have to keep hands off. But I'm not through. One day, we'll have it out."

"Thanks," says he. "Whenever you're ready, I'm ready. Day or night, morning or evening, foot or horseback, fist, or knife or guns, I'm your man, Jacks. But as for what happened between us that other day, I'm really sorry about it. Except that the idea would never have entered my head, even, if it hadn't been for the way that you were holding out your jaw asking for a punch!"

And he began to laugh like a child.

It made me pretty mad, but I held onto myself. It didn't pay to lose your head, when you were on the trail for the Colonel.

Says he:

"I wonder what the old goat wants of me?"

"Who do you mean?" says I.

"The Colonel, of course," says he.

That took my breath a little, because you wouldn't refer to the Colonel like that, not even if you was the president of these United States, you wouldn't.

"What he wants of you, I don't know," says I. "All I do know is that he's amazing kind to you, after what you've done."

"Not at all," says he. "I've kept any number of his riders and hunters in good trim and fighting shape. Not enough of a war to put a drain on his resources, but just enough of a war to keep his men and horses exercised. The Colonel is really under a great obligation to me, as I see it."

You would think that he meant what he said, to hear the calm way in which he said it. The nerve of him would of stocked up the supply of a thousand book peddlers.

"All right," says I. "Anyway, you have the plum."

"Not yet," says he. "And when he offers it, I don't think that I'll bite."

"Don't you?" says I.

And I couldn't help laughing again. He was so sure of himself, I mean, and so set and confident. And him with the Colonel in the offing!

"I don't," says he.

"Well," says I, "I'll tell you what I'll do. I'll bet you a cold thousand that you'll take a job with the Colonel rather than split with

71

him—and get yourself shot by me an hour later!"

He turned his head in the darkness and studied me for a moment, and then he said quietly:

"You don't seem to understand me, Jacks. I really never hunt for trouble, but it's impossible for me to run away when trouble comes hunting me. Is that clear to you?"

I admitted that it was, and he went on:

"As for your bet, I'll take you up."

"If you have a thousand you will," says I.

"Oh, yes," says he, "I always make it a point to have plenty of ready cash about me!"

He was like that, I mean. Not exactly fatheaded, but just satisfied and sure of himself, and now he struck up a tune and began to sing in one of the best voices that you ever heard in your life. I forgot how much I hated him, while I listened to that voice.

When he was tired of the singing, he unlimbered a guitar and struck up a tune on that, and I never seen the hours and the miles fly as fast as he made them do with his music.

I took him up to the house and we got there about midnight, and when I asked, I heard that the Colonel was still up, so I brought my man right to the door of the study. The Colonel called us in.

"Well done, Jacks," says he. "Now go to bed and sleep tight."

I went out. But I was aching clean to the bone to hear what was happening between the pair of them, and finally, I slipped outside the house and climbed up to the little ornamental stone balcony that passed under the windows of the Colonel's study.

It wasn't honorable, but, somehow, honor was the last thing that you thought of, when you were in the employ of the Colonel.

Anyway, there I sat up, as big as life, and I could see and hear them both. They were talking about cigars, when I arrived, and I heard the Colonel switch off by saying:

"What was your college, Lamb?"

"An Eastern one," says he.

"Thank you," said the Colonel, not peeved by being dodged, apparently. "One of the big ones?"

"A famous place, but rather provincial," says Lamb.

"Princeton, perhaps?" says the Colonel.

"Perhaps," says Lamb, and smiled again.

"I am glad to know," says the Colonel, "that you have such an excellent educational background. That always helps. Particularly in view of the work that I have in mind for you."

"And what is that work?" says Lamb.

"Something with a sufficient remuneration," says the Colonel.

"Ah?"

"Let's say—five thousand a year?"

Smiling Charlie didn't smile. He simply laughed.

"Did you say sufficient remuneration?" he remarked.

"I don't know just on what plane you've arranged your ideas of money," says the Colonel.

"My ideas of life," says Lamb, "are not ideas of money. But where there is nothing but money to attract one, the money payments would have to be large to make up for the rest!"

"To make up for what?"

"For freedom, sir."

"I intend to give you a very free hand."

"No doubt you do. But still you would hold the reins."

"A position in my establishment, Lamb, is one that makes you a literal prince."

"I suppose that I understand you now," says Lamb. "I am to be one of your hired gunmen and general lieutenants, like Billy Jacks, for instance?"

"Is that beneath you?" asked the Colonel, curiously, but not in a heat.

"A great deal," says Lamb, in exactly the same manner.

Well, I wasn't much surprised. Some surprised, but not much. Because after you'd been with Lamb for a while, you expected him to answer just the opposite from everybody else.

"Ah, well," murmured the Colonel, "there are other ways of arranging the matter. As for the salary——"

"Let that subject drop," said Mr. Lamb, "until I hear what the work is to be."

"In the first place," said the Colonel, "it would be in the nature of a secret commission."

"Ah? That, I suppose, means something a little shady?"

"Are you particularly interested in such matters?" said the Colonel.

"Terribly," said Lamb, the fugitive and horse thief.

The Colonel looked for a moment at the end of his cigar.

"I believe that I must lay my cards on the table, face up," said he.

"Perhaps that would be better."

"Very well. You know that I have a daughter, of course?"

"I do."

"You know that my daughter is engaged to be married?"

"I do."

"And that the man is now in my house?"

"I do."

"It is about her that I wish to talk to you."

"Yes?"

"About my daughter Olivia, and Baron Wakeness."

The Colonel seemed to find it very hard to go on, but finally he brought out with a snap:

"My friend, that marriage must not take place!"

CHAPTER 10

Now, TO ME on the outside of that room, hanging onto that balcony, it seemed that suddenly things was clearing up.

I mean, everything was as mysterious as possible, but just the same I could begin to follow the drift of the Colonel a little. All of this elaborate scheming of his was to get his hands on Charlie Lamb and then use him as a tool to separate the girl and her fiancé. Other things were lying behind and ahead of that idea, so that it was easy to guess that the devil would be at work with all hands, before very long.

I had looked on my stay at the Colonel's house as a sort of a fairy tale, up to now, but after this, I could see that I was apt to get into active service. Nothing was clear before my eyes. But I done some of the world's tallest guessing, for a while.

I was curious, too, seeing the way in which Charlie Lamb took this last speech from his host. He didn't seem shocked. He didn't seem surprised. He just sat and looked the old Colonel in the eye, and both of them smoked their cigars, and the clock began to tick steady and loud from the corner of the room. After a while, Charlie Lamb knocked off the ashes from his cigar.

"I think that I'd better be starting on," said he. "It's already rather late."

He got up and went to the door, without the Colonel stirring.

"Good night," says Charlie from the door as he goes out.

"Hold on!" barked the Colonel. "Come back here, sir, if you please!"

He'd thought that it was a bluff, and his face was black enough as he half raised himself from the chair. Charlie closed the door and stood with his hand on the knob.

"I don't think that there's any use talking the matter over," says he. "I never change my mind, sir."

The Colonel had to get his wind before he could answer. He was thunderstruck. Finally he got up and took Lamb by the arm and led him back to the opposite chair.

"Neither do I," said the Colonel. "I never change my mind, sir, and since I'm an older man than you, I have the greater right to maintain the habit."

Charlie Lamb sat down, agreeably enough, and very polite. But you could see that he was as steady and as hard as stone in his determination not to give way.

"Now, sir," said the Colonel, "let me ask why you've jumped so far to a conclusion?"

"Colonel Stockton," said Smiling Charlie, "I'll give you a few of my reasons, the first of them being that no man has a right to interfere between a man and the woman of his choice."

The Colonel was silent for a while, and then he smiled rather grimly.

"May I ask you, young man," says he,

"what would have happened to the lives of several girls if you had not been interfered with once in a while during your life?"

Charlie Lamb smiled in turn and yet he grew a little red, also. I was glad to see that there was some shame in him.

"I've been a particular sinner," he admitted.

"And yet," said the Colonel, "I suppose that most of the time you've actually felt that you were really in love with the girl of the day?"

"I suppose that I have," said Charlie, growing still more red.

"But on the whole, you're rather glad either that you were interrupted, or that you grew tired of the lady yourself?"

"I suppose so," said Charlie, frowning a little, as though he did not wish to have the talk kept on this most painful subject.

"And yet," said the Colonel, coming suddenly back to the point, "you feel that one should let a man alone to have the woman of his choice?"

Smiling Charlie frowned again, but then he added sharply:

"Do you think that the Baron is the same sort of a sinner that I am?"

"Not a bit," replied the Colonel. "Not a

bit! I shouldn't worry so much, if that alone were the case! But the fact is that I haven't yet decided that I must tell you of what I suspect him. There are no established crimes that he has committed. On the surface, his character is as attractive as one could wish to have it. But what lies beneath the surface counts most with me. Give me a habitually gloomy man, if he can be cheerful in times of danger. That is a rule with me. It is the man inside that counts!"

You could see that Charlie had forced the Colonel to come down to his own level and talk man to man, but you couldn't help wondering which of the pair would win out. I felt that the Colonel was the strongest and most commanding personality that I'd ever met. And still, I didn't see how he could overcome Smiling Charlie.

"I suppose," said Charlie Lamb, "that I may as well cut the matter short by telling you that I don't care for the assignment."

He said that in a very final tone.

"And what would you leave this house and go towards?" asked the Colonel.

"You are fond of the Sierra Blanca, aren't you?" asked Lamb.

"Certainly. The happy part of my life has been spent here."

"I agree with you," said Charlie. "Because the happiest weeks in my life have been spent here, also!"

You couldn't help believing him. When his big, brown eyes looked straight at you, there was no dodging them.

"I wish you'd explain," asked the Colonel, behind his cloud of tobacco smoke.

"Certainly. It's the perfect freedom. The jolly days. And the uncertain nights. I've never had so much fun in all the other years that I've lived. Besides, the girls in the Sierra Blanca won't see a poor fellow go hungry!"

And he laughed deep in his throat.

Yes, he certainly meant what he said, and I was surprised to see that the Colonel was chuckling, also.

"You infernal young scoundrel," says he, "I should like to know just how much devil you have raised in my country. However, that's aside from the point. But tell me, Lamb. Have you never cast eyes at a married woman?"

"Never," said Charlie Lamb. And he said it so quickly and quietly that I was startled, because I knew that it was true.

"And you've never even interfered when a girl was engaged?"

81

The answer came just as pat, and was just as much of a shock to me:

"Never!" said Charlie. "That is, when she was really in love with the other fellow."

"And you're an unfailing judge of such things?"

"I think I am," said Charlie calmly. "I've had enough experience," he added, coloring a little again.

"Ah," said the Colonel, "I think that I understand you fairly well, now. As a matter of fact, when I sent for you, I thought that you were a worthless rascal. Now that I find you are not, I see how absolutely essential it is that I make you one of my men!"

"Thank you," said Lamb, "because I know that is meant as a compliment. I should be a thousand times happy to have you as a friend—but never as a master!"

"Very free and frank and open," said the Colonel. "However, I must have you know that I always have my own way. In important matters, always!"

"I should hate to break a precedent, for you," says Charlie, stiffening a bit in his chair.

"You won't, my dear young man," replied the Colonel. "We'll get on famously, and along the lines which I lay down."

Charlie leaned back in his chair and smiled.

"You intrigue me, sir," said he.

"I knew that I would," said the Colonel. "And there are a great many people who cannot escape the service of the devil, simply because they're so eager to see his face at first hand, as I may say."

There was just enough truth about this to give a point to what he said—a sort of stinging point, you know. And he did look rather like a devil just then, with his bushy brows drawn down to a point over his nose, and his eyes glittering like cold stars on a winter night.

"The game is still to be won, I may remind you," said Charlie Lamb. "But in the first place, may I ask you what service, exactly, you would expect of me?"

"The same service that you have performed before, without any reward other than your own pleasure in doing it. I mean, young man, that you have a particular talent for making a girl forget other men, and I intend to use you as a taste of Lethe to make my daughter forget the Baron. And, after that, you will fade unexpectedly from the picture!"

I've never seen such a look as that which

came into the eyes of Charlie Lamb. No, I'm wrong. For there was just such a flash in his eyes the tenth part of a second before he knocked me down—me with my drawn gun covering him!

"Do you expect that any man can play the part of a hired cad?" said he. "But I don't intend to draw out the conversation, sir. I think that I've said enough to let you know my position, and you've certainly said enough to let me see yours. I find it—unattractive!"

He talked like that. I've remembered all of the words, because each of them jumped right through me like an electric spark. I almost expected to see the Colonel throw a blast of lightning at him, but the Colonel was merely sitting back and smiling.

"My dear Mr. Lamb," said he, "I've never enjoyed anything more than my conversation with you—which is not yet ended. And I assure you that you need not feel insulted when I say that I call in your services not as a cad, but as—let me say—a medical man, who I hope will remove from the mind of my poor daughter a dreadful hallucination. But, in the first place, you would expect me to give you reasons connected with the case. I'm very willing. But to begin with, you have seen my girl?"

Charlie shook his head, and the Colonel took a little leather case from his pocket, opened it, and passed it to Charlie Lamb.

"Darking painted it," said the Colonel.

Charlie didn't answer. I suppose that he didn't even know that the Colonel had spoken. He was lost, like a man in a dream.

CHAPTER 11

HE FINALLY CLOSED the case softly, handed it back to the Colonel, and stood up.

"I thought that I should be able to hear you out," said he. "But now I find that I'm afraid to stay to hear another word on this subject."

"I thought you would feel that way," said this devil of a Colonel. "However, you will nevertheless hear my reasons. Because if you were once convinced that my girl was about to make a gross mistake in her marriage, then you would be even keen to stop the affair."

"Keen sir?" said Charlie. "I should kill the dog with as little feeling as I would pistol a wolf!"

"Excellent!" said the Colonel. "However, you would require stringent reasons?"

"Entirely so!"

"In that case, I think that I must ask you to stay here a few days—on trial, as I may say. And then I shall arrange matters so that you will see a good deal of young Baron Wakeness. In the course of your meetings, I'll manage it so that you may look beneath the surface. Does that appeal to you?"

I thought that Charlie Lamb was the strangest figure that I ever saw, at that moment. He had been such a cool master of himself, all the time, but now the Colonel had found the right touch to completely shake him.

He was fighting a losing fight with himself, and his face was white with it.

"I suppose that I shall stay," says he. "I suppose that I'll stay. But mind you—I shall expect sheer proofs!"

"Exactly," smiled the Colonel. "Proofs that you yourself shall help to demonstrate, I hope. In the meantime, you'd better go to bed, I think. Your rooms are waiting for you——"

I didn't wait for any more, but I snaked down from the balcony and I skidded around into the house by a side door and got up to my own rooms.

I was barely in time to peel off my coat

and light a cigarette and look sleepy, when there was a knock at the door, and Charlie comes in. He said:

"What do you know about the Colonel, partner?"

"I know he's a clever old devil that always has his way," I ventured on him.

Charlie bit his lip.

"At least," says he, "the devil part of it is true enough."

And he turned on his heel and went back to his own rooms, without even saying good-night. The last thing that Charlie would ever have been was discourteous. So that I knew his brain was in a real fog.

I could hardly sleep that night, of course, now that I felt that things was gathering to a head so rapidly. But though I got up early, Smiling Charlie Lamb was ahead of me, and I found him talking to Albemarle.

Old Albemarle was just as hostile to Charlie as he'd been to me, and, as a matter of fact, the story was that he was always deadly afraid that by accident somebody might lay hands on Albemarle's own pets—the best in the bunch of horses, though nobody but him knew it. What ones was his favorites, not even the grooms in the stables could tell. What good they was to him, nobody could tell, either. But the fact was that he hated to see another gent get the cream of the lot.

"Well," says Albemarle to Charlie, "do you know horses, Mr. Lamb?"

You see how quick they got to know about the Colonel's inside men! Even a gent that had been there only one night!

"Not a great deal about them," says Charlie. "I like 'em, though. May I have a look?"

"Look as long as you like," says Albemarle, with a satisfied smile.

And he stood by the fence still smiling to himself and snapping his long fingers, and making them pop like whips. Because you could see that he was sure that his pets would be safe as could be while Charlie was picking.

Charlie walked around through the drift of horses, taking his time, and whistling, and smoking, and never stopping long to look over any one horse.

"Mr. Lamb," says Albemarle with a sneer, "seems to think that reading a horse is no harder than reading a novel!"

He was plumb filled with disgust, was crusty old Albemarle.

Charlie leans an elbow on the fence.

"What are those in that field?" he asks. "Work stock?"

For down in the hollow there was a few horses, too.

"Just weeds," says Albemarle. "What the devil is he up to now!"

That last was to me, because Smiling Charlie had vaulted over the fence and was now sauntering down into the hollow.

"Maybe he found nothing to fill his eye here!" says Albemarle, with a snort.

"He's simply taking his time and missing no bets," I told Albemarle.

"Humph!" says Albemarle. "Looking at a draft horse, now!"

Because Smiling Charlie had stopped and was patting the neck of a big Percheron and talking in his ear.

"He's a heavy man," says I, to put in my hook, and get on the right side of Albemarle. "So maybe he needs a heavy horse."

"Hell!" says Albemarle.

I stared at him, because he wasn't the sort that did much cussing. But there he was, stiff and red.

"Hell!" says Albemarle. "What does he mean by that?"

Because Smiling Charlie was coming back up the hollow leading a rusty looking old chestnut by the mane—a long-headed, down-headed, high-withered brute.

"He likes a horse old enough to get its character established," I suggests.

But Albemarle, he paid no attention. He just lighted a pipe. And he seemed so excited and disgusted that he bit off the stem right away and cut his lip, and that made him damn in earnest.

Charlie opened the gate and came through to us with the veteran.

"How old is this one?" he asks.

"Seventeen years," says Albemarle.

"Hello!" says Smiling Charlie. "As old as that? Well, well!"

"Why?" sneers Albemarle. "Do you like him?"

"Well, he has a sort of a comfortable look," says Charlie.

"He has enough stomach, at least," says I, standing back and laughing.

The chestnut cocked his ears forward and began to fiddle at the pocket of Smiling Charlie's coat with his long upper lip. The upper lip of a horse, it's sort of like the trunk of an elephant, only shorter, of course. But it can take hold of things fine.

"Well," says Charlie, "I'd like to try the gaits of the old boy."

"You can't do it!" says Albemarle.

"I can't? I thought that I could make my

pick from the whole bunch of horses?" says Lamb.

"You can. But you have to make your choice before you get into the saddle. However, if you want that old stallion, you can have him. Shall I call a boy?"

He whistled, and a little groom come running. There was nobody under the orders of Albemarle that ever walked when they heard his voice sing out.

"This gentleman wants old Cringle," said Albemarle.

"Wait a moment," said Smiling Charlie. "Don't rush me. Let me have my time."

The stable boy stood by, grinning behind his hand. But I was grinning openly. When you took a good look at the chest and legs and the bone of this old veteran, you could see why Charlie might really like him pretty well. But of course—to prefer him to the beauties in the other fields——!

Suddenly Charlie stepped back and snapped his head up.

"All right!" he said. "Put a saddle on this horse. I'll take him!"

I was really staggered, and the stable boy turned his back to hide his laughing, and comes out with Charlie's big range saddle.

"Not that infernal monster of a saddle,"

says Charlie. "Can't you lend me an English saddle, Albemarle?"

"I'll lend you nothing!" snaps Albemarle.

Why, I look at the man and thought he'd gone mad, for his face was white and his lips was quivering and twitching.

"I'll lend you nothing, and be damned to you!" says Albemarle, and he turned his back and went to the fence and leaned there against it. Even in the distance, you could see his body shake.

I couldn't make it out, but Charlie, slipping a bridle on Cringle, nodded and whistled to himself.

"I half guessed it!" says he.

Then he jumped onto Cringle's bare back, twitched the reins up, and took a sort of hard-pulling grip on the reins.

It was a quite amazing thing to see what happened then. That old stallion thrust out his head and his tail arched, and his neck bowed, and he busted out into a gallop with a stride so long that it made you dizzy to watch.

Charlie turned him sharp around, and Cringle floated over the fence of the paddock and then dipped out again and stood dancing beside us.

"I thought so!" cried Charlie Lamb. "I thought that this was the one!"

Poor Albemarle, he turned around and he threw up both hands into the air.

"You damned impostor, you only guessed! You only guessed!" he shouted, and then he turned on his heel and ran into the stable and out of sight, half crazy.

"You might have picked one of the others," says the stable boy, sort of scared by the way that old Albemarle carried on. "This here old nag, he's just what old Al hacks around the country on."

"Exactly," said Smiling Charlie. "I guessed that this was his chosen horse!"

CHAPTER 12

WELL, IT ONLY dawned on us by degrees.

You couldn't believe it, at first. But then the cat come out of the bag. They say that poor Albemarle, he sat with his head in his hands, for about a month, groaning because his horse was gone, because of all of the fine horses that was raised at Stockton House, there was never a one that was worthy of being mentioned on the same page with Cringle.

You could see how poor Albemarle would of worked it. You see, Cringle wasn't seventeen years old. He was only seven, but he'd always been kept rough, and his mane was in no sort of order, and he was gentled till there was no shine and show in him, and the feed that he got was so coarse and poor that it kept him pot-bellied, and his neck and his sides didn't get a chance to gloss over.

Well, Albemarle had picked that horse out as a colt, and watched him. He'd looked like a weed, with his long, ugly head and his high withers. And he never could flesh up well on the back, except right across the loins. And there's nothing much uglier in a horse than a ridgy back, like a water-divide.

And Albemarle watched that colt like a hawk, and must of trained him by night. And then when he seen what was in the stallion, he put him in with the hacks and the buggy horses, and he let him roam around with the draught stock that done the ploughing and the hauling.

So Cringle, with his dub of a name and his dubby looks, he was left alone, and never bothered, and Albemarle made him even more common by riding him around for a hack, in all sorts of weather.

But when he was out of the sight of the

rest, and let that horse feel the touch of the hands of a real rider, how many a fine spin he must have had across the countryside, over the fences and through the woods!

Yes, when Cringle really got into action, you could see the picture of the horse that he was intended to be, but you only got a mere flash of it; but when he was glossed up by the right sort of feeding and grooming, and when he'd lost his pot-belly and got his true lines, even then he didn't look anything better than just a very, very plain thorough-bred. Thoroughbred he looked, and thor-oughbred he was, but it took a grand expert to see the facts about him, which was that he was a horse in a million.

I never knew whether Charlie Lamb knew or guessed. But then, there was a lot about Charlie that nobody could really fathom. He kept his life and his thoughts to himself, most of the time, and he didn't open the door and ask you in to sit down with him and his thoughts.

I couldn't actually believe that Charlie had picked a speedster. I dared him to try paces with my bay.

"I've never seen your horse," says Charlie, "and I won't bet with you, unless you'll put up the thousand that I owe you."

95

"Because you're going to work for the Colonel?"

"Yes, it seems that I am—for a while!"

"All right," says I. "Here I am in another thousand!"

And I was laughing myself almost to death as I got out my gelding. I called him Vincent and told my servant that I had named the horse after him, and he was the most tickledest man that you ever saw in all your life long days.

Well, there I was in the saddle on Vincent, and, in the meantime, Charlie had had an English saddle strapped on the stallion. In another minute, off we sailed down the road, with Vincent going first. I saw the stallion go back behind me at every stride. Then I turned Vincent loose at full speed to let Charlie really taste my dust and see what a fine horse I'd picked out.

I looked back, after a minute, and nearly dropped out of the saddle, because there was old Cringle rocking along behind me with his head on the hip of Vincent, as comfortable as you please. Before I could get my wits back, Charlie sailed past me calling out:

"Come on, Billy!"

I tried to come on. But Vincent seemed to have ten pounds of lead on each leg, all at once, and Cringle walked away down the road until I gave up.

When it was over, I stopped Vincent and damned him a little—I couldn't help it. He was a fine horse and a stayer, but he was blown by that long sprint against a better horse than himself. You take horses, they're usually that way. They shine till they meet a champion, and then they look like fools. Same way with prizefighters. The second rater looks better than the champion—until the first round begins! And then he seems to be standing still saying his prayers.

Smiling Charlie came back to me, patting the neck of Cringle and talking soft to him, and well he might, because Cringle had just dropped a thousand in cold cash into his pocket. But somehow, you could see that Lamb wasn't thinking about the money. He says:

"The lovely part about it is that this fellow is going to improve at least a hundred per cent, after he's put into training and handled properly. Why, he's as rough as a rake, just now. But what a working stride! What a God-given stride!"

It was, too. It was like wings, you know. And then he broke out:

"I think old Albemarle has lost his heart

as well as his horse. But he certainly lied when he said seventeen!"

He had, too, as we learned afterwards. Lied by ten years, as we all heard.

"Where did you learn about horses?" says I.

"Oh, I just picked it up, while drifting around the world," says Charlie, and smiled at me.

You never could tell what was in his mind, when he smiled. It locked up his mind, and you couldn't read his thoughts a bit.

A little later, the Colonel heard that Charlie had unearthed a diamond among the horses—a diamond in the rough, in more than one way. He came right out to see and to admire.

You would expect that he would pull inside his shell and be offended with Albemarle for having kept such a horse in the dark, but he wasn't a bit.

"Every dog has its tricks," says he to the trainer. "This is a rare one of yours, you rascal."

"Every dog has his day, too," says Albemarle, too heartbroken to be ashamed of what he had done. "And mine has ended."

"Tush!" says the Colonel, and he puts his hand on the shoulder of Albemarle. "Your day is just beginning. You're going to raise finer horses than Cringle ever dreamed of being, and the next time you'll have your pick to keep for yourself!"

Which I sort of admired the Colonel more for that speech than for any of the sharp, smart things that I ever heard him say, before or after.

Baron Wakeness was out with the Colonel to see the horse. He looked him over and admired him a good deal. And he hoped that Cringle would be in shape to try out the speed of the Baron's own best horse which he had brought over from England and which was expected out West at almost any moment.

"What's this, Wakeness?" says the Colonel. "Are you suggesting a match between your crack horse and this old fellow?"

And he patted Cringle's head.

"Certainly not," said the Baron, flushing a little. "Except with a sufficient handicap for Cringle, perhaps. That is, if the idea were attractive to you!"

"But," said the Colonel, "your animal is a stake horse, isn't it?"

"Quite so! Quite so!" says the Baron, flushing a little more. "Of course I only threw out the suggestion. You can handicap any horse to equality."

"Humph!" says the Colonel. "What do you say, Albemarle?"

"With a week's training," says Albemarle, very cold and cool, and looking at the sky-line, "I think you might venture on Cringle, sir."

But under the coolness of his tone, you could guess that he was fair quivering.

I happened to look at Smiling Charlie, just then, and he was watching the Baron the way that a hawk watches a field mouse. There was no doubt that he was seeing something in him. What it was I couldn't guess.

"In that case," says the Colonel, "we'll call it a match, Baron."

"Very well, sir," says Wakeness, smiling at once. "We'll arrange the handicap on your own terms."

"Handicap? Handicap? Not at all! We'll run even, sir. For the honor of Sierra Blanca, if you please!"

"Ah?" says the Baron. "We'll leave it that way, then. But under my protest, of course. Inverary is a proved runner, as you know!"

"We'll call it ten thousand a side, then," said the Colonel. "How does that fit in with your idea?"

There was a spark in the eye of the Baron. His lips set a bit and his nostrils quivered.

"If that pleases you, sir," says he, "of course we'll arrange it in that manner, exactly!"

And he turned his head to give another rather anxious glance to big Cringle.

In that minute the look of the Colonel flashed across to Charlie Lamb, and he nodded a little, as much as to say:

"Write that down among your notes, because it's worth remembering."

There was no need of pointing anything out, however, for Charlie Lamb obviously hadn't missed a trick.

The only trouble was that I didn't see just what the game might be. Something was up that meant a lot to both the Colonel and Lamb, but what the game could be was beyond me.

However, I've always been willing to wait and watch, and I just felt that this was another rumble of thunder while the storm gathered. Pretty soon, we'd be seeing the lightning, too. And maybe it would be striking near-by!

CHAPTER 13

THERE WERE OTHER affairs going on in Stockton House, along with the things that I've been talking about, and, among the rest, there was one thing that mattered a lot more to me than almost anything else. Most likely you would guess right away what it was. Which you would be right, because it was Betty.

There was a lot of things about Betty that I didn't like and that I didn't approve of. She was a terrible flirt. That was one thing. She was one of the world's most champion liars. That was another thing. But the worst of all was that she could bamboozle a man so that he didn't know what to think while he was with her. When he was away, he could see through her pretty easy. But when he was with her, I'll tell you that it was hard to make out what was going on in the head of Betty.

If you had seen her on the morning when she come up to talk to me about the new job, you would of knowed what I mean by all of this.

As a matter of fact, sometimes I wonder

how it comes that the whole world, it don't know about Betty, and how pretty she is, and how gay, because to hear Betty laugh, it would make you happy for a month, even if she was to be laughing at you. And to see Betty just wrinkle her nose at you would be enough to keep you jolly for a whole day. But mostly I notice that women is known in their own home towns, and not outside of them. Because every man thinks that his own women, they lead the world. It's strange how even a wise man would think that way.

But you take Betty, there was something about her. Not that she was the most beautiful girl in the world, but the hotel that she worked for in town put the other hotel nearly on the rocks, because all of the boys, they wanted to eat where they had a chance to watch Betty walking around, and talking, and laughing, and sometimes she would come and put a hand on your shoulder and look down into your eyes.

There is a fish called the electric eel that paralyzes you when you touch it in the water. Betty was like that.

And when she stopped being a waitress at the hotel, the other hotel picked up business right away and got the best half of the trade, because the boys didn't like to go into the place where Betty had been. It seemed sort of empty and useless, without her.

This all I've had to explain, because otherwise maybe you would think that I was more of a fool than I am. Which I am not.

She comes up to my room, this morning, pretty early, before I got my hair combed proper. I felt pretty silly, because my hair is uncommon balky in the morning and makes my head look like an old thistle, where half of the down has already blowed away.

Anyway, she came up and sat down in the big chair by the window and she slumped over to one side of the chair and buried her face in her arms. Her back humped and quivered a little.

I went over and stood beside her.

"Look here, Betty," says I, "do you want love or comfort?"

She let out a gasp.

"Are you crying," says I, "or just trying to cry?"

"Oh, Billy," says she, "you're gonna break my heart!"

"Hey! How come?" I asked her.

"Because you're grinding me down," says Betty.

"Hold on," says I. "I got you your place

out here. Wasn't that giving you a boost in the world?"

"You want to see me a common chamber-maid all the rest of my days!" says Betty, boohooing.

"No," says I, "I want to see you married to myself, and I will hire you a servant, and all that you will have to do will be to sit still and be a fine lady the rest of your life."

"Humph!" says Betty, and she gasped again. "How—how could I marry a man that shows he despises me?"

"Will you stop biting your arm and look me in the eye, Betty?" says I. "Because honest to God, I can't tell when you're crying and when you're laughing at me. You just sound all sort of choked up! Only, you explain to me where I can find the person that ever dared to tell you that I despise you!"

"You would want to lift me up in the world if you loved me," sobs Betty.

"For God's sake, Betty," says I, "how can I lift you higher than to make you my wife?"

"You want to grind me down and break my spirit being a housemaid!" says Betty, "when there's plenty of finer things to do right here!"

"Betty, stop blubbering, and talk like I

can understand you. What else could you do here in Stockton House, will you tell me?"

"There's the job of maid to Miss Olivia!" says she.

It staggered me.

It was true that Miss Olivia's maid had just left, but that maid, she could speak French and other things, and she had read everything, and she was sort of a lady herself. At least, you couldn't tell her apart from one, unless you could look closer than me.

"Why, honey," says I, after I'd settled the idea inside of me, "are you clean rattled?"

"I know! I know!" sobs Betty. "It just shows! You're not happy unless you're keeping me down!"

I hit the ceiling at that. It made me wild. I said:

"Betty, name anything a man can do that I won't do for you!"

Her answer knocked me right out of time.

"Go to Olivia and tell her that I want to be her maid!" says she.

"Me! Go to Olivia! Good God Betty, what have I to do with her? How could I talk to her?"

"I knew it! I knew it!" says Betty. "You just want to keep me down! You don't want me to rise!"

"But Betty, can you speak French? You got no more education than me! Could you be a companion for a baroness?"

"I could try!" sobs Betty. "But you haven't any faith in me!"

It stopped me short. I says:

"Betty, you really want me to make a fool of myself by going to that girl and asking?"

"Yes," says she. "Only, it won't make you a fool. It'll only show me that you love me!"

And she begun to cry so hard that I could hardly think.

"I'll do it! I'll do it!" says I. "Only, stop yapping, will you?"

"Will you do it, Billy darling?"

"I'll do it."

She jumped up and threw her arms around my neck and kissed me.

"Billy, you're such a darling dear," says she. "Will you go right this day?"

"I will," says I, paralyzed, like I was saying a while back.

And Betty went away before I could count ten, and left me wondering why it was that after she's been crying so long and so hard, there was no tear-stains on her face at all, and it wasn't a bit swollen and red. No, I could hear her piping up with a song, as she went down through the house. You couldn't beat that girl. At least, I couldn't.

I was faced with my promise, then, and it was a pretty hard thing for me to do, but that afternoon, I took hold of myself, and I seen Miss Olivia sitting out under a tree in the garden all alone. I walked up to the gate and took off my hat.

"Do you want to see me, Billy?" says she.

"If you please, ma'am," says I, very polite and miserable.

"What's wrong?" says she. And she comes right over to the gate.

"Nothing wrong with me," says I, "but a friend of mine has got a terrible wild idea, and is afraid to talk to you about it, and so I'm elected!"

"Dear me," says Olivia. "What could it be?"

"The idea," says I, feeling hard for the words, "is that she wants to be——"

"What? A lady?" says Olivia, and all at once she smiled at me. "Is it that very pretty girl who's already here?"

"Yes," says I, my Adam's apple beginning to work like a rusty hinge.

"I'm sure that whatever is wanted can be arranged," says Olivia. "Won't you tell me what it is?"

"I mean," says I, "that she's extreme ambitious. And she knows that your maid has just left——"

I stuck.

"Oh," says Olivia.

And she looked at me, rather thoughtful. Then she smiled, and her nose wrinkled a bit, almost like the way that Betty sometimes smiled.

"After all," says Miss Olivia, "why not?"

"She don't speak French nor nothing!" says I.

"Well, my own French conversation is hopeless," says Olivia. "I've given it up, practically. And—I suppose that your friend will really have to have her way!"

And that was all that there was to it.

She said for me to send Betty around to talk to her right away. So I went to see Betty and told her.

"Billy darling," says she, "you can always manage just anything that you put your mind to. You see, I knew that you could do it for me!"

And off she went in a whirl, and from a window I watched her talking with Olivia, until pretty soon I heard them both laughing like a pair of birds, a wonderful thing to see.

And then I knew for sure that Betty had her place.

I felt pretty puffed up by what I had managed to do, because naturally it made me feel that I amounted to something at Stockton House, but just then, that very day, Inverary arrived, and we all had something to think about besides Betty and her affairs.

CHAPTER 14

BY THIS TIME, as I was saying, the Baron's horse, Inverary, had arrived on the train and been brought out to Stockton House. And after we had had a good look at him, we didn't have to wait for the running of the race before we were sure that poor old Cringle was in for a beating.

Mind you that Cringle had been coming along, all of this time, and he had been groomed and worked over and slicked up until now you could see the lines of speed and strength in him, but still, he was nothing compared to that Inverary.

Just the way that a wedge makes you know that it can go through water, so Inverary made you feel that he could fly. He wasn't only a beauty, but he seemed everything that

110

a horse should be for covering of ground, except maybe that he seemed a trifle leggy.

We all looked him over really careful, and no sooner was he there, than the Baron got him out and took him for a little exercise canter.

Inverary had been on the track, first on the flat, and then steeplechasing, and after that, he'd been used as a hunter, by Wakeness. And you never seen anything in your life so pretty as him sailing over the big jumps which the fences and the wild hedges give him around Stockton House. It seemed to me that Cringle was a tramp, by the side of him. And when they danced the pair of them out, side by side, it was wonderful to see what a lot of style that Inverary could show!

The Baron, he proposed, everybody said, that the match should be called off, because now there had been a chance to see what his horse was really like, but the Colonel, he was just as cheerful as ever. He only said:

"Suppose that we make it a rather long trial, if you please?"

"Certainly," says the Baron, "and with a weight no greater than mine in the saddle, distance is really nothing to him. I should warn you of that, in the first place."

"Thank you," says the Colonel. "However, I've always preferred a long race to a short one, because it gives a chance for the ponies to stretch themselves, and the quitters are shown in their true colors. I've always detested a quitter, Wakeness."

The Baron said that he did, too.

"I mean," says the Colonel, with a good deal of point, "the horse or the man that can't stand the rub, but quits in the middle of it—or loses its head!"

"Quite," says the Baron. "I understand perfectly!"

So they laid out the course, and it was a humdinger. It was sketched out in a great circle, all around the house. It was about three miles around, and they was to make it twice. The Baron, he seemed hot for a lot of fences, and finally it was agreed to have four in every mile, which made twenty-four jumps during the course of the whole race.

Twenty-four jumps taken at high speed squeezes a lot out of a horse, of course, and I wondered how poor old Cringle could manage to stand the work. I was given to understand just what the two of them wanted, and a gang of twenty men was turned over to me to put that course in order, with a week to do it in. I slicked it up fine, and every day

Smiling Charlie rode out Cringle and put him over a few of the fences. And every day the Baron, he would come out and exercise his flier.

I had to notice that the Baron didn't take anything for granted. He went over that course with a fine-toothed comb, and he spotted every streak of soft dirt, and every place where the ground was too hard or too rough. And he measured all of the fences, and located the easiest places for clearing them.

You could hardly blame him, because it was a killing course, up hill and down dale, over rough and smooth. It would be easy to watch, too, because the folks could just keep on the inside of the circle, fairly close to the house, and work their horses around slowly, and keep their glasses fixed on the runners, if they wanted to see every detail.

Albemarle was to put up a fine stable boy to ride the old timer, but three days before the race, there was a bomb dropped into the camp, when the stable boy got into the saddle and got out again, without asking to be put down. Then they tried the gamest of the rest of the boys, and they couldn't handle the horse. Then old Albemarle himself damned a little and climbed into the saddle, and doggone me if Cringle didn't pile him on his head quicker 'n you could say Jack Robinson.

I was standing by and offered to take a try, and it was a hard go, but I managed to stick the thing out. Only, they had to give me a range saddle, because I wouldn't try to ride even an old cow with nothing to grip but one of those English saddles.

Well, as things was going along like this, I seemed to be elected for the race. I was about the weight of the Baron, and I was used to riding, of course. I'd laid out the track, and therefore it was taken for granted that I would be accustomed to it. The main thing was, how was I to get accustomed to the horse? I tried hard, but he wouldn't do anything but fight me, except when Smiling Charlie was walking along at his head, and then he was as sweet as pie.

I think that that was the first time that Olivia ever took a good, full look at Smiling Charlie, because, up to that time, she'd been hypnotized, and all that she could see was the lean, aristocratic face of the Baron, that looked like a picture torn out of a history.

But I remember when she came tearing up on her horse, after I had been trying my hand with Cringle, and the old fool had acted up, until Smiling Charlie showed up. She had the Baron and her father with her.

"What *is* it that the man does?" says she.

"You'll have to ask the horse, my dear," says the Colonel, "because it seems to be a secret between the two of them."

I got out of the saddle, about done up, and Cringle leaned up against Charlie, puffing hard.

"Another ride like that and my horse will be beaten before it's entered," says the Colonel, with one of his wicked smiles. "What are you doing to the horse, Lamb?"

"I appeal to his sense of humor, sir," says Smiling Charlie, as serious as could be. "And then he hasn't the heart to fight with me."

The Baron bit his lip and looked sideways at the Colonel, because he was a lot too polite to laugh, but the Colonel seemed as cheerful as ever. It took a good deal to upset him, except when somebody presumed on him.

It was Olivia that got excited. She began to laugh, very soft, and then stopped, and then laughed again, and looked at big Charlie Lamb, and laughed again like a chattering bell, very sweet to hear.

"What a delightful idea!" says Olivia. "And really, old Cringle looks like a smiling horse! Don't you really have some tricks to make him so decidedly a one-man horse, and so quickly!"

"Not at all," says Smiling Charlie, and you can believe that he didn't smile a bit, but was as grave as though his face was made out of stone. "Not at all. But we talk a good deal together."

"Ah," says Olivia. "Of course that's it. You've won his confidence!"

"Perhaps. Or stolen it," says Smiling Charlie.

He seemed to have an answer for everything, that fellow Lamb. And much as I hated him—with that little lump still on the point of my chin where he'd hit me, still I couldn't help sort of admiring him standing there, as wonderful big and powerful and masterful and handsome, being a man, as Olivia was small, and made like a clock, and delicate and dainty, being a woman.

Mostly, it was sort of delightful to see the way that she marked him, seeing him for the first time, and looking deeper and deeper into him, and seeing that there was more to him, every look. Well, it would of beat you, and made you want to bubble over with laughing, too, to watch that girl, she was so plumb beautiful and delightful.

"Stolen his confidence, of course," says

she, and looks to the Baron to have him share her pleasure in this chatter. The Baron laughed, too, but only skin deep.

"But how do you manage to talk to him?" says she, not willing to let the subject drop.

"He understands whispers and nudges very well," says Lamb.

"Oh, I've no doubt," laughs Olivia.

"And then, you see, when I was a young-ster I learned the Indian sign language, and of course Cringle and I get on well in that."

"Of course!" cried Olivia Stockton, and went off into another peal.

Charlie hadn't cracked a smile all the time, and the Colonel was twisting his moustaches. He says:

"And now you have a horse which won't run except with you in the saddle, young man!"

"Infernally awkward!" says the Baron.

But I couldn't help noticing that he didn't offer to call the race off, again!

"Very well," says the Colonel, "I suppose that the only thing to do is to weight your horse up to the riding weight of Lamb, Baron?"

The Baron passed a hand across his face.

"A heavy weight kills Inverary," says he. "Frightfully sorry. Simply frightfully!"

"Ha?" says the Colonel. "And what do you weigh, Wakeness?"

"A hundred and fifty, sir."

"And you, Lamb?"

"Just under two hundred."

"Stripped?"

"Yes."

"The devil!"

"It is the devil," agreed the Baron. But he doesn't offer anything.

"It seems to me," says the Colonel, "that poor old Cringle is handicapped enough without the extra weight. But if extra pounds kill your horse, suppose that we split the difference. You carry twenty-five pounds of lead. That will still leave you twenty-five pounds to the good!"

"Exactly," says Lamb.

The Baron bit his lip again, for another reason, and hung fire, but Olivia broke out thoughtlessly:

"Of course that's perfectly sporting."

Then the Baron had to say:

"I suppose that it will have to be arranged along those lines."

But you could see that he didn't like it. It upset him a good deal. And for the first time I guessed how extremely keen he was to win that race!

It shocked me a little. It was something that I wouldn't have guessed. Of course, though, ten thousand dollars is a good deal of money. But then, it looked like he had the race in his pocket, as you might say! However, things was arranged like that, with poor Cringle to carry twenty-five pounds more than that speed-burner.

I said to Albemarle:

"Now you'll sweat, old fellow, and wish that you hadn't put up that five hundred on Cringle!"

He was sweating, all right. But he set his jaw and wouldn't give way. He says:

"It's a long race, and you have to remember that these horses are not quite clean bred. There's a dash of Indian blood in 'em, a long distance back! And they're apt to wear like hickory!"

CHAPTER 15

HAVE YOU EVER had much to do with hickory? It bends hard, and even when it breaks, it breaks mean, and slow, and turns into splinters at the break, like the end of a broom, and there's no doubt that old Albemarle had actually bred some of that strain

119

into the horses. They were tough as could be, and at the time when other strains were just thinking of quitting, they were only beginning to run, as you might say.

I remembered that, and when I looked over old Cringle again, and calculated his chances, I took the toughness of him into account, and I looked at the power in his shoulders, and the driving strength in his quarters, which looked able to shove tons of weight across fences all day long. However, then I stepped out and saw Inverary working out with his scale weight of a hundred and seventy-five pounds, and he managed it as slick as you please.

I wanted to bet on Cringle. My heart was all with the home horse, and besides, I was a little cut up about the way that the Baron had acted on the question of the weights. However, there was no use throwing money away, and so I said to Smiling Charlie. He was a cool devil, as usual.

"I don't know," said he, "but what odds do you think one could get on the chances of my horse?"

"Three to one, I suppose," said I.

"Short odds, short odds, kid," said Smiling Charlie. "Considering that they're running the old plough-horse against a stake racer, I'd call three to one very short odds. A man with blood might run those odds up to five or ten to one, and still feel that he was putting his money in the bank. But I'll tell you what, my son, I'll take three hundred of your money against a hundred of mine."

I closed the bet, then and there, but afterwards, I was a little uneasy. It wasn't that I had any doubt about the superior speed of the English horse. And it wasn't that I doubted that Wakeness was a fine, brave, steady rider. But there was another thing that had to be counted in the race, and that was Smiling Charlie himself. You never could tell about that man. I'd had him under the nose of my gun, and I'd waked up on the ground, with him gone. And after that, I'd seen other things that he could do. So had the other people in the Sierra Blanca, and there wasn't one out of hundreds that would of put much past Charlie Lamb.

He was the sort of a man that did what he started out to do, and he usually did it so that he made it look easy. If you saw another man doing tricks with a rifle, you'd find him all tense and unsteady with the effort, but when Charlie tried anything, he did it so smooth and frictionless that it was wonderful to watch. The same with a rope. He could make a rope tie itself in knots in mid air and untangle them before the same rope touched the ground. But when he was putting a rope on a cow, it never looked as though Charlie was showing any particular skill. You would hardly say that he was daubing on the lariat in fine style. You would simply feel that the fool cows was running themselves into the noose of their own accord. And after you'd been living with Charlie for a few days, you began to feel that he was just lucky. Just as though he had been given everything, and that he didn't have to worry about his life.

I mean this way, for instance. You take me, I'm pretty strong. Nothing to shout about, but able to stand up and take care of myself with other men as they come. But every bit of muscle that I've got, I had to work for it. I've bucked hay, baled and loose. I've sweated on a baler, and I've put in hours in the hell of a hay mow, when you're up against the roof, and the hay dust is choking you, and the sun has turned that roof to a blazing fire just above your head. And I've slung a single jack and a double jack in mines, and I've broken all kind of ground, and worked in lumber camps, swinging an ax, and done a lot of other miserable hard things to do. But you take Charlie, you could see that there was hardly anybody in the world as strong as he was, and yet he'd never done anything in his life that he didn't want to do. He had taken things easy, and everything had come his way. He was given that strapping big body of his all equipped with the same sort of muscles that a panther cat has. And if you've ever noticed, there's a difference between the muscles of a cat and the muscles of a dog. A cat can be killed by a dog. But you make the cat just half the size of a dog, and then see which one is going to win.

Take a good, upstanding, seventy-five pound fighting dog, and then match it up with a forty pound lynx. Did you ever see a forty pound lynx? Well, it's a whale—a giant of its kind. And I can promise you that it would tear the innards out of any dog in the world. Or take a big Great Dane; it might weigh a hundred and seventy-five pounds. So does a leopard. And how many Great Danes would you turn loose in the ring with a leopard? I would hate to see the fight, because I love dogs.

Now it was the same way with Charlie. I mean, that he done things just so easy that you would never believe it. They put him up on a tough, mean, half-broken roan horse that was famous for the hardness of its mouth. Nobody would touch that horse except with a heavy Spanish curb—a regular torture bridle. But Charlie, he took a plain, straight snaffle. All he done was to put on double reins, so that they would stand the strain. And after he'd been riding that roan for five minutes, it was the tenderest mouth horse that you ever saw in your life, and ever after, a baby could of pulled it right back on its haunches. Because it never felt a hand on the reins without fearing that it might have the jawbreaking strength of Charlie Lamb behind it.

I saw Charlie Lamb lift a two hundred and seventy-five pound bale of hay with one hand and throw it up four high with his hook. If you've ever handled baled hay, you know what that means. But you never would of picked him out in a crowd as being anything but the most graceful man there.

I mean, altogether, that after I had come to know Charlie Lamb pretty well, I was fixed in my mind that, one of these days, him and me would have to have our fight out, but all the time I kept hoping that the date would be postponed for a long time— to let me practice up. But even while I was slinging my Colts every day, and working out with my rifle, I had a sneaking idea that I would never be able to stand up to Charlie, man to man.

That was what kept the odds down on the race. Everybody in Sierra Blanca had either come out to see the horses training, or else they had been on hand, and heard others tell about how they looked. It seemed hard to believe that Cringle could win, but I knew that the Sheriff, who was a pretty shrewd fellow, and who ought to of knowed a good deal about Charlie Lamb, had got down half a dozen bets that added up to nearly two thousand dollars. He got odds of between three and four to one, and there was others in Sierra Blanca was willing to back Charlie, no matter what horse he might sit on.

So, as the day of the race came, I found myself sort of edgy. Not that I minded losing three hundred dollars in a lump, now that I was making so much money regular, but because I didn't want to see Charlie distinguish himself none too much. I still wore that lump on my jaw.

The Baron, it seemed to me, was getting a little nervous, too. It was said—and I don't know how true it was—that he had put ten thousand pounds (which means around fifty thousand iron men, if you don't happen to know) with a commission man in town, and that he had put it out at odds of anywhere from three to five to one.

And that gave the Baron his tense look. He could stand a ten thousand dollar side bet, but fifty thousand maybe would strain even a Baron a good deal. And you could hardly wonder.

This was the way that the stage was all set when the day of the race came, and the Baron and Charlie got onto their horses with something like two thousand people to watch the race. Most of them had to watch the race from the outside of the circle, but there was about a hundred on horses inside the circle, ready to ride in the short swing around the house and the grounds, and so keep a close eye on the pair all the time. And nearly all of us had glasses. The Colonel had seen to that.

CHAPTER 16

I GOT AN IDEA of what the Colonel's thought was just before the race come off. And it was a real sassy, nasty idea, at that. He comes up to me and he says:

"You have a glass, Jacks?"

"I have, sir," says I.

"My daughter doesn't want to be bothered with one," says he. "Because she wants to keep her hands free for managing her horse, and she thinks that she can see clearly enough. However, it may be that the race will turn out quite close. And if old Cringle can manage to get up close enough to give Inverary a challenge, perhaps my girl will really want to see how Wakeness is riding. In that case, you might keep close to her and hand her the glasses to look through. You understand?"

I looked straight back at him and kept my eyes as blank as possible, because I could see what was in his mind. He was a foxy one. In the first place, all the fuss about that race, and the money that was bet on it, and the test of the Stockton stables, didn't amount to anything to him, though he pretended it did. But what he wanted was to convince Charlie that the Baron was a poor sport, and after he's convinced him of that, he had another idea—maybe he could show his girl that her Baron was not quite perfect!

That was why he wanted me handy with the field-glasses.

I understood, but I tried to make him think that I wasn't bothering my head about such things at all. I just took the extra pair of glasses that he handed to me, and I set sail to keep close to the girl.

It was a grand day for the race. The sky had some big sailing white clouds in it, that went voyaging across like ships, with all sails set. But, what was more important, the air was cool, with a little breeze setting in from the north and west. The Baron had spoke about the hot Western sun maybe would be too much for a horse raised in the bracing air of England, and used to racing in it, but he wouldn't have no excuse like that, just now.

Before the start, the Baron come up and spoke to Olivia.

"I'm like the poor girl in King John," says she. "I don't know which side I should put my sympathies on."

"Now, what might she mean by that?" says I to Dick Wace.

"Shut up, kid, and don't show your ignorance," says Dick. "That's Mr. Shakespeare that she's referring to."

And then Cringle went by and got a cheer from everybody. He didn't go fussing and prancing by, the same as Inverary did, but with his head stuck out straight, switching his tail at the flies, and cocking an ear back, now and then, to listen to what his boss was saying to him. And Charlie was talking all the time!

They got down to the start, where the Sheriff saw them lined up, and fired the starting gun. The start didn't amount to much, but we couldn't help being pleased, even in such a long race as that, to see that old Cringle was away first, and on the inside of the circle. He floated across the first couple of fences in perfect style, and it seemed to me that, barring accidents, all he had to do was to keep on like that, and the race would be over. Then I took a look through the glasses at Inverary, and I felt relieved a good deal, because I could see that the Baron had him under strong wraps, that was nearly pulling him double. And just then there was a squeal of excitement from Olivia, for the Baron had taken off some of the wraps, and that long-legged English horse, he just floated up and past Cringle without half trying.

And there he went half a dozen lengths in the lead! The boys let out a groan, but the Colonel said:

"It's a six mile race, and it's not over yet!"

I fixed the glasses on Charlie. He was steady as a rock, his talking to Cringle going on all of the time. Then I looked at the Baron just in time to see him glance back and then laugh, and take another pull at the head of his racer.

Cringle was a good horse. But here was the difference between a good horse and a great one. You sort of felt that. Because they hadn't yet gone far enough for the extra weight to of killed off Cringle.

They wheeled around the circle the first time, both of them turning black and shining with sweat, and things was getting sort of monotonous, because their positions never changed a bit, and when they come to fences, they sailed over them like nothing at all. There was nothing that compared with Inverary getting over an obstacle, because he sailed high, wide and handsome.

But old Cringle, when he come along, he just bobbed over each hedge and fence and ditch with barely enough to spare, dragging his heels through everything where it was safe to drag them, and fair brushing his belly on the tops of the thickets. He was over a fence and on the ground running again so quick you could hardly see what he'd done. It wasn't a beautiful thing to watch, but I must say that it didn't look like he was wasting much strength at the jumps!

Well, they had turned the first three miles, and then they peeled over another mile and a half, when Olivia cries:

"There he goes!"

I looked and there was the Baron with all the wraps off of Inverary, just fairly letting him sail along.

You could see what he meant, because he'd been sitting back, riding with a pull, all of the time, but now he meant to go to work and show the Colonel just what sort of class there was in Inverary.

I laughed, and then I heard Betty yip:

"Go it, Cringle! Good old boy!"

I looked at her and frowned, but she was too excited to notice me. And then a shout went up from the others, and I stared back at the race.

Well, it was worth seeing, just then, because, though Inverary was cutting loose, Charlie Lamb was sitting well forward, swinging himself with the stride of Cringle, the way that he had been doing all through the race, and that horse was keeping right up with Inverary!

By that time the English horse had an advantage of about twelve or fifteen lengths, but he hadn't been able to stretch it out any. And there was Cringle, plodding along the same as ever, not seeming to be running any harder.

But when you looked closer, you could see a difference, all right. I never seen such strides. He was hopping along like he had wings to help him between the spots where he hit the ground. Yes, it was a right pretty thing to see.

But in the meantime, there was only a last mile to go, and the fifteen lengths began to amount to something. Only one thing you could be sure of, and that was that, with the extra pounds that he was packing, Cringle was not disgraced. Not by a jugful!

However, I let out a cheer for Inverary, seeing him clipping along so fine. Flecked with foam and running with sweat, still he seemed to be running as strong as ever. And his ears was pricking, which made my three hundred seem safer than in a bank.

However, the race wasn't quite over. No, along comes Charlie Lamb and settles a bit lower to his work, and begins to rise from the saddle, and as he did it, Cringle began to gain!

Yes, sir, it was a hard thing to see and to believe, but there the old rascal was creeping up on Inverary with every stride. He had his ears back, but that simply seemed to mean that his fighting, mustang streak of blood was up in him. His mouth was wide open. He would of been a terrible mean horse to see charging down at you, at that time.

And still he ate up the distance until he wasn't more than two lengths behind Inverary.

And a good quarter of a mile to go.

Then the Baron seemed to wake up. I suppose that he'd been sailing along thinking about the money that was going to be bulging his pocket before nightfall of that day. But now he jerked his head around, took one look at Cringle, and snatched out his whip.

I seen that the time had come when I was to do what the Colonel wanted. I handed the glasses to Miss Olivia.

"Maybe you'd like to see the Baron ride it out?" says I.

She was so excited that she snatched at them without saying a word and clapped them to her eyes.

I turned and took a squint at the Colonel. Well, sir, that old rascal, he was sitting up there on his horse with his glass cocked up against the pommel of the saddle, and looking around over the field, something like a general at a battle, and from his face you would of said that the battle was going just the way that he had planned to have it go.

And sometimes, he smiled to see the way that the folks outside of the fences was hollering and throwing up their hats and yelling like mad because Cringle was making such a wonderful run. And sometimes, he turned his head and let his hawk's eye rest for a minute on Miss Olivia. And then there was just a trace of a frown on his forehead.

But the Colonel's frown meant the same as a smile, in any other man!

But by about this time, I didn't give a rap what other folks might be thinking about, because what was commencing to worry me was whether or not my three hundred dollars was going to be safe. And I clapped the glasses to my eyes and I kept them there until the finish, while I watched that pair of horses strung out straight as a string, and rushing for the flag.

CHAPTER 17

THERE WAS AN English flag on the one side of the finish, and there was a big American flag on the other side, and, bunched around that finish, there was a couple of thousands of the wildest gents that ever walked, all whooping it up for Cringle.

There was still a furlong to run, and that infernal Cringle had his head on the hip of the English horse. But it was a caution to see the way that the Baron was riding.

I was interested in the saving of my three hundred dollars, as maybe you've been able to guess for yourselves, by this time. But just the same, I wasn't any too pleased to see the way that the Baron was lighting into Inverary. If the winning of that race was hidden away any place in the innards of the thoroughbred, you could make sure that the Baron was going to have it out where folks could see it.

His whip came down with every stride that Inverary made, and the flank of the racer was all covered with a growing pink blotch, where the spur had been rammed home again and again, as deep as it would go.

I have seen Mexicans and Indians race their horses. But you don't mind, so much, when they're doing it. It was different to see a white man acting like that! Because, after all, money is only money, and a horse is always a horse.

But the insides of Inverary was being torn out. His mouth was wide open with foam

135

dripping. His ears was flat back, and that whip was slashing him harder and harder at every stride. Poor Inverary!

And still that devil of a Cringle was sneaking up little by little and inch by inch, and gaining and gaining, until his head was at the hip, the saddle, the shoulder, the neck——

Wouldn't that infernal finish post ever come? I never have seen such long seconds in my life!

But fifty yards from the finish, it seemed to me that the head of Inverary went up and began to bob like a cork. And that instant he seemed to go staggering, and Cringle went by to win by half a length.

I couldn't believe my eyes. Olivia was what I first looked at. And her face was as white as you please. I looked at the Colonel, and nobody could of told that he had proved that his string of horses was as good as could be found in the world—at least, for long distance racing! His face was just a polite blank.

As we started down to reach the horses, Betty came by me with a rush and slapped me on the back.

"Wasn't it great?" says she.

And her face was bright and shining enough to make you pretty near agree with anything that she wanted to say. However, I was three hundred dollars out, and that stuck in my crop like a burr.

Well, we rushed down to the finish, and there we saw the Baron just in the act of dismounting, while Charlie Lamb was already down and walking Cringle up and down.

I can tell you that though the thoroughbred from England looked the worst beat during the race, it was Cringle that seemed about dead after the finish. You could never believe that a horse could be so tired without actually falling down dead. He staggered along up and down behind big Charlie Lamb, his ears flopping, and his knees sagging, and Charlie Lamb all the time talking to him. Nobody else could get a word out of Charlie, and when the Colonel came up to congratulate him on the wonderful ride that he had made, he just turned his back on his boss and began to rub Cringle down.

Olivia came up, just then. Says the Colonel in a voice loud enough for anyone to hear:

"I don't exactly understand how you could have made that ride without a spur or a whip, Lamb!"

And Charlie Lamb answered:

"Well, that's a secret between me and

Cringle. I say, half a dozen of you turn to, here, and help me swab the old fellow down, will you?"

There were plenty of willing hands for that, you can bet, because after the way that they had seen old Cringle run, I suppose that half of the men in the county were willing to die for that old timer. And as a matter of fact, I think that they might have counted me in the list.

I'd lost some money, but I'd seen a dead-game horse at work running, and that was worth a good deal to me. More, somehow, than I had counted on before. But seeing him close up, with the sweat running off of him, and him all done up, it rather went to your heart.

The thing that made me the maddest, was that Charlie should of come out on the top of the heap, so high. Up to that day, most people had been saying that it was a howling shame for the Colonel to import his fighting men, and specially a no account fellow like Charlie Lamb, when there was plenty of the right sort to be had already right in Sierra Blanca. And then it was said, in addition, that the Colonel had had to spend several thousands to square the old accounts that Charlie had against him in various parts of the country, and it was wondered why the Colonel should have done it; but after the exhibition that Charlie gave of bang-up riding, on this day, there was nobody to ask any more questions, and they all agreed that for a fine rider and a clean horseman, Charlie Lamb was the king. He was pretty near more important than the Colonel, for that one day.

I made it a point to stick rather close to the Colonel while he was around Charlie, during the swabbing down of Cringle, and I managed to hear Lamb say:

"Worthy of her? Not worthy to so much as own a good dog!"

And I knew that the Colonel had made his point.

After that, I would of been pretty glad to see what was to happen in the near future, and I felt that a man didn't have to be any fortune teller to guess that Charlie would soon be playing his hand with Olivia as high as possible.

As for the Baron, his stock was only down for a moment, as you might say. The moment that he was off his horse, he waltzed up to Charlie and congratulated him in fine style because of the fine horse he had been riding, and the fine way he had handled him.

I was curious to see how Charlie would

receive him, but Charlie he had his smile ready, as usual, when it came to the pinch, and he merely said:

"I'm afraid that you took the thing too much for granted, sir. And you left the speed of your horse behind you when you kept him under such a strong pull for so long."

"Very likely! Very likely!" says the Baron, and seemed rather pleased to hear it.

So that my own impression of him took a jump upwards. I felt that a man who could stand such money losses as he had stood on this day without flinching, must be the right sort, after all. It was only when I turned and looked at Inverary that I wanted to change my mind again. He was covered with welts on the shoulder where the whip had cut home, and both of his flanks was stripped and stabbed by the spurs, so deep that he was still bleeding a trifle an hour after the race was finished.

Now, I don't think that the others paid much attention to these details, because it would simply of looked, to most, as though the Baron had just ridden his horse out with a stirring finish, but the Colonel had managed things so that the attention of me and Charlie Lamb had been focused on the job.

It wasn't so much what had happened as

it was that the Colonel had prophesied the thing. That was what made it bad. He had said: "This fellow Wakeness is no good, and I'll prove it to you by showing you what he does when he comes to a pinch in a race."

And what the Colonel had said had worked out to a T. So that it looked as though he must have had the inside information; and I, for one, began to discount everything favorable that I had known or thought of Baron Wakeness before.

But mostly I wondered at Colonel Stockton. The longer I stayed around that man the more I felt that I could understand why it was that he was the owner of Sierra Blanca. All that was strange, really, was simply that he didn't own about half the world besides.

Well, the great race was over, and Cringle was recovered, at last, and went up the hill, walking behind Charlie like a dog at the heels of its master, and I heard Miss Olivia say:

"Isn't it touching, really, to see that a common cowpuncher has such a wonderful ability to control a horse—and make a horse love him!"

And at that the Baron chipped in with:

"One of the finest exhibitions of riding that I've ever seen. Inverary was all out and had no excuses—except that perhaps I kept him in my lap through the middle of the race when he wanted to gallop. I can't think that it was only Cringle that beat us. It was the man on Cringle's back. And, as Olivia says, it's a wonderful thing that an ordinary cow-puncher should have been able to ride such a race."

"You and Olivia each make a very serious mistake," says the Colonel gravely.

"Really?" says the Baron.

"Certainly. For you must never imagine that Charles Lamb is a common or an ordinary man. I've known a great many people in my life, and I should say that Charlie Lamb is as far as possible from anything common. I think he's the most unusual person I've ever known!"

Perhaps you've guessed that the Colonel didn't often praise people, to any extent. And I don't suppose that he would have done it that day. But if the race hadn't attracted Olivia's attention to Smiling Charlie strongly enough, he wanted to put in his recommendation to make the matter sure.

I could see what he was driving at, and I almost smiled when I saw Olivia turn again in the saddle to look after Cringle and Charlie. But I had to shiver, too. Because though the Colonel could control everyone else in the world, I wondered what real luck he would have when it came to controlling Charlie Lamb.

It's easy to drop a match in dry grass on the prairie. But it's hard to pay for the consequences.

CHAPTER 18

ABOUT THIS TIME, I was feeling pretty much on top of the world, as you might say. I was sitting pretty, with a perfectly good job that brought me in four thousand a year—more than I'd ever dreamed before of having. I had a horse under me that beat the style of any horse that I'd ever hoped to own. I was looked up to and respected a lot by all of the punchers that had knowed me in the old days before the Colonel discovered that I was on the map, and in addition I had fine quarters that not even a prince would of turned up his nose at, and though now and then some of the boys had a nasty job handed him to do, our work came only at wide intervals.

We never had to ride night-herd and sing the cows to sleep. We never had any of the sweaty, dirty work of a round-up. We never had to take orders from some pernickety straw-boss. But the jobs that we had to handle was all the sort of things that you would be glad to tell your grandchildren about. Yes, or anybody's grandchildren.

We had only one boss, and that was the Colonel himself, except when he had to send out more than one of us at a time. And that didn't happen very often. When a party of us went out, one of us was always the commander—but who would of minded being under a man like Dick Wace, say? But, usually, there was never more work than the Colonel thought that one of his men could tackle. He considered that any one of us was good enough to eat up three other men, and he acted on that principle day in and day out. And the queer thing was that other folks was willing to take his word for it. For my part, I was as happy as though I was really three men rolled into one. But, the best part of all, I had Betty in the same house with me, and sort of under my thumb.

It's all very well to leave a girl free and easy. But Betty was always free enough and easy enough. And now that I had her at the house of the Colonel, it pleased me no end to have her look up to me. I'd found her her place in the house to begin with and then it was me that had got her the job as maid to Miss Olivia, though that wasn't hardly a job—it was just a cinch. She could loaf around with nothing on her mind. She was dressed like a queen in clothes that Olivia was tired of, and Miss Olivia herself was too like a doggone saint to ever ask that girl to do anything low or ornery.

So, when I met up with Betty, here or there, you could be sure that she would have a smile for me. And it was always "Billy darling!" when she talked to me. Not so bad I can tell you. Not that I took it altogether serious. I wasn't fool enough to think that Betty meant everything that she said, by a long margin, but as long as she would keep on looking up to me as the boss, until a day come along when I could marry her and have her for keeps, I didn't much care. Once she was roped and tied, I could laugh at the world. So I talked to her about it, and she agreed that we had to get married and she said we had better wait until the next spring, because that was the best time to get married, and maybe the Colonel wouldn't like to have me get married before that date.

I agreed that that was sensible, all right, and we left the matter like that, but I sort of shied when she said that she wanted to keep the engagement secret. However, I put up with that because you know how a pretty girl is. She doesn't want the rest of the boys to stop paying her attention until she's really delivered for keeps. So I swallowed down the things that I had thought of saying, and let the matter go as though I didn't care, much. In the meantime, I was watching for Charlie Lamb to start playing his hand with Olivia, according to his agreement with the Colonel, but though I watched and listened all of the time I couldn't see or hear anything that was really worth repeating. Then one day I says to Betty:

"Where's Miss Olivia?"

"Down riding by the river," says she.

"With the Baron, I suppose?" says I.

"No," says she. "The Baron was writing letters pretty busy, so she took Charlie Lamb along."

"Ah!" says I.

"What are you 'ah'ing' about?" says she.

"Nothing," says I.

"Why shouldn't she take Charlie along after him turning out such a real hero in that horse race?"

"Well," says I, "horse race heroes ain't hard to find, you know."

"Except on the day of a race," says she, very sharp, "and then they ain't on hand."

And she threw a mean look at me, but I didn't mind, because you know how it is with a girl. She's always running down her best man until it comes time for a marriage.

"Besides," says she, "what more proper man could she find than Charlie Lamb? Are you jealous of him?"

"You mean," says I, "that I ain't got the face to be jealous of Charlie Lamb?"

"Never mind what I mean," says Betty, on her high horse.

It annoyed me a mite, to hear her talk up like this, because I'd had her eating out of my hand for so long. And I says:

"Well, the time might come when folks wouldn't be so proud and fond of sending Charlie Lamb off riding alone with a girl!"

She give me a sort of frowning look.

"What do you mean? You don't dare to mean anything wrong," says she, "about a angel like Miss Olivia!"

"Sure I don't," says I, "except that she's human the same as other girls that I've heard of that have made Charlie Lamb make eyes at 'em!"

"I don't know what you mean," says Betty.

"I didn't guess that you would," says I.

"Remembering sometimes is a right mean job, even for a man on horseback."

"You're referring," says she pretty icy, "to the day that I fed the poor, hungry fellow?"

"Aw, I ain't referring to you only," says I, "but to the hundreds of girls that has broken their hearts over him."

"I could laugh at you, Billy," says she, "if I didn't feel a sort of pity for you."

"Well," says I, "I suppose you know better than me about Charlie?"

"Be that as it may," says she, very lofty.

"And where might you of found out, Betty, if you're so wise?"

"What about finding out from his own lips?" says she.

"He admitted that he wasn't a low down philanderer, I suppose," I remarked, very sarcastic.

"There is something that you oughtn't to be," says Betty, "and that's sarcastic, because it doesn't become you none. Not with your face! But I don't mind telling you that Charlie Lamb is a terrible misunderstood man, and that he's never tried to deceive no good girl."

"Well," says I, "I suppose that you got all of the facts and that there ain't any use for me to talk and give figures, because I've always noticed that the figures you've got is worth ten times the ones that I know. But I would like a lot for you to explain to me why it was that he was drove out of four states by gents that wanted to lynch him because of him breaking the hearts of nice girls."

"It's false!" says she.

"How come?" says I. "What was it that drove him up here, in the first place, into the Sierra Blanca? And didn't the Sheriff go back over his record and find out that all his life he'd been just drifting around and making love to pretty girls?"

"I don't believe a word of it!" says Betty. "Just because some brazen hussies would throw themselves at his handsome head——"

"All right," says I, "but I've heard you say a dozen times that where there's a lot of smoke there's apt to be some fire, too. I would like to have you remember that old moth-eaten saying of yours, just now!"

"You are simply amusing yourself with gossip," says she, getting a little pale.

"And right this minute," says I, "I'll bet you dollars to doughnuts that he's sitting his horse under the shade of some tree beside the river and telling Miss Olivia how his life has been turned into hell, and how the pretty girls has all united to drive him around the country, telling fibs about him, while the only thing that he wants is to find just one girl that is quiet and faithful and gentle and true that can understand him, and maybe let him offer her his heart——"

She busts out at me suddenly:

"Billy Jacks, I hate you, simply!"

"Hold on, Betty," says I. "Why should you hate me for telling you the facts about Charlie?"

"She would slap his face," says Betty. "She would have her father shoot him!"

"There ain't likely to be more than one man in the world that's got the nerve ever to stand up to Charlie Lamb," says I.

"Do you mean yourself, by that?" says she, very wicked. "Because he would eat you up—bah!"

"What's got you so excited?" I asked her. "Who's stepped on your toes?"

"Miss Olivia!" says she to herself. "No— he wouldn't dare!"

"What is there that he wouldn't dare?" says I. "He dared to laugh at the Colonel and chase around over the Sierra Blanca for weeks just for the fun in the thing, didn't he?"

150

She took a thought about that, for a time. Then:

"I never heard anybody talk so disgusting as you, Billy Jacks," says she, and all at once she flings around and goes bolting out of the room where we was.

It surprised me a good deal and I sat down and smoked a pipe over it, but the pipe didn't appear to do me no good at all. There was nothing in it but smoke.

However, I've made it a rule that when any woman upsets you, even your mother, you mustn't take it too serious. Because women, they ain't serious. They're just sort of narrow-gauge, you understand?

However, I was in love with Betty, and one thing that worried me was wondering whether or not I would be able to handle her until the next spring without her raising ructions about nothing, like she'd done to-day.

And five minutes later I got marching orders from the Colonel. Three reservation Indians had gotten away and come through the mountains and they was living high, wide and handsome on whatever they needed. I was to go and round them up.

CHAPTER 19

DID IT EVER happen to you on some dark, windy, December night, when you was a kid, that there was a spooky sound in the attic, and your father says:

"Son, take a lantern upstairs and see what's moving around up there——?"

Or did you ever go out with your best girl, and a runaway horse come smashing wild down the street with a screaming girl falling out of the saddle, and your girl says:

"Oh that some brave, brave man would stop that terrible brute——?"

But you can believe me when I say that runaway horses and spooky sounds in the attic is nothing to stop compared with three Indians off of a reservation, all hell-bent for death or fun, because if they wasn't hell-bent that way, they would of stayed at home.

They have educated Indians up into football teams and such civilized kinds of murder, these days, but in the old times of the reservations there was no way that they was able to take out their meanness, except by gambling and throwing knives at a line, and so they sat around and shivered and damned the Great Father back in Washington, and stewed around and got up a fine heat dreaming about the good old days when grandpa White Eagle, and uncle Charging Bull had used to come swooping down on the white settlements and never go home without a half dozen good scalps—some of them made of nice long, silky, shiny hair.

And finally the pot would boil over, as you might say, and three or four of the wildest and the meanest of those redskins, and the most straight-shootinest, would swipe a rifle and start out to get famous and die young.

These bucks had sashayed across about five hundred miles of prairie and mountain, and finally they come down into the Sierra Blanca and there they settled, like folks that said that that country was good enough for them. Well, and it was a good enough hole-in-the-wall country, at that. Those Indians had three fine, up-to-date Winchesters, besides which they had a plenty of good ammunition, and they had the best horses that they could pick up in their five hundred miles of traveling, all Indians being nacheral stealers of horses. On top of all that, they'd had a rattling good time, and they hadn't taken any scalps, but they had gone into a house and killed an old settler and murdered his wife and three children of his son. That made five scalps that they *might* of taken if they had been real ambitious, but they wasn't. They only wanted a little blood, now and then.

So the Sheriff's posse run them up into the mountains, and there the head of that posse was blown to kingdom come, by those three repeating Winchesters. Two men died and seven more was bad hurt.

So that it was plain those red men knew that, when they was cornered finally, it would pay them to die on the spot rather than linger things out. Because they had done more harm than their three murdering lives could ever repay ten times over!

I heard all of these details from the Sheriff, and old Steve Ross says:

"I would like to help you out, old timer, with a few men to round up those skunks, but it ain't according to the way the Colonel wants the game played!"

"No," says I, "I wouldn't want any help to round up a handful of copper scum, like that!"

I talked up big, y'understand, so's I would maybe hearten myself some, but my knees, they was no stronger than the little finger of a week-old baby.

Then I oiled up my guns and cleaned 'em and started for the danger line, and maybe it should of done me good to see the way that folks pointed me out; and when I got into the danger region maybe it would of made some men feel fine to have gents walk up to 'em and say, "God bless you, old fellow! And thank God that Sierra Blanca has got men like you in it to clean up their messes!" But it didn't hearten me none at all, because all the time, I was daydreaming about what a pity it was that Betty wouldn't even be a widow, on my account. And the worst of it was that I couldn't really tell whether she'd be glad or sorry when she heard about the news of my death. No, I couldn't tell. That girl, she was always the buried card to me. The buried card—in the other man's hand. You keep worrying a lot more about it than about all the ones that lie face-up.

I rode on, feeling certain that some minute three red devils would rush me from behind some hedge. Or, better still, three thirty-two caliber bullets would go through my head and heart and backbone—smack, crackle, bang!

Yes, I was feeling pretty neighborly with the devil and dear departed, I can tell you. And mostly, I wished that the Colonel had dropped dead just before he spotted me, that day when he offered me the horse.

Anyway, here I was on the spot, and without courage to turn back, when the thing happened. You wouldn't believe how it happened. It was like this. I was having bedtime coffee at the house of a farmer, and he was telling me how, not a mile away, six men had run the three red men into a covert three days before, and how three of the six was shot, but none fatal, thank God, and the other three had remembered that it was about chore time at home—and while this was going on, thank God that the Colonel had sent one of his right hand men to fix everything—and what a comfort it was to have such a man as me under his roof, which his wife and three kids, they would sleep tonight for the first time in a week—God bless me again!

I was listening to this here talk when the back door of that kitchen opened with a sigh and three copper-faced devils, uglier than the heart of hell, come side-stepping in, with their rifles ready, and the first of them was a plumb educated Indian because he hollers:

"Hands up, you white swine!"

And he turns the muzzle of that rifle straight at us. But only with half an eye, because the other eye was lingering over the good things that was simmering for my supper on the top of the old stove.

I have always believed in two revolvers in the place of one, because revolver work is sort of like guess work. Some guess close and some guess wide, but it's always better to have two guesses than one. And just as that copper-face barked out his command, I slipped out my pair of guns from my holsters, which I always wear extra low, and without bothering to lift those guns above the table, I slid down underneath, and with my neck on the edge of the chair, I fanned both of those guns at the three of them.

The educated Indian had time to pump a bullet through the side of the house where I had been leaning a minute before, and then he folded his hands over the place where his stomach had been, and sat down. I mean, two forty-five caliber slugs had tore most of that section of him away.

Indian number two yelled and started to shoot, too. But he got his right between the eyes, which was a couple of feet higher than I thought I was aiming.

And Indian number three, he leaped back for the door, and I got a holler of pain out of him as he went through.

I sort of half scrambled and half rolled into that doorway, and, lying on my belly, with both gats stretched out before me, I seen that red man heading for the tall timber and not more than twenty-five yards away.

There was a broad, bright moon blowing up like a soap-bubble over the tops of the trees, and if I had missed such a target at such a distance by such a light, and with two good guns to work on it, I would of been a candidate for the booby class, and no mistake. Well, I didn't miss. He had gone twenty-five measure paces when I seen him. The next time he hit the ground was five paces further ahead, but his soul had departed this earth while he was still in the air.

After that, we all sat around and fed the Indian without a stomach whisky, and he got happier and happier till the whisky jug was empty. Then he went on the long trail after his pals.

After that, I went to bed, and when I woke up about noon, from a sweet dream of Betty with a golden ring on a finger of her left hand, I found that I was a hero, and that there was about a hundred people in that farmhouse to tell me so.

I let them talk. I felt sort of sneaking, because I was the only man in the world that could tell how really scared I had been when those three red ghosts slipped into the kitchen. But that was not the first time that self-defense was called heroic, so far as I can judge. But there is no time for a man to act up proud and bold like the times when he feels that he's a cornered rat.

Anyway, the red peril was over, and I started back for Stockton House hoping that I had finished that year's work, and wondering how young a man could retire from that business for a measly four thousand dollars a year!

No, sir, there was never anybody that despised easy money as much as I did on the way back to the Colonel after I'd proved myself a hero. But on the way, things sort of changed me.

You see, we think of ourselves half by what we know ourselves to be and half by what other people tell us that we are, and it takes a pretty good man to untangle one idea from the other.

By the time that I'd had my hand shaken five hundred times and had five hundred slaps on the back, and five hundred drinks offered to me, I begun to feel that what was three or four redskins between a real man and his friends? Why, hardly worth mentioning! And I'd begun to think that the way that I'd slid under that table so quick was not because I was scared limp, but because I'd thought it all out and decided that that was the best way to fight the three of them. It ain't so easy to say this even to a piece of paper, but a man rests sort of easy after he's confessed.

Anyway, finally I got back to Stockton House and drifted in to the employees' dining room just at lunch time, and there I had the pleasure of seeing all of the gents stand up and come around and shake hands with me, and tell me that they was damned glad to see me back.

But what made the most special difference to me was big Charlie Lamb. Because he come around and he shook my hand extra hard, and afterwards he couldn't hardly keep his eyes off of me. There seemed to be a good deal of liking in those eyes of his, and there seemed to be a shadow of trouble, too. And for a time I sat there and says to myself that at last I've showed Lamb that I'm an enemy worth considering.

That was how much I'd been puffed up!

CHAPTER 20

YOU TAKE STRANGERS when they come out of the East and usually they consider the Westerners a pretty silent lot that particular don't like to talk about themselves. But as a matter of fact, I suppose that people from one part of a country are not very different at heart from those in other sections. It's just the face that looks queer. One section sips its coffee and the other gulps it, and the manners of each section looks pretty queer to the opposite folks. Now we Westerners get pretty quiet when a stranger comes around because, take us by and large, we ain't used to people. We spend a lot of time in the desert or the mountains and we are more used to being alone than with folks, so that when a stranger comes around we wait and let him do the talking, mostly. But take us among ourselves, when we know the men or the women we're with, and we talk pretty near as free as anybody outside of Mexicans.

Them that think that Westerners are a measly lot, they should of been inside that dining hall after I come in and heard the boys pelting me with questions. I kept away from them for a while but pretty soon I couldn't stand it, because it's all right to let outsiders praise you up for nothing, but it's pretty mean to be living on a lie with your everyday friends. And I whacked on the table, and all of those boys was silent as the tomb. I says:

"Partners, I come back here through a lot of talk and praise, and I thought that I could swaller it and digest it, but I see that I can't. So I'm gonna give you the lowdown on just what happened up the line, there."

Well, it would of surprised you to see their eyes sparkle and shine, so that you could see that they expected to hear something pretty exciting. I just said: "The back door opened and those three Indians, they come in with their rifles before you could say Jack Robinson. I was wedged into a corner behind a table, so's I couldn't get away. I was about paralyzed, as a matter of fact. I was so scared that the best I could do was to slide down under the table, yanking out my gats automatic as I slid under. The first buck, he missed me with his bullet, most likely because he wasn't used to seeing the Colonel's men disappearing under tables like scared kids. So all that I had to do, then, was to lie there on the floor nice and comfortable and fan two guns at those thugs. Nobody could of missed at that range. Two of them dropped and the other one was nicked and legged it and all I had to do was to scramble over into the doorway and bring him down at twenty-five yards—with a nice bright moon to show me the target. No, boys, that's all that there was to it. I thought that I would make it out sort of wonderful, but I ain't got the nerve to. Them are the facts. You corner any ten year old kid, and he would of done just as much rather than have a scalp took off!"

They listened to me telling my story out to the end, and after that there was a little silence, with all of them looking down, as though they was ashamed. Then big Charlie Lamb says with a grave face but with a smile in his eyes:

"It looks as though our partner has only done something to be ashamed of!"

Dick Wace up and says:

"Yep, it sure looks as though there was a yellow streak in Billy Jacks!"

I couldn't hardly stand for that and I says:

"Dick, you ain't a man that I'd pick any trouble with, but I can't sit here and take that sort of talk from you, even if I ain't no hero!"

"I dunno," says Champ McGinnis, "that I would waste my time fighting a gent like him, Dick. A gent that takes to hiding behind tables because of a measly three or four buck Indians."

I glared at Champ. I couldn't fight everybody in the world. But I begun to think that pretty soon I would have to have my guns out to save any sort of a name for myself.

Says Hal Doolittle:

"Well, boys, I never heard of anything like it! I supposed that everybody in these parts got his shooting eye in shape by gunning for Indians."

Chet Murphy with a grin on his Irish face went right on with:

"And think of lying out there all comfortable under the table with two good guns to shoot with and then letting one of the three get away from the house! It's a damn disgrace!"

I sat back with a sort of a gasp. I seen that they was maybe stringing me a little, and as I begun to get red, the whole lot of those gents let out a whoop that you could of heard for a mile. Because there ain't nothing that cowpunchers like so much as stringing somebody. They whooped and they yelled again.

"Nothing but three Indians, and he got

scared!" says Lord Marvin, pointing his forefinger at me.

"I give up, boys," says I. "I ain't gunna talk no more—damn all your hearts!"

And they roared some more, but I felt pretty relieved, because I would of hated to stand up to a dead shot like Dick Wace, or a hell-bender like Champ McGinnis.

They made such a disturbance that pretty soon word come in that the Colonel would like to have the roof kept on the house, and they told the servant that brought the word that the Colonel could go to hell, which made him back out of that room on the jump.

It didn't take long before the Colonel himself came into the room with a black face and his eyes like bits of steel polished bright. But before he said a word he seen me and that seemed to make him understand. He comes right for me and when I stood up to meet him, he says:

"I expect my men to report at the end of an expedition, Jacks, even when they're successful!"

And he shook hands with me, a good hard shake, and you could see by the warmth in his hard face that he was pleased. He says:

"I wanted to talk to you in private about this, Jacks, but since there seems to be an audience, here, I have to say that this is one of the finest things that has ever been done in the Sierra Blanca, and such work as this is what scares out the thugs and murderers and gives all the valleys a quiet secure life!"

"Colonel," says I, so red and hot that I could hardly see, "the fact is that it wasn't wonderful, but that I was cornered and sort of had to fight—and——"

I couldn't get no further. There was another wild yell from all of the boys.

"That's what he was explaining to us!" sings out McGinnis.

Well, the Colonel, he give me one long, steady look, and then he nods, as much as to say that he understood and that he was satisfied with his understanding.

Then he went out of the room, and left me to be tortured by them hounds worse than mosquitoes ever tortured me in any river bottom at night.

I seen that there was no use talking, and I shut up, because they'd made a fine, large joke about my true story, and now I knew that the truth would never get around, because if these fellows was wrong about the yarn, everybody in the Sierra Blanca and outside would be wrong. But now I have wrote down the whole story exactly as it happened, and you can see for yourself just how it all come about that people begun to make a hero out of me in spite of myself.

I can't help admitting, now that I'm about it, that it was sort of good, in a way. I used to feel guilty, right enough, but at the same time, I was pretty pleased when one of the boys would say:

"Did you hear about the three Mexicans that kidnapped young Cleveland?"

And then somebody sings out and says:

"Yep. We'll have to send Billy Jacks down there to attend to them. Because three is just his number."

"Yes," says another, "when he gets cornered!"

"But not more than three," says somebody else. "Otherwise he would get a little rattled."

Well, it was all pretty fine. It warmed me, y'understand, the same as whisky does after a long, cold ride. But right after lunch trouble started for me again, and it was the trouble that I had been waiting for and sort of expecting for a long time.

It was one of the important days of my life, and a lot more worth dwelling on than the time that I happened to pot three Indians by luck. Because about this next trouble, there was no luck at all. It was just all schemed and planned out beforehand, as you might say. It was the sort of trouble that you see ahead of you, but you can never dodge it, because your conscience makes you go to meet it!

Well, now that I can look backwards and see everything the way that it actually was, I can understand that I might of taken a different line. But that day when Charlie Lamb come up to me after lunch, I thought that I was doing only what every honest man would of had to do, by telling him that him and me could never rest until one of us had killed the other one!

CHAPTER 21

I HAVE GOT to expand things and explain them a little, however.

I might begin by saying that the boys had scattered to do one thing or another, here and there, and that I had gone and sauntered off by myself and Betty comes running out of the garden and stops me.

"Wait a minute, Billy darling," says she. "Somebody wants to speak to you!"

Wait? I would of waited for a century to

hear her say nice things to me. And she had a flock of them right at the tip of her tongue about how proud and how happy she was, and how she'd lain awake and cried herself to sleep after I'd left on that terrible job.

Somehow, I couldn't hardly believe that about crying herself to sleep, because there was only one kind of tears that come easy and nacheral, as you might say, to Betty. And those was tears of anger.

But just then up comes Miss Olivia and shakes my hand in both of hers and tells me how happy she is to have me back home. Why, you could just see that she meant all that she said and more, and that she sort of loved me, the same as she loved all the boys on the place that she'd had a chance to know. And then, seeing me all tongue-tied, and reaching for words but not able to daub a rope on none at all, she got herself and Betty away as slick as a whistle before I should have a chance to make a fool of myself, and left me there staring after her, and wondering how God had ever managed to make such a sweet woman.

Well, while I was standing there doing the admiring that most folks leave for Sundays and Christmas, up comes big Charlie Lamb. Before he spoke, and before I turned, I knew it was him by the softness combined with the weight of his step. Because he walked like a cat. Like a big cat, I should say maybe a lion slouching around the floor of his cage in the zoo, and despising the folks that come to admire him. Charlie Lamb, he says:

"Billy, I want to know if you and I cannot be friends?"

I turned around and gaped at him. He knew that I had a grudge against him. And just then, after what the folks were saying about me, some folks might of thought that he'd been scared into trying to make up with me, but I wasn't any such a fool as to think that. Low and mean as I figgered that woman-killer to be, still I knew that there wasn't no cowardice in him. So I was all the more staggered. He says, to begin with:

"In the first place, Billy, the time that I knocked you down I had to do it. Otherwise it was jail for me, and I can't help hating jail, you know. Afterwards—well, I've played a low part to you, and I freely admit it. But today I've had to admire you such a lot that I can't help asking you if I can't make up for what I've done, in some way?"

I tried to gather in what he was saying, and while I paused, he went right ahead in his smooth, gentle voice—that voice which always opened the hearts of the women. And he says:

"That was a grand fight you made against the Indians. But it didn't give me the same fine feeling about you as I had during lunch just now."

"During lunch?" says I. "Yes, I suppose that it pleased you a good deal to see me made a fool of!"

He only smiled at me, not contemptuous, but kind, and understanding.

"I should have known that you wouldn't understand, Billy," says he. "So I'll drop that, if you please, and go on to something else."

"Before you go on," says I, "would you mind holding your horses until I can understand how come that you've injured me any way since the first day that I met you? Have you been talking about me?"

"Talking?" says he. And then he stopped for a minute.

"No," he says at last. "I haven't been talking. However—suppose that we let sleeping dogs lie?"

"What I don't see," says I, "is why you should want to come to me like this?"

"I'll tell you frankly," says he. "It's because I like you, Jacks. Because I want to have you down in the list of my friends."

"You've got the whole valley on that list, just now," says I. "Ain't that enough?"

"Friends that are easy to get are easy to lose," says he, as gentle as ever. "But the fact is that the hard friends to secure are the ones who last the longest."

Now, I stood there for a minute and I thought this over carefully, because I wasn't fool enough to underrate him in any way. He was the strongest, the smartest, and the bravest and most skilful fighting man that I'd ever met in my life, and in my life I've met some hard cases, I can tell you.

But then it seemed to me that there was only one thing for me to do, and I done it. I said:

"Charlie, I dunno that I know everything about you, because you got a long history. I know that you got a lot of good points behind you, but I know some of the bad ones, too. But I'll tell you this. Ever since I was a kid, I've aimed to treat all my friends like they was kings and all of my enemies like they was devils. And that holds for you, too. You started in by hammering me on the chin in front of the girl that I was in love with. You made a fool of me before her. And I ain't going to forget it in a hurry."

"Consider this, old fellow," says he. "I didn't know you. I only knew that there was a gun pointing at me and that there was a jail door open in front of me, and if you put yourself in my boots, you'll see that I had to get away if I could. But I'll admit that if I had known about you then what I know about you since, I should never have had the nerve to tackle you in that open handed way."

"You're a talker that I can't compare with," says I. "And there's a lot of other things about you that I can't touch. But as a matter of fact, Charlie, though I ain't sure death with guns like you, and though I ain't strong as a bear like you, and though I ain't no hero like you, the day has got to come when you and me stands up to one another and fights it out, and God save one of us!"

He looked at me very curious, as though I was standing a long distance away.

"I think you mean that," says he.

"I do," says I.

"If I thought that there was any way of changing you," says he, "I should try it, but one reason why I want you for a friend is because I know that you have a mind of your

173

own, and not simply a head packed full of the opinions of other people."

"Thanks," says I, "and cutting out the fancy stuff that you put in, you can lay to it that I won't change none."

He frowned down at the ground. Then he looked up quick, with a sigh.

"If you take this attitude," says he, "I want to tell you that I put a higher and a truer value on you than you put on yourself. I've been hated by a good many formidable men, old fellow, but never by one I took more seriously than I take you. I'll be ready for you, then, day or night."

"Thanks," says I. "I would sure appreciate that. I dunno just when the good opportunity will come. But when it does, in a way that folks won't have a chance to call either of us a murderer, then we'll have our little party."

He seemed to be a little sad. But then he shrugged his shoulders and tossed up his head.

"I've taken more from you," says he, "than I've ever taken from any other man. But there's a limit to a fellow's patience, and I think that I can fairly say that mine has been reached. I wanted to be a white man to you, Billy. I wanted it as I've never wanted the same thing before. Well, you've wiped the dirty shoes of your bad manners on me as a reward. Now, my friend, I can only advise you not to marry Betty before we've had our little settlement, because I hate to make a woman a widow."

He turned around on his heel and marched away. And then he paused and threw over his shoulder:

"And I'm very sorry to say that I've made widows in my day."

It didn't occur to me to doubt him as he strode off. There was never a man so soft and smooth in his ways. And there was never a man so devilish and dangerous as him. It sickened me a little. And yet I dunno that I ever admired anyone so much as I admired him just then. I mean, for his courage, and the wonderful bigness and grace of him, added together. Because you don't often get hold of a man that has both of those things— bigness and self-control. But he was always like a cat. Even when he was asleep, you could see that you couldn't start to take no advantages.

I watched him go right out of sight. And I remember that afterwards I took a long, long look around me, because I half felt that it might be the last time that I would see

such things—I mean the sky, you understand, and the shadows under the trees,
pointing east, now, and stretching out like a
cat before the fire—and such things that
don't matter very much, except at the thought
of leaving them.

Well, when I had had a chance to turn
these things over in my head, I decided that
I was now committed. I had dived into the
water where the stream was the quickest.
And I couldn't expect any mercy from big
Charlie Lamb.

I was half of a mind to hurry after him and
have the thing over with in one flurry. But
then, after thinking the thing over, I knew
that I would never have the nerve to up and
face him until I had my back to the wall, the
same as when the three Indians had come in
and cornered me.

It was a queer thing that life, that had
looked so fine and bright and warm just a
little bit before was now as dark as December. And all that I could do was to wait. It
was like being sick and the doctor saying that
he couldn't give you any hope until the crisis
come—and he can't say when that will be.

Well, I had a sinking feeling. I knew that
sign of sickness at the least.

CHAPTER 22

BUT WHAT HAD been happening with big Charlie Lamb and Miss Olivia while I was away?

There was only one person around the place that I could talk to and that was Betty, and talking to her about Charlie was hard, because she couldn't seem to see much that was wrong about him. However, I tried her out, but all she would say was that Charlie Lamb did go out riding with Miss Olivia now and then, but that was only because the Baron often had a lot to do in the line of writing letters, because he had a bunch of business on his hands back in England about selling off one of his castles.

Maybe you would get a little excited to hear about a castle, because so was I when I heard about it. But after a while I got it explained. The Baron, he was a good deal heated up about the thing, and I heard him talking to the Colonel about it and asking would his honor really be compromised if he was to sell this castle?

The Colonel says no he didn't hardly see how a few piles of ruined stones would really make or mar the honor of a family. And it turned out that that was all that the castle was.

It seems that it had been a pretty upstanding place until along comes a gent by the name of Cromwell with some old-fashioned guns and blows most of it down. And after that it comes with the land into the hands of the ancestors of Wakeness.

But there was a history behind that pile of stones. It seems that there had been a couple of young nobles knifed in it once, and there was an old duchess that was poisoned at the table one day, so that even a pretty sketchy history of England had to mention that castle a couple of times. Besides that, being blowed down by Cromwell was quite a feather in its cap, though it appears that he done the same honor to a lot of other castles in the old country.

"The ruffian Cromwell," the Baron called him.

But anyway, there was a retired pork packer from Chicago that wanted to buy that old castle and rebuild it, and leave not much of the old stuff except some climbing ivy and the traditions, and the Baron he didn't know would it be honorable to sell so much history for dirty money?

Well, the money won out in the end, like I notice that it generally does when it only has honor to play against, because money works with marked cards, as you might say, and honor usually has all of its cards face up.

Now, I took note of this here, and it pleased me a good deal to notice how things went, but all the same, while Baron was sitting in the house so many hours writing letters about the honor of his family and the price that it would take to buy that same, I couldn't help wondering might he not be letting the Stockton millions slip out of his hands?

Yes, there was Miss Olivia going to climb Mount Christy and Charlie Lamb was going along to carry the lunch basket, him being so strong and so—good-natured!

And Miss Olivia wanted to go out on a horse that wasn't quite safe for her, and who was there that could make a horse safe so well as Smiling Charlie? Particular when there was a girl in the saddle!

And I wondered, too, if he got out of Miss Olivia as much sympathy as he could get from Betty about how the cruel world had gossiped about him?

Well, I didn't have long to wait before something happened. One evening the Colonel started out for a ride and the Baron went along with him, because he had finished writing about castles, for that day, and as they went, they passed me exercising of my big bay and the Baron he says would I accompany them, which I would.

We rode along at a good windy gait until we come bang over a hill and there crossing the creek below us was Miss Olivia and big Smiling Charlie. You could tell him even at that distance by his shoulders and the way that he had of holding his head, which no other man was ever like him in that way.

They was going across the stones that stuck out above the top of the creek, with the rapid water showing its white teeth against the rocks, and Charlie, he was steadying Miss Olivia and helping her across, by holding her with one hand.

It was fine to see them. We pulled up and watched, and the Baron, he couldn't help smiling a little to see how graceful she was and how the tinkle of her laughter come up to us like the sound of a bell, almost lost in the wind.

They got to the farther side of the bank, and there she seemed to lose balance, and she tipped into the arms of Charlie Lamb— who was steadying her, y'understand? And if she stayed there just a minute, you might say that she was only righting herself and catching her breath a little. And still it made the Baron get red and set his teeth, because I was specially keeping one eye upon him.

But as if for fear that the Baron might not be noticing everything, the Colonel comes out with:

"Well, well! They seem quite friendly!"

And just at that minute, pat, as Miss Olivia stepped back from Charlie, she seemed to trip again, and to fall back into his arms, and her face raised, and his lowered—

And even in a Sunday school it would have had to pass for a kiss I suppose!

"Friendly!" says the Baron. "My God!"

And he started to spur his horse forwards, but the Colonel caught the reins of his bridle and stopped his horse.

"Let me go, sir!" says the Baron. "If you have no manner of controlling your daughter, at least I have the right of protecting the honor of a girl who's engaged to a Wakeness!"

"Honor is a splendid thing," says the Colonel, extreme dry. "But it doesn't decorate the breast of a dead man. And a dead man you will be, Wakeness, if you go down to that creek, just now!"

Nobody ever said a truer thing since the world began, I suppose, but still it was pretty hard on Wakeness. I was glad to see him show so much spunk, because he must of knowed what sort of a fighting devil Charlie Lamb was—the whole world knew it. But he seemed rearing and tearing to get at him.

I admired to watch him! That was honor working in him, I suppose, like yeast in bread.

I thank my good God that it wasn't Betty that I seen down there. It gave me a shiver. Because there wouldn't of been nobody to hold the bridle of my horse, me not being a baron by some miles!

"Is nothing to be done?" says the Baron. "Your daughter—disgraced before the eyes of the entire world?"

And he looked at me.

The Colonel looked at me, too, and nodded a little. So I says:

"Beg pardon, sir. I ain't the entire world, if you please. Besides which, I've always been a good deal near sighted!"

"Ah!" says the Baron. "Ah," says he, "I believe you, and don't think that I shall forget what you say, my good fellow!"

I didn't mind that much—being called my good fellow, I mean, because the Baron was so heated up that he might of said a lot worse things.

And just then the pair of them, down there by the creek, they looked up and seen us, just as they started to get their horses, which they had left behind them when they crossed on the rocks. They seen us, and they stood still, and stared.

And all at once it hit me like a thunder-clap—it didn't matter so much about the Baron and his damn honor. It mattered a terrible lot that even Miss Olivia hadn't been above the oily tongue of Smiling Charlie. It hit me, and it hit me like a bullet and tore through the heart of me, and made me sick.

"What is to be done?" gasps the Baron.

"I think," says the Colonel, "that we'd better start back for Stockton House. We may as well, you know!"

I knew that he had wanted just a thing like this to happen, but it never occurred to me for a minute that he would take the thing like this—so dead easy! As though his girl was no better than dirt, I mean.

He turned right around, as cool as you please, and rode back over the hill. And I followed, and the Baron couldn't find any-thing to do except to come along after us, because, mad as he might be, he sure didn't want to come down the hill and mix up with big Charlie Lamb. Few men love duty well enough to want to die for it more than once a day.

Says the Baron, flying up to us on his horse:

"I've heard of such a thing as a lynch law in this part of your country, Colonel Stockton. And I hope that I shall have a chance to see it working!"

The Colonel looked him over very deliberately. He says:

"I've always frowned on the lynch law in the Sierra Blanca. And as for Charlie Lamb, I don't know that he has committed any very vital crime. He has kissed a pretty girl. And what's fatal about that?"

The Baron grappled with his horse's mane as though to keep himself from falling, and then he says:

"Are you speaking in this fashion about your own daughter, sir?"

"I am," says the Colonel.

"This is very hard to believe," answered the Baron. "If I were in control here——"

"Suppose that you were, what would you do?"

"Hang him up for the crows to eat!"

"No, you say that because you are a fairly

young fellow. But if you had a chance to think these things over, you would agree with me, I have no doubt, that it is not a crime worth hanging to kiss a girl."

"My God, sir," cried the Baron, "the betrothed wife of an English peer?"

"She is even more than that," says the Colonel, steady as a rock. "She is the daughter of an American citizen. Nevertheless I don't feel that I have the right to shoot the man who puts his arm around her waist."

I wish that I could give you a real idea of the way that the Colonel said all of these things. He wasn't mean about them, and he wasn't hasty. He was just sort of good-humored.

But I was able to look a little behind the scenes, because I happened to know more about Colonel Stockton's mind in that business than Baron Wakeness did, and I could guess that the Colonel was just on the point of being the meanest man that ever lived.

He was smiling too much, you understand!

CHAPTER 23

"MIGHT I ASK," says the Baron, "what, if anything, you intend to do about this affair?"

"You are quite free to ask," replied Colonel Stockton. "I recognize that you have a peculiar interest, here. I suggest that the thing should be first approached through an interview with Olivia."

"Thank you," says the Baron, and suddenly he gave the rein to the stallion, Inverary, and he flew away before us.

I suppose that he would of regretted doing a thing so childish as that, afterwards, but at the time, all that he knew was that he had had more than he could stomach, and he had to be off by himself for a while. I just sympathized with him a good deal.

In fact, I didn't blame the Baron and I didn't blame Olivia and I hardly even blamed that damned philanderer, Charlie Lamb, because it was pretty plain to me and it would of been plain to any man able to look for himself that nobody had any real control over anything except the Colonel himself. He had made everything happen.

For you can see for yourself that he had been playing the part of God, and you may think that he had been playing it pretty successfully, but at the same time, there was never anything that I liked less than his attitude.

He scared me. All at once, riding back towards the house, he seemed to me like a great big giant, bigger than any in a fairy tale, and in the palm of this giant's hand Miss Olivia and Baron Wakeness and Smiling Charlie Lamb and me and all the rest was running around, and all thinking that we had a good deal of free will to lead our own lives, but always likely to have those big fingers close down upon us and end everything.

Yes, it scared me to think about the power of that man. Always up to then it had seemed a sort of a miracle that anybody could of built up an estate for himself like that Sierra Blanca. But now it didn't surprise me any more and it only seemed wonderful to me that he hadn't gone on and just used Sierra Blanca for a starting point, and rolled it up like a snowball going down a slope until the whole country was sort of soaked up by him.

But you felt that though he could of done all of this, he didn't because he was interested in something else, more important, and that he knew life and the world too well to want to have very much of it.

Maybe I ain't making this at all clear, but I mean that behind his smiling and his kindness and his anger, and everything else, there was a sort of a sneer that was a damned black thing and that made your heart all curl up inside of you.

It was almost as though the Colonel knew what was going on inside my mind, because now he turned to me with a terrible kind smile and he said to me:

"This seems a very confused affair, Jacks, doesn't it?"

I hardly knew what to say, and I blurted out:

"No matter what it may seem to be, I'm sure that Miss Olivia is right, sir!"

The Colonel nodded and lighted a cigar and went along puffing at it, and more interested in his own thoughts than he seemed to be in me or the sky, or the trees, or the horses, or the thing that had just happened. He says in a quiet voice:

"Perhaps she is right. I cannot tell. The women are closed away from us behind a veil. God, perhaps, understands them. We cannot. More mysterious than Egyptian goddesses, wouldn't you say, Billy?"

I agreed with that. I didn't know much about Egyptian goddesses, but I knew Betty, and she was enough to make me agree with both hands, as you might say.

"Yes," went on the Colonel, who of course wasn't paying any real attention to whether I agreed or not.

"Yes," says he with a sigh, "more mysterious than the goddesses of Egypt, or the goddesses of the Hindu. Bloodstained goddesses, Billy, stained with blood of sacrifices. Not of mere women and children. But the blood of strong, brave men, in the strength and the bravery of their life—their blood, their brains, their noble hearts poured out before the shrine of woman—woman—woman!"

He said that word three times in such a way that you would begin to think that any girl, even Betty, was a sort of a Juggernaut.

"Why should it be?" went on the Colonel. "They are the sphinxes. They are the mysteries. Man has stronger hands, but he does not use women. She uses him. She makes him the tool with which she makes her way through life. Sometimes an edged tool cleaving a clean, easy way. Sometimes a blunt instrument, hacking and hewing brutally. But the brutality, the bloodshed, the crime-stained hands, what becomes of them, in the end? They vanish like thinnest water vapor, and they reveal to you the picture of what? Of an ogress? Of a living sphinx, licking guilty lips? No but of a tender young mother with a babe at her breast."

Colonel Stockton, as he said this, let his horse come to a pause and went on smoking his cigar slowly. He would turn it a little in his lips and blow out a little cloud, tasting every bit of the fragrance and the strength and the beauty and the poison of his thoughts.

Me, I got a little more scared than ever. I could feel the fingers of the giant wriggling a little, and I hated the sight of his infernal smile worse than anything that I knew in this wide world. Much worse than Charlie Lamb, for instance.

"We grow old," said the Colonel. "And just before the end we may see the flash of truth about two things. About what two things would you say, Jacks?"

"I don't exactly follow you, sir," says I.

"God bless you for that quality of incomprehension," replies the Colonel. "For if I had more men like you about me, Jacks, men on whose incomprehension I could depend, I would eventually learn how to live an innocent life. But as it is, one dares not be free. One respects and bows before the stupid face of society. One dares not strike! One dares not strike!"

He had a long-fingered, slender hand, and now he curled up the fingers of it a little. Not into a fist, but as though there were something more than thin air in his grasp. Well, it made me a little giddy to watch him.

"I shall tell you what the two things are at which the old may guess just before they die. One is God, and the other is woman. God is sometimes nakedly revealed. And the wise and the aged stretch out their arms to Him with a smile. But as for woman—no, man dares not understand her. We shut our eyes upon the true vision. And we shrink from the facts. We put the ugly nightmare behind us—we throw it over our shoulder, so to speak, and in our thoughts we go on, like the Creator, making her in our image, endowing her with our thoughts, breathing into her our soul, because, forsooth, she walks erect and speaks words!

"Oh God, oh God, Billy Jacks, that ever we should see the blood upon the lion's claws and the blood upon the lion's lips and nevertheless let the guilty beast creep into our hearts!

"But in the end, our eyes are fixed in death, and our hand is being chafed by the widow of our grandson, and only after death our souls are free at last to rise above the dust—to soar—to swing through the glorious ether. Ha, Billy Jacks! Is not this true?"

"I don't know, sir," says I, "that I actually follow much of what you been saying. I never had much education, but stopped off short in the eighth grade, just when we come to the Merchant of Venice!"

"Ah, Billy," says the Colonel, "and have you met Shylock, then? And the overwise Portia? And the gentle and doomed Antonio? Well, there was a wealth for you, was there not?"

"Sir," says I, "there was something about a Jew, but I forget his name."

The Colonel turned a little in his saddle and looked at me in his queer way that I think I've described before—I mean, as though he was seeing a man for the first time. Then he says:

"You are a help to me, Billy Jacks. You help me to think clearly, and hereafter I must see a great deal of you. Yes, I shall insist on that. Seeing a great deal of you. I hope that you won't object?"

"I'm always here to be commanded, sir," says I.

"Exactly," says the Colonel. "Always ready to be commanded. And how few there are who realize that there is no obedience where commands are given! The greater the king, the more perfectly he fails to reign! Irony, all is irony! However, I begin to feel that I may have been talking nonsense, Billy Jacks."

He wasn't confused, but he looked me gravely in the face, and it bewildered me, a good deal. Because, usually, you know how you feel a little superior to a gent that hasn't been able to understand things? But the Colonel, he wasn't feeling superior because he'd been able to say things too hard for me to follow. No sir, he wasn't set up at all, because he was so much smarter than me. No, at the time it just seemed to me that all of his smartness and his seeing through things didn't give him a great deal of happiness. Yes, sir, he says suddenly:

"Billy Jacks, I think you are the only person I've ever known whom I've envied a great deal!"

"Sir," says I, "I'm a very simple man. I hope that you ain't laughing at me!"

"No, Jacks," says he, "because you would promptly shoot me if I did. But I envy you because you are contented with the truth of the world, the world which can be so majestic, so grand, so eternal, so gloriously strong and beautiful. That is to say, unless one looks behind the curtain! And why look there? No, let the play go on. Never wish to get behind the scenes. And really, it is better never to get behind the footlights, even, because those who go that far, as they come on, or as they go off, may have glimpses of the wings, and of all the strange, fantastic brutal machinery which lies behind fairyland. Do you understand, Billy?"

"Sir," says I, "doggone me if I understand a single word of the whole thing!"

"Good!" says the Colonel. "Confoundedly good, by Jove!"

And he reached out his hand and let it rest for a moment on my shoulder, while he smiled into my face.

CHAPTER 24

WELL, I WAS pretty glad when we got to Stockton House. The Colonel told me to put up my horse and wait for orders. I done just that, and pretty soon word comes to my room that he wants me and I go down and

I'm brought into the big library where I heard the Baron saying, as I went in:

"You really think it essential that we should have him?"

"Exactly, Wakeness. We must have him to keep us in our proper places. There is no greater danger than that of being too familiar in our treatment of our problems. How rarely is a father just to his wife, or to his son, or a girl to her lover, or a brother to his younger brother. We need perspective. We need nothing more, really, than the ability to treat our nearest and dearest as a stranger would treat them. But, on the whole, we are apt to lean too heavily upon love and forget that he is only a blind boy, whose shoulder is easily put out of joint. Let us not presume too much upon those who are dear to us, but let us try to act as much like judges as we can, when we have judicial work on our hands. And as for Billy Jacks, well, he was present. He saw what we saw. And his impersonal point of view ought to be illuminating. I want him here. In the first place, he is not a talker. In the second place, he is honest. By all means let's have him."

And here I came into the room, feeling a good deal out of place as I walked across that big, shining floor.

"I don't know that it's good taste, sir!" blurted out the Baron, very red.

"I don't know that it is, either," replied the Colonel. "Just now, I'm not thinking about good or bad taste, you know!"

He had me sit down with them, and he said:

"You have seen what we've seen, Billy. I wonder if you mind being here with us while we talk to Olivia?"

"Sir," says I, "I'd be best pleased not to be here. But when Miss Olivia comes, I'd rather that you asked her, because I would like to please her!"

"Ah," says the Colonel, "you see that one of the three judges, at least, is ready to review the case with a prejudice in favor of the criminal!"

And he chuckled a little, and seemed pleased with me. All at once I wondered did he really love his daughter. But there wasn't a great deal of chance for wondering, now, because there comes a light step on the floor outside the door, and there was Miss Olivia.

There was no doubt about *her* being upset. Her head was down a little, and she had to bring it up with an effort so that she could look at all the three of us.

I couldn't stand it. I says:

"Miss Olivia, if you'd rather that I shouldn't be here, nothing'll keep me. Nothing in the world."

And I turned and glared at the Colonel and the Baron.

"I don't mind you, Billy," says Olivia. "I'm rather glad to have you here."

"Sir," says the Baron suddenly, "we must be alone with Olivia."

"As you please," says the Colonel. "You step into the next room, if you please, Jacks."

I went quick enough, and glad to get out of the business. But that next room was just a little sort of an alcove, and the door had a great big crack all the way around it, so that there wasn't any way for me to escape from hearing all of the voices in the next apartment, where they was talking. But why should the Colonel have wanted me there at all? Pretty soon, I began to wonder when they would start in, because there was quite a long silence.

"I don't know where to begin," says the Colonel, at the last. "Where do you suggest, Wakeness?"

"At the beginning," says the Baron coldly. "When did this sort of thing begin, Olivia?"

"What sort of thing?" says the Colonel gravely.

"I think she understands what I mean. Olivia, will you answer me?"

"I understand," says the faint voice of Olivia. "I'm to explain when I first began—when I first noticed Charlie Lamb?"

"The cowpuncher—yes!" snapped the Baron.

"Ah, well," says the Colonel, "I hoped that we would not have to be bitter."

Says the Baron:

"Sir, I have to get at the bottom of this."

"Very well," answered the Colonel. "I can assure you that Olivia is my daughter and she is much too proud to lie."

I could hardly hear what Olivia said. I suppose that if I'd been a perfect gentleman and not strained my ears, I wouldn't of heard her at all. But I couldn't help listening. She says:

"You've been very busy, Peter."

"Yes," said the Baron. "I must plead guilty to that!"

"And Charlie Lamb has been taking me about the place—and, really, I didn't know that I was paying much attention to him!"

"Ha!" says the Baron, with a sort of a groan.

"Except," says Olivia, "that he was always gentle and very thoughtful and courteous. And after that magnificent race that he rode—why, one couldn't help noticing him a little more particularly."

"Talk up, my dear," says the Colonel. "I can hardly hear you."

"I mean," says Olivia, "that I haven't much to talk about, but when we walked over the rocks across the stream today, suddenly—why, you were there and watched."

"Was that the first time that he—er—touched you?" snapped the Baron.

"Yes," says the girl.

There was a little silence. Maybe they all sighed. I know that I did.

"And that is the truth?" asked the Baron.

"Yes," says she.

There was another silence.

"And may I ask what was in your mind?" asked the Baron.

"I don't know," she answered. "Except that—it seemed—natural. I couldn't well tell why!"

"Great heavens!" says the Baron. "Natural to—er—kiss a cowpuncher—a common cowpuncher?"

"I think that he's not a common man," says Olivia. "Is he a common man, father?"

"I don't know," says the Colonel. "I don't know that I can very well answer that. What would you say, Baron?"

That was pretty mean, handing that question back to the Baron, who just went on:

"After all, that is not of the first importance. However, it seems to me that I am not called upon to act like a hasty fool or a bigot. It seems to me that I should remember that you are extremely young, Olivia. And the fellow is handsome, and I believe his manners and his English are well enough. I think I can conceive how you might have been carried away by the folly of a moment.

"Suppose that we begin by discharging the man? Are you willing to do that, sir?"

"Why, certainly," says the Colonel.

"Very well," remarked the Baron, "then we are making progress. And as for Olivia, I suppose that she already repents her folly a good deal."

It seemed to me that that ended the thing, but Olivia now spoke up as quietly as ever and replied:

"I don't really know that I repent, Peter."

"Eh?" gasped the Baron.

"I mean just that. I'm sorry to say that I'm terribly unsettled. I don't think that I repent. I'm ashamed. Yes. I feel that I've done what I ought not to do. But—I'm not sure that I wouldn't do it again."

"My God!" gasped Wakeness.

"My dear," says the Colonel, "do you know what you're saying?"

"I'm afraid that I do, exactly!"

"Are you canceling our engagement?" says the Baron.

"Oh, Peter," says the girl, "I don't know what to say. I thought—I thought that I loved you, and that I could never care for any other man!"

"But you find that you care for the cowpuncher?"

"I don't blame you for being bitter," she said, "but when I try to think of him banished from Sierra Blanca, somehow I can't manage that little trick of the imagination."

"I see that you're frank," says the Baron in a shaky voice.

"I have to be," says the girl. "Because I'm not sure of myself, and I'm just fumbling along and trying to feel my way to the truth!"

"Olivia, dear!" cries the Baron suddenly, and certainly there was something in his voice that had more than a love of her millions in it. "Olivia, let me help you to think your way through the horrible tangle."

And I heard him step on the floor.

201

"Please don't touch me, Peter," says she.

There was another ghastly silence. It seemed pretty ghastly to me, too, because, from what she had said before, you could guess that maybe this fellow Lamb didn't after all mean so much to her. But suddenly you guessed that in spite of her quietness she might be all wrapped up in him.

"Olivia," says the Baron, hoarse and deep. "This is the most awful day of my life. I thought that I knew before how much I cared about you, but I see that I didn't. Now I think that I have the right to ask you if you have stopped caring about me."

"I don't know," says the girl, "I only know, really, that all at once—I don't want you to touch me, Peter!"

That was what you would call a facer. It made me shrink. It must have torn the heart out of the Baron, and when I thought of what a girl she was, I could see that the poor Baron must be in hell. Because believe me, there was never nobody else at all like her.

"Colonel," says the Baron, "I think that this is the end of everything!"

"Ah, don't say that!" breaks out the Colonel.

Why I hated him worse than you would

hate a snake, when I heard him say that. Him that had planned and managed everything.

"I'm afraid that it is the end of everything," repeated the Baron. "And yet—God knows how my pride lets me say it! But—I wish that I may have the privilege of staying on for a few days—to see what can be done!"

"Oh Peter," cried Olivia, with a break in her voice. "Oh, don't ask such a thing. Stay forever, if you wish. And I've given you my sacred word to marry you; and I would never break it! You can keep me if you will!"

CHAPTER 25

WELL, SIR, IT took my breath a little when I heard her call out that way. It was just the thing that the Colonel hadn't been planning on. He'd beaten the Baron, already. All the game was in his hands, and suddenly his daughter turns around and throws herself back into the Baron's hands, not through love, but through pity, and because of her sense of honor.

Well, it beat me. Because, somehow, you don't figure on a woman's sense of honor ever getting very seriously between her and her way of living. But everything about this here girl was queer and different from other women. She was a purer quill, as you might say. She was a hundred per cent pay.

While this pause lasted, and while my heart hammered and I wondered what the Colonel would have up his sleeve to meet the emergency, the Baron must have been doing some thinking on his part. At any rate, he said suddenly:

"It's all horribly mixed up. I don't want to play the part of a cad. I—confound it, Colonel Stockton, I wish that you could give me your advice in front of Olivia. Should I withdraw in favor of the cowpuncher?"

That word, you could see, stuck a good deal in his throat. He didn't like it, and he couldn't help showing that he didn't like it. And who could blame him? It looked like it hardly paid to be a baron, in the Sierra Blanca. Everything like that seemed sort of wasted.

The Colonel, I could see, had his opening now. But doggone me if he would take it. He wanted to keep right in the background. He had brought Smiling Charlie into this business at a great cost to himself. And it was plain that he was going to keep Charlie in to handle the matter by himself. As a matter of fact, by what Lamb had managed already, it was a pretty good guess that he wouldn't need any even of the Colonel's backing to beat the Baron.

The Colonel just said:

"I only wish for the happiness of both of you. I don't wish to speak rashly. I have given the best of my thought all my life to the forming of Olivia's character and providing for her happiness. I cannot feel, now, that I should interfere. In such matters, even a father is a distant relative."

He'd hardly got through talking, when I could see that he was right, and that he would have been pretty foolish to commit himself in this matter. How would the Baron act, now that everything was placed in his hands? Well, anything that he did would be wrong, unless he just withdrew on the spot. He said at last:

"I suppose that I must make up my mind about this. I don't want to drag an unwilling wife to the altar. I don't want to play the part of a rotter. And at the same time, it's terribly hard to give up Olivia. And this thing has happened so suddenly—confound it, you know, it's hard to realize it! Olivia, may I ask you a frank question?"

"Yes, Peter dear, of course."

And the gentleness and the pity in her

voice, oh, that must have been hard on the Baron.

"Then tell me—do you love this man Charles Lamb?"

She was a slow-talking girl. It always took her a time to make up her mind. But that was because she was so honest. It ain't hard for a liar to talk fast. She said:

"I don't know, Peter."

"You don't know, Olivia?" cried the Baron. "Ah, my dear, then that means that you don't really love him, for if you did, you would surely know!"

"No," she said, "perhaps I don't. Only— I feel differently towards him than towards other men."

"How many men have you been very fond of, Olivia? Is that too intimate a question to ask you?" says the poor Baron.

"No—I'll answer that. When I was fifteen, there was a great, wild, fighting man on the place. He was the chief of father's knights, you know. His name was Creegan. I dreamed about Danny Creegan. I used to wake up at night and admire the thought of him. When I heard his voice, it sent a tingle through me, and if he had ever asked me to marry him, I'm sure that I should have said yes."

"Go on!" said the Baron, his voice sharp and high.

"He had to go away on some sort of dangerous business."

"It was an unlucky affair," says the Colonel in his smooth way. "I had to send poor Creegan off on an expedition against some Mexican raiders. He acquitted himself handsomely, as he always did, but in the end, they killed him."

I wondered how much that was an accident, and how much of it was caused by the Colonel's own planning.

"Afterwards," said the girl, "I was very much grieved. But a month or so later, I remember that Father gave me a fine horse for my own, and I was so pleased with it that it rubbed Danny Creegan out of my mind for an hour or two. Afterwards, I was shocked when I thought of my lack of faith and strong feeling. But when I pondered about it, I had to decide that I had never really loved Danny. That troubled me a great deal, because it made me see that perhaps there was more than one kind of love. Then, I don't think that any man ever interested me again until I met you, Peter."

Says the Baron:

"Now that we're on that subject, do you

mind telling me just what your attitude has been to me?"

"It's so hard for me to say," says she. And gad, she had a kind and gentle voice, aiming not to hurt him. "But when we first met at the tennis courts, and afterwards at Lady Welhurst's party, I felt that you meant more to me than other men. Oh, a lot more than Danny Creegan had in the past. So I was sure that that was love. And I *am* terribly fond of you, Peter. I like you a great, great deal, and please you will believe that!"

"I want to believe it," says the Baron bitterly. "But that brings us back to the point. What is the difference between your feeling for the Creegan person, and your feeling for me, and your feeling for Mr. Charlie Lamb?"

She said after a minute of thinking:

"Suppose I put it this way. Danny Creegan was like some splendid young man going dashing and smashing and crashing and laughing through the world and making lots of enemies and laughing at them and heading straight for destruction, before very long. You really couldn't imagine that Danny would last very long, because he loved war. And because he was so young, it gave one a

208

melancholy sort of an interest in him. One wondered what went on in his mind. He was not like others. And somehow, one wanted to give him a little happiness before the end."

"A sort of pity," says the Baron. "Isn't that it, Colonel?"

"I can't pretend to be an expert critic in such delicate matters as a girl's fancies," says the Colonel.

"And then," said she, "I met you, in England. I always loved England and the English. There's something clean and fine and self-contained and complete about them. They're whole men, educated without being stupid bores about their knowledge, and all good at games, and all without self-consciousness. And when I met you, Peter, it seemed to me as though I were meeting everything that was best and cleanest and truest about England. Then there was your title and all——"

"My dear! My dear!" groans the Baron. "Don't tell me that that had anything to do with it!"

"It did though, honestly," she replied. "It helped to make you a little different from other men. The title, and the long line of your family, and the oldness of the castle, and everything! It all went into the making of the picture. I suppose that I've been almost as much in love with the deer park as with—no, I don't mean that!"

"It's all right," said the Baron. "We're getting to the bottom of things. I've asked for truth, and I'm getting what I want. You've loved the deer park about as much as you've loved me!"

"Peter, now I've insulted you!"

"Not a bit. As a matter of fact, that's a jolly old park. I like it a lot, myself. No, I'm not insulted. I can see that you may have cared for a good many things about me— enough to make you think that it was love, when it wasn't at all!"

"I don't know. Perhaps that was it. And then I met Charlie Lamb. Well, he was someone to notice, right away. They said that he was a great flirt and a great fighter, and then I saw him ride that wonderful race. I don't like a man who's a philanderer. I hate that sort of thing. But I suppose that I like a man who's been noticed by the world. Perhaps it helps *me* to notice him."

"Perhaps," said the Baron, "he knew how to put his best foot forward."

"Not that. He never claimed any attention from me. He never talked about the great things he had done. He never told of fights or rides or races. But he was simply kind and pleasant and always ready to show me tricks about fishing, or riding, and then he told me a lot about how to shoot with my rifle. And behind it all, I felt that he was watching me. I felt that he was—enjoying me, you know."

"It's all right, my dear," says the Baron. "You don't have to be afraid to talk frankly."

"It was fun to be—enjoyed," says she. "And to be always looked at as though one were—oh, well, as though one were worth seeing! I think that other men had flattered me about silly things. But Charlie Lamb didn't flatter. He never said a single complimentary word, and yet I just knew that he liked me. He was other things, too. Of course, it's easy to think about a man who's so wonderfully good-looking. I remembered about Danny Creegan that I used to have to think of him as a sort of a blur, he was so extremely plain. But Charlie Lamb can jump up into my mind just as he is, and seem more wonderful each time. And then I feel, somehow, as though there is a tremendous lot behind him. As though he's never done all that he could do. As though there's a great reservoir of strength in him, and even more than that, he has a charming voice, and I love to hear him sing silly songs while he plays his guitar. It's really wonderful what he can do with the idlest sort of music. He makes it important, I mean, so that it stays in one's thoughts for a long time and seems worth remembering.

"But I never expected that anything would happen—I mean, such as happened today. But it just *did* happen. And—I suppose that the worst part of all is that I'm not very sorry that it happened. Except that I hate terribly to hurt you, Peter dear."

"Tell me this!" he broke in. "If we had not seen you, would you have gone on planning on our marriage?"

"I think that I should," said she.

"Well, Baron," said the Colonel. "The matter is in your hands. You decide, and my girl and I shall do what you wish."

"That seems a handsome thing to say," muttered the Baron. "Just let me have a day or two to think over the things that I might do, will you?"

CHAPTER 26

ABOUT THIS TIME, I noticed that there was a door on the farther side of that little room, locking on my side. I unlocked it, because I'd heard enough, and I didn't want to go on feeling like an eavesdropper if I could help it.

Why the devil had the Colonel brought me into the thing? I couldn't tell, unless he wanted to make the Baron feel, you see, that the matter was already public property, and that what had happened was right in the eye of the world. And I suppose that he *did* manage to get that effect, pretty well.

There was never a keener old fox than the Colonel!

I got through the next room, which was a sealed up chamber that was never used, to a little hallway, and by that I got back into the part of the house that I knew, and so outdoors, at last, and mighty glad that I wasn't back there listening to the unravelings of that miserable affair.

I was glad, too, that *I* didn't have troubles like that. I met Betty coming in from a ride, with a fine color in her brown cheeks. I said to her:

"Betty, we'll have some smashing rides together when we're married."

"Will we?" says Betty. "Well, if we can afford to keep such horses, I suppose that we will! That is, except on baking and washing and mending days——"

"Damn it, Betty," says I, "be a little bit easier on me, will you? I don't intend to make a slave out of you. I'm going to keep a servant for you, of course!"

"Oh, I know men!" says Betty. "They're one thing before they're married. But they ain't interested in a poor girl after they've caught her. It's just the chase that amuses 'em!"

"Well," says I, "you've had plenty of chances to know all about men, I got to admit."

"What do you mean by that?" she snapped at me, getting pretty red.

"You look the part right now," says I. "There was never a time since your dresses was down to your knees that some boy or man ain't been breaking his heart after you. And you look like I'd caught you right in the middle of an affair, now!"

"Bah!" said Betty. "I never heard such a silly ninny as you, Billy Jacks! It's just

214

disgusting to hear what you think about the mind of a poor girl!"

"I run you down a lot, I suppose," says I. "But who is it now that you've taken a shine to?"

"No one!" she banged back at me.

But she got tremendously red and her eyes glittered, so that I could guess that maybe I was right.

"It's maybe the Baron," I told her.

"I hate him!" says she.

"The fine old castles and the good English accent," says I.

"The frosty old sap!" says Betty.

That dismissed the Baron.

"It's Dick Wace!" I jumped at her.

"Dick? Good old Dickie!" says she.

And she laughed, so that I guessed that if it wasn't Dick now, it had been sometime. Well, I didn't care much. It made me not very mad. I knew that a hundred gents had been in love with her, but Betty was a good girl. What counted was not the loving her, but the marrying her. A fish in the basket is worth a thousand that you can't have for dinner, says I to myself.

"If it ain't Dick Wace," says I, "then it's——"

"Stuff!" says she, and jumps past me, and

gets away, because she was as quick as a wink, and when I grabbed at her, she just faded away. It was like beating at a dead leaf, that a wind whirls away from your hand. And away she went into the house and gave me a laugh over her shoulder as she got through the door and slammed it in my face.

I leaned up against a tree, after that, and smelled the dinner that was seeping through the air, and watched the shadows curling like purple cats around the feet of the mountains, and altogether, I thanked God that I wasn't in the boots of the English Baron, with all of his castles and his ancestors.

No, I preferred being just as I was—the boss-to-be of my Betty, with all of her sassy ways. She was a great girl. If you could of seen just the way that she walked, never having to look at the ground for fear of stumbling. Or if you could of seen her laughing and smiling, which she mostly always was doing one of the two——

Well, she satisfied me. Not the best girl in the world, but one of the prettiest. And as for understanding her, why, even a deep gent like the Colonel had admitted that you can't know about women. You can just guess about 'em.

I remember that that night everything was

pretty gay in our dining room, because Roger Bartholomew and Joe Laurens had just come back from a trip up to the headwaters of the river, and there they had found what do you think? Why, it was the whole layout of a set of counterfeiters that was making ten dollar bills up there in a sort of a trapper's cabin. They had everything fine. One of 'em was a real trapper. And they caught things, too, and now and then they come down and sold pelts. And that old cabin was all filled up with hides and stretchers, and rusty traps, and what not. But it struck the Sheriff as queer that they should be able to live without selling *more* furs than they brought down. Which shows you how close everybody was watched in the Sierra Blanca. So he got the Colonel to send the two on a raid. They had a neat little fight on their hands. They got off clear, except that Joe got a scratch of a bullet across the back of his neck. And they caught one of the counterfeiters, and down through a trap door into a cellar they found the layout, where they made the stuff, and a lot of the queer, too, such good work that it would of been easy to push it right through the cash window of a bank, y'understand? Well, it did give my fingers an itch to see that good stuff—and know that it all had to be turned in as evidence! Because it was really almost as pretty as honest money.

But it was a big haul. Counterfeiting is a pretty low game, when you come to think of it, and we all praised Joe and Roger Bartholomew, and the Colonel sent in some wine out of his deepest cellar, and it was a rousing old time during dinner, I can tell you.

But that was only part of what interested me the most, because, as dinner was breaking up, big Charlie Lamb, he comes by me and he says:

"Look here, Billy. What's happening in the house?"

"You damned hound!" says I aside to him. "This here is one more reason why every decent man should hate your guts!"

He only laughed at me and went on. You couldn't reach Charlie Lamb very easy. And as for me, I stared after him hardly knowing whether to hate him most or just wonder at him, because that day he had been making love to the girl that would some day own the whole Sierra Blanca, and yet he took it as easy as if it had been nothing at all. You couldn't beat that man. There was Charlie Lamb all by himself and nobody else like him.

I wanted to get off by myself, however, and think things over, so I went outside in the dusk and rambled around the place. The whole back section of the garden up to a big stonewall hung over with vines belonged to us to walk around in. And pretty soon, off in a far corner of the garden, I could hear the tinkling of a guitar through the dusk and the murmer of a voice. When I come closer, I could make out, of course, that it was Charlie Lamb, singing very soft. All by himself, maybe?

No, that wasn't likely. And neither was it likely that Olivia Stockton would be sitting out there in the dark of the night even with Charlie Lamb. It must be somebody else, and I was rather anxious to find out who, I don't know why. So I sneaked up on them, and, after a while, I saw Charlie Lamb sitting on a bench against the wall, with a girl beside him, and her head on his shoulder, while he sang to her. It was sort of funny to listen to the clever way that he had of making the songs over and singing the words, so that they all talked about the girl that was with him. It must have tickled her a lot, but at the same time it disgusted me a good deal.

I sort of wished for the moon to show me her face. And then I told myself that there was a scare coming to them. I twitched out a Colt and put in a bullet not six inches over their heads.

I heard a squeak from the girl, and she went over that wall like a cat with nine legs and headed for the house, and then I faded out back the way that I had come, but behind me I could hear, a couple of times, the soft sound of a man brushing through the thickets of the garden.

Once I pressed back against the wall, and Charlie Lamb came by me as silent as a shadow, with the glint of a gun or a knife in his hand. And I was scared, believe you me! They could all talk as they pleased about dangerous men, but I knew that no man was half so dangerous as Charlie Lamb. He was off in a class by himself.

Still, it pleased me a good deal to have throwed that scare into the pair of them, and I wondered, sort of dim, which of the pretty housemaids had been the one whose heart Charlie was busting. As if Miss Olivia wasn't enough for him! No, he had to have plenty of work along that line to keep his hand in.

Well, I went along up to my room, and stood there in the window, that night, watching the moon rising late, and wondering what other eyes were watching her. It might be Betty, for instance, thinking maybe a little bit about me. And it might be Olivia worrying over the tangle that she had got things into. And it might be the poor Baron.

I had a lot of sympathy for the Baron. I can't say that I would of liked to see him marry the Colonel's daughter. But I had to admit that he had been acting like a man. It may have been that during that horse race he had showed enough yellow to make Charlie Lamb decide to treat him like a dog. But just the same, there was a good deal to the Baron, and I felt that he had been pretty white in the way that he had handled the ruction that evening in the house. He had acted fair, and a fair man always has me on his side.

But what the deuce would tomorrow bring to that house of Stockton?

CHAPTER 27

YOU TAKE THE English, there is some that like them and there is some that don't, but take them by and large and I should say that they got one good thing that can be said about them—they're dead game. Which worked out in the case of the Baron, as I'm gonna show you in detail. Yes, the Englishman will fight, when fighting counts the most. I mean, in the quiet times, where there ain't nothing but a man's honor to be considered.

The Baron, he sent word up to me early the next morning, and I went down as quick as I could and found him looking a little gray and peaked.

"I am going to need your help this morning, Jacks," says he. "May I count on you for an important service?"

"I'll do my best for you, sir," says I.

"Then may I ask you to get Charles Lamb and bring him over the hill, yonder? I'll be waiting for him down by the river edge."

I suppose that what he wanted was just to talk things over, and so I got Lamb and asked him to come out with me, without explaining a thing.

He came along, asking no questions, and yawning a good deal, because he wasn't one of these early birds. About sunset was the time when Charlie mostly woke up. We walked together over the edge of the hill and down to the trees by the river, and there was the Baron.

When Charlie saw him, "Hello!" says he, under his breath. "What does the little beggar want?"

He looked at me.

"I don't know what's in the deal," said I.

The Baron walked up to us.

"I've lain awake thinking this matter over," said he. "If I were in my own country I might know more clearly what to do. But I'm not in England, and it seems to me that every country has its own important customs, which should be followed by visitors. Now it seems to me that if a Westerner had been treated as you have treated me, Lamb, he would act as I intend to act. I suppose that you have a Colt with you?"

It dazed me. It seemed to daze Charlie Lamb, too, but finally he woke up and nodded.

"Yes," said he, "I have a Colt with me."

"Good!" says the Baron. "And I am armed, also. And we have Billy Jacks, an honorable fellow, to stand by and see fair play and report to the world what happens. I propose that we fight this matter out on the spot!"

Why, I couldn't catch my breath. Of course the Baron was a good shot and a sportsman, and all that. But even against a gent like me, that worked my two hours a day with shooting irons, what chance would the Baron have stood?

And against Charlie Lamb——

Well, it was like leading a man up to a slaughter.

"I don't need to tell you that I can shoot both fast and straight?" said Charlie Lamb.

"You don't need to tell me that. I have heard enough about you. But with your permission, we'll stand close together. I suppose that eight paces will be far enough apart to make a man miss. And that will leave the thing to speed of hand and, to a certain degree, leave things on the knees of the Gods. Here is a mark where you can stand. And my position is here."

He stepped off eight paces, very brisk, and heeled a deep line in the ground, and stood with his toe on it.

Yes, he was a game one, very pale, but steady as a ticking clock, and ready to fight till he died.

I looked at Charlie. He hadn't made a move to step to the mark. I even wondered if this quiet way of the Baron's might not have scared him a little, but it hadn't. Only, he was a little curious, and watching the Baron every minute very hard.

"Are you ready, sir?" says the Baron.

"I'm afraid that I'm not," says Charlie Lamb.

"May I ask you why not, sir?" says the Baron.

At that, Charlie let a faint smile come on his lips.

"Ah, well," says the Baron, as cool as you please, "if that's the case, I presume that I can remedy matters."

He walked straight up to Charlie and struck him with the flat of his hand across the face!

God bless me! I jumped both guns out and trained 'em on Charlie.

"Steady!" says I.

But Charlie wasn't making any move towards a draw. He just lifted his hand and wiped away a couple of drops of blood where the ring on the Baron's finger had cut his mouth. But you could see that he was raging. He'd got white, with one bright spot in the middle of each cheek, and there was a little trembling all through his whole body.

"Have I supplied you with enough cause to fight?" says the Baron, standing back on his mark again.

"You haven't given me enough cause to do a murder," says Charlie Lamb. "Almost, sir, but not quite enough."

Then he turned on me, with his jaw muscles bulging.

"Did you know about this, Jacks?" said he.

"No, so help me God!" I couldn't help busting out.

"Then see that you forget it," said Lamb, "or I'll break you in two and throw the pieces in the river. I'm a bit tired of matters in Sierra Blanca, and I think that I may as well begin to make a little trouble on my own account!"

And with that, he turned his back on the two of us, and he walked on back to the house.

The Baron was somewhat flabbergasted. He had come out there all set on killing or being killed, with the odds about twenty to one that he would take the bullet through his head. And now he was partly relieved and partly beat, relieved to find that he was still alive, after having done what he believed to be his duty, and beat because Charlie Lamb hadn't fought. Because you could see clearly enough that Charlie had *wanted* to fight after being hit.

"I really don't know what to make of it," says the Baron.

"You can thank God that you ain't already in heaven," says I. I kicked a stone away in front of me, and then pulverized it with a forty-five caliber bullet, because I was feeling sort of edgy and mean.

"I suppose that I can," said the Baron. "I admit that I'm glad the thing is over. But still I'm troubled. He allowed me to strike him!"

"He could break you apart worse than any doctors would ever mend!" I couldn't help telling him. "He could kill five like you while they was drawing their guns!"

"I half believe that he could!" murmured the Baron.

"You take it straight from me—because I know!" says I.

We started walking slowly back towards the house.

"Ah, well——" says the Baron a couple of times, but whatever was on the edge of being said, he didn't say it, but finished the trip in silence except that at the end he said:

"Thank you a great deal for helping me out, Jacks."

"Don't thank me," says I. "I wouldn't of been in on it for a million, if I'd knowed the crazy idea that was in your head."

"At any rate," says the Baron, "I want you to get some trifle by which you can remember me."

And he passed me a fifty dollar bill!

Well it came over me with a sort of a hot rush, and for a minute it was hard for me to hold myself in, but finally I just said:

"Out here, sir, a cowpuncher ain't no damned valet nor houseservant. I don't want your money!"

He took it back, looking pretty sick, and I went on, feeling more easy:

"It's all right. Only, if you have to spend much time around these parts, it'd pay you to study the natives a mite. Because it is really a great saver. Sometimes it saves you money. Sometimes it saves you blood. I know you didn't mean no harm, so it's all right, and we part friends!"

"I feel a complete fool!" says the Baron. "Thank you for teaching me the correct thing!"

And as I went off, I could hear him saying: "Extraordinary!" But nothing ever beat that—I mean, up and handing me fifty bucks! If it had been anybody else, even the Colonel, I would of chucked it back into his face and told him which way hell was planted. But a stranger like him, me knowing him beforehand, why it sort of was different.

Only you see the trouble sometimes is that your hand is faster than your thought, and a man's hand, in those days, was always hanging close to the butt of a Colt. I've seen men die just because they didn't have time to finish a sentence, and the first part of the sentence was all misunderstood. I've seen 'em die because they laughed at the wrong place in a story. And take it by and large, there was more work for the spinning cylinder of a revolver, in the Sierra Blanca, than there was for a normal set of brains.

However, I was sort of glad that the Baron had come through those two bad scrapes in one morning, and I didn't bear him no malice. As for him getting me in wrong with Smiling Charlie, why, Charlie and me was such perfect enemies already that there was nothing more to be wished for in that direction.

I went on up to my room, threw some water at my face, and then come down for breakfast and there is something sort of friendly and smiling in the face of ham and eggs. I waded through a couple of plates of them, and felt better all around.

And then I went out to take the air and see if there was any orders. But there wasn't none. There was too much trouble inside for the Colonel to pay much attention to what was going on outside. Too much trouble in the inside of his family. And I wondered what sort of an earthquake it would be to the minds of men, if they was ever to wake up in the Sierra Blanca and know the inside truth of what was happening in Stockton House.

Another thing sort of bothered me. It was the girl that I had seen with Charlie the evening before, because that squeak she let out as she went over the fence, it had sounded sort of familiar to me, though I couldn't yet locate the voice.

CHAPTER 28

IF YOU FEEL about these things the way that I did, maybe you think that it was all enough piled up and complicated before this, but it was to get more tangled still, and all of the trouble was to be brought to a head, and it was me that done it!

No, of all the bad things that I've done in my life it was the worst. A woman was what done it. And there ain't any resisting a woman. No, sir, they're the real poison, mostly, that turns a man's life bad for him.

Well, it was like this: I had gone strolling down to the river in the noontime, after lunch, thinking of looking over the spot where that little game-cock, the Baron, had stood up to terrible Charlie Lamb in the morning of this same day. I aimed to look the spot over and to stretch myself out in a place where there was half shadow and half sun, and take a nap, being always partial to a snooze after lunchtime. But when I got down there, I forgot all about sleeping, for there was Betty, and no matter what else could ever be said about her, she was a sure cure for sleepiness. You could wager that something exciting would be happening every time that Betty come around.

She maybe had seen me coming, and got into position when I arrived, but anyway, when I got down there, she was sitting on a stone at the edge of the river, and her chin was on her fist, and she was staring into the water, very gloomy looking, and very pretty looking, too.

Well, I walked up behind her until the shadow of me stood down in the water beside her.

"What are you fishing for, Betty?" says I.

She didn't answer. She pretended like she didn't hear.

"Betty," says I, "what's up, please."

"If I knew," says she, "wouldn't I tell

you? I would consider that it was my bounden right to tell you—the man that I'm practically engaged to marry!"

"Hey, wait a minute!" I called to her. "How come you to say that you're only practically engaged? Ain't I got your word?"

"Not before no witnesses," says Betty.

It jarred me, that did. I never had even had that sort of a thought.

"I didn't think that you would work it out that way, Betty," says I to her.

"Never would of come into my mind," says Betty, "except that I see how mean and light you treat me, like I didn't matter to you, and it makes me wish that I had had you speak before witnesses."

"Witnesses?" says I. "Look here! Come up to the house, right now. There's a lot of the boys there, and nothing would please me more than to give you all of the witnesses that you want. Why, honey, I never heard of such an idea. You know that you can have all of the witnesses that you want."

"You say it just to please and flatter me," says she. "But after I got up there with you, you'd find some way of slipping away from your contract. Oh, I know you! And I know other men! But never any that would treat me the way that you do!"

I stood back a little to take another look at her. I couldn't make her out. And the reason, of course, was that she didn't want to be made out, but I couldn't see that at the time. Back sight is always a lot clearer than front sight, when it comes to women and their affairs.

"I dunno what's got into you, Betty," says I.

But she had started staring down at the river again, and I couldn't get a word from her until I touched her shoulder. Then she raised her head and let me look down into eyes more mournful than the eyes of a dying calf.

"What do you want of me, Billy?" said she.

I said to her:

"Now, Betty, come out in the clear with me and tell me what's wrong?"

"Oh, Billy, Billy!" said she. "Ain't you ashamed to ask me? You know. And the others know. And I'm almost the only person in the house that doesn't understand what's wrong, or why Miss Olivia sits so much looking straight in front of her, and why she spends so much time in her room, and why the Colonel is so gay, and why the Baron is so down! You know! Because you're on the inside, and everybody trusts you! Oh, but I wish that they could know as much about you as I do, and they wouldn't be trusting you so quick!"

I saw where the shoe was pinching, and I wished very hearty that I hadn't kept up the subject so long.

"I got no idea what you mean, Betty," I told her. "How should I know the private affairs of Miss Olivia and the Colonel and the Baron?"

"Is there any other man on the place that's taken into their confidence as much as you are?" says Betty.

Why, that appealed to my pride a good deal. I couldn't help admitting that probably there wasn't.

"And isn't there some reason," said Betty, "why everyone is saying that the Colonel is going to make you a permanent manager of the estate after he's dead and gone?"

"Hello!" said I. "Do they say that?"

"Do they!" said she. "Oh, Billy, you know right well that they do. And you don't tell me—your own wedded wife!"

"Hold on, Betty, you ain't my wedded wife, yet!"

"I'm just the same, really. I've told you that I love you. I've promised to marry you."

"Yes," I couldn't help putting in, "but not before witnesses!"

"I knew it," says Betty, her lip beginning to twitch. "I knew it. You just been playing with me and making a fool of me!"

"Don't cry, Betty, for God's sake!" says I.

"And now you won't tell me even the least little thing!" she said, half sobbing.

"I will!" said I. "I will tell you everything that I can!"

"Then tell me what you and the Colonel and Miss Olivia and the Baron was talking about in that room yesterday!" she snapped back at me.

It made me dizzy. I looked around me.

"Don't wait to invent something!" she said. "You just tell me the truth, because that'll be good enough for me!"

"It's a matter of honor," says I.

"Honor!" cried Betty, and quick as a wink the fire was out of her eye and she was on the edge of tears again. "Honor! And therefore I ain't good enough to hear it! Oh, I know what you are now, Billy Jacks! You're just a mean, low philanderer!"

I couldn't hardly stand that.

"It ain't true!" said I.

"It is! It is!" said Betty. "Nothing with honor in it is poor enough for me."

"Betty," said I, telling the truth, "you're just talking plain nonsense!"

"I'm a fool, too!" sobbed Betty. "Oh, why don't you beat me, too! That's all that's needed! I can see the kind of a life that I'm going to lead with you! But I won't lead it! No, I won't! I'll find some man that has a decent respect for me, even if I don't care two snaps of my fingers for him!"

I was getting deeper and deeper into the mire. I didn't know which way to turn or what to do. I could only stammer: "Will you please listen to me?"

"Oh, you've thought up your lie by this time, I suppose!" said she.

"What do you want me to do?" I asked her. "Give away the honor that I pledged to the Colonel and to the Baron and to Miss Olivia?"

"Oh!" gasped Betty. "It's as important as all of that?"

"It is!"

"And you'll let me break my heart for not knowing? Oh, Billy, ain't it just the same as you knowing for me to know? Ain't we just one and the same person?"

I hardly knew what to say to that. I knew

that there was something like that in the marriage service. You couldn't expect a girl to be reasonable about such things.

All at once she broke out:

"It's just because you don't trust me! It's because you think that I couldn't keep a little secret! A little, silly, unimportant secret!"

"Silly and unimportant!" I snorted. "I tell you, it's the most important thing that I ever come across. It may send the Baron back to England and put another man here as the husband of Miss Olivia to be the heir to the Sierra Blanca."

She couldn't even speak. Her eyes, tears and all, was like saucers.

"Billy!" she gasped. "It ain't true!"

"What ain't true."

"Miss Olivia—she *couldn't* of got compromised with another man! I know her!"

"You do, eh?" says I, very grim.

"I know her. You're simply dodging me—and I say it's pure cowardly to put the blame onto a beautiful, perfect girl like her!"

"Is it," says I, very hot. "I'm dragging her down, am I?"

"It couldn't be! Not something that she did in England!" gasped Betty.

"No," says I, "it's someone right here in the valley!"

At that she rolled her eyes, and she turned actually white.

"Someone—here—in the valley! I don't believe it!"

"Someone right here in Stockton House!" I said, taking a sort of vicious pleasure in convincing her.

"I don't believe one single word of it!"

"No," said I, "you always know everything beforehand!"

"Because there isn't anybody!" said she.

"My God," said I, "you're just blind! Ain't I warned you before about a man that's right here in Stockton House? Ain't I said beforehand that he was a hound, and ain't you stood up for him, and said that the world has abused him? And now he's dared to make love to Miss Olivia herself. That shows you how much you know about——"

I stopped here, because Betty had jumped up and caught me by the hands and she shook them, crazy with a sort of fear.

"You don't mean Smiling Charlie!" she whispered to me. "Dear God, you don't mean him!"

"Don't I? But I do. Him that you think so much of! Him that the world has mistreated so bad!"

"It's a lie!" whispered Betty, whiter and sicker looking than before.

"Is it a lie? Then you that know so much, here's something else for you to know: I seen him kiss her—with my own eyes I seen it!"

CHAPTER 29

WELL, THERE IT was out—the thing that I had swore to the Colonel that I would never say. The thing that I had promised the Baron was dead, so far as I was concerned. More than that, my own honor should have kept me silent, even though I had never promised nothing to nobody.

But it was out. It was said. It couldn't be taken back!

Maybe it don't seem so terrible to you that hear about it now, but that's because you're most likely accustomed to the cigarette-smoking, bobbed-haired, short-skirted girls of these days, that would about as soon kiss a man as say good morning to him. Kissing ain't a crime, these days. It ain't even a luxury! It's just taken for granted.

But it was different in those times. And Miss Olivia, why you didn't think about such things when you looked at her. She was that much above other women!

But what mattered just then was not Miss Olivia and her honor and mine. No, what mattered was just Betty. I'd seen her in tantrums before, and wildnesses, and hysterias, but never in anything like this, because she kept on getting whiter and sicker, and she put back a hand and rested it against a tree and leaned there with her eyes closed.

"Betty! Betty!" says I. "Don't take on so! It just proves that Miss Olivia is only human. There never was a girl that could resist him. He's got a thousand girls, scattered all over the country!"

She says:

"Don't touch me. I don't want to be touched. I want—to go away!"

And she did turn away from me and she started for the house. I caught up with her. She looked like a sleepwalker, with her great, staring, scared eyes fixed on me, but not seeing me.

"Betty," says I, "for God's sake, what's wrong?"

"Nothing," says she. "Only let me go—I want to be alone! I want to be alone! I want to die!"

And she burst into a sort of a little choked

wail and ran away from me through the sunshine and into Stockton House, with me too flabbergasted to follow her, even, or to stop her from going in.

Well, I went back and sat down by the river. I figgered that what had happened was about as bad as if the duel had taken place there that morning, because on this spot I'd given up my honor and throwed away my word of honor. I'd let a girl wheedle it out of me! Ah, that was a damn mean moment. I didn't much care whether I lived or died.

And then I took a grip on myself and I turned around and starched up my back, as you might say, and I marched for Stockton House.

I went up to the main entrance, and a servant with a turned-up nose come and looked me over.

"Have you mistaken the door?" says he.

He was new to his place and his job, and he didn't know me.

I says:

"Go tell your boss that Billy Jacks wants to see him, will you?"

"To whom," says he, "do you refer?"

"You flat-faced son of a fool!" says I, a trifle peeved, "Go do what I tell you!"

He acted like I had pulled a gun on him

and faded away from that door instanter, but in a minute he come back and very polite and he says:

"Mr. Jacks, excuse me for not recognizing you, sir. And would you step this way, sir? Colonel Stockton is coming down immediately to see you, sir."

I didn't talk back to him. It didn't even give me much pleasure to put a worm like that in his right place—which is under a gent's feet.

I'd no sooner sat down than the Colonel come in, and he takes his cigar out of his mouth and drops his hands into his coat pockets and spreads his legs a little apart.

"Ah!" says he. "You have been raising the devil, Jacks, I see!"

I looked at the little puffs of smoke that he had blowed out through the cigar in speaking. I watched 'em float up and turn thin and brown.

"Yes, sir," says I, "I have raised hell!"

"You've killed someone, I suppose," says the Colonel, not seeming terrible shocked.

"Killed somebody?" says I. "No, sir, I wish that it was only as bad as that! I ain't killed a man for three years."

"Barring a few Indians," says he. "But go on. You interest me a good deal!"

He took the cigar out of his mouth.

"Colonel Stockton," says I, "I have throwed away my honor. I am standin' here no better than a dog!"

"Hello!" says he. "Hello, Billy! I'm terribly sorry to hear you talk like this. Sit down, my boy, and tell me about it."

"I can't sit down, sir," said I. "I'm gunna tell you what I've done, and then I'm gunna take myself out of Sierra Blanca."

"Tush, man!" says he. "Not until I release you, surely? And if it's a mere matter of protection—I may tell you, Billy, that I have learned ways of turning the law into a very tame dog indeed!"

"Sir," says I, "it's you that I've wronged!"

He waited.

I says:

"I have let a girl worm the facts out of me. I let her find out what I'd seen—I mean, sir, about Miss Olivia and Charlie Lamb!"

I heard a click as his jaws set, and his eyes sent out a couple of sparks. It made me sick, but I had to stand and take it. I looked him in the eye and waited for hell to open. How many things he said to himself before he spoke to me I never can guess, but I do know that in the end he only said:

"Well, Billy, a good man can do no wrong.

And you're a good fellow, Billy, and therefore it will turn out that you've done no great harm. But about the girl—who is she?"

"She's Miss Olivia's maid, sir."

"Betty? Ah, yes, and I've heard that you're rather fond of her, haven't I? Well, perhaps for once in the world we can keep a woman's tongue still!"

"Perhaps, sir," says I. "And perhaps she won't talk at all. She seemed wonderful upset by what I told her."

"She did, did she?"

"Yes, sir. The idea that Miss Olivia—her figgering Miss Stockton for a kind of a saint, y'understand——"

"I understand perfectly. But more womanly than saintly. Therefore more blessed, my boy, though perhaps you hardly follow that. Let me see—we'd better send for Betty straight way!"

He rang for a servant and said for Betty to be called. While we waited he went on very gentle and quiet:

"How long ago did this happen?"

"Between five and six minutes," I told him.

"Tut, tut!" says he. "It didn't take you long to see that you had done wrong. You didn't have to wait for the consequences to develop."

"I wished that I had tore my tongue out by the roots," says I, feeling pretty bitter.

"I believe it! I believe it! I believe it!" says he, three times over. "And now let me tell you another thing, my lad. Since you've made this one little slip, I'm prepared to find you perfect in all matters of honor from this time forth, and I'm more willing to trust you than ever before. You haven't lost ground with me. You've gained."

The servant came back into the room, looking sort of puzzled. He said that Betty couldn't come down, because she was sick in bed, and Miss Olivia was very busy taking care of her.

That staggered me a good deal. It put out the Colonel, too.

"Damn me!" says he. "It doesn't matter if she only talks to Olivia. But—who would think that any such bouncing country girl would have such a stock of sensibility?"

"Sir," says I, "I can't make it out at all. She ain't a flighty kind. She ain't no sentimentalist, I can tell you."

"All right," said the Colonel. "I don't have to tell you never to forget this affair. I know it will be a lesson to you. And even the best horse will need a touch on the rein, now and then. Good-by, Billy!"

Well, I went out of that house sort of feeble and blinded, and worshiping the Colonel, you had better believe. There was a saying that nobody that had ever started working for him had ever stopped off, and I could understand that, now, because he was just hard and mean and calculating and smart enough to set off his kindness, when he felt like being kind. And when he put his trust in you, you felt richer than a bank.

He was a great man, was the Colonel, as more men than me could testify, and he never really deserved the end that lay ahead of him, it seemed to me. But it ain't my duty to talk about that.

Anyhow, when I went out of that house, I was so relieved that I could understand why the Catholics have confession. Because it's pretty good for the soul to talk out the things that are pressing on your mind. And there ain't anything worse than to take your sins home into your mind and lock the door on them.

I went out into the open. I got my big bay, and I took him for a ride with a pipe between my teeth, and damn glad that I could hold up my head again. I still felt a mite sick, but I was determined to play so straight and square all the rest of my life that I would make up for what I had done on this day.

Afterwards, I loped back to the house, and on the way, a big hawk sailed out from the top of a scrub oak. I slipped my rifle out and took a quick bead and fired. And down come the hawk head over heels. It was a pretty neat shot. And it pleased me, because with the tense feeling that I had, I had begun to think that maybe I would have to shoot my way out of some of the difficulties that might be lying ahead of me.

In that, I was a true prophet, and I was never righter than in being glad that my shooting eye was in good trim at that moment, because, when I come back to Stockton House, I found that the old place was wearing just the same fine, dignified, satisfied look that it always had, but the insides of it was changed so's you could never of recognized them.

Things had been happening, since I left, and it was me that had been the cause of the happenings.

I hadn't more than got to my room when a knock come at my door.

"Come in," I sang out, and in comes Dick Wace.

"I was looking for you, Old Timer," he says. "Here's a note Charlie left for you." And he holds out an envelope with my name on it.

CHAPTER 30

I TOOK A LOOK at that note and then at Dick.

"Why didn't Charlie wait to tell me what he wanted to say?" I asked him.

"I dunno," says Dick. "Charlie's mind ain't mine. There you are!"

And he went off and left me with the note. Which I was sort of glad afterwards that nobody was there to see my face as I read it. Because it said:

Billy, I didn't realize that there was so much snake in you. As for the harm that I've done you, I've been half sorry about it. But now I'm damned glad.

As for the further harm that I intend to do you, you can make up your mind that it will not be long before I come on your trail. And when I come, have your guns ready, because I intend to kill you, Jacks, as sure as there is a God in heaven.

Charles Lamb.

Yes, that was serious. Nobody leaves a note threatening to kill a man unless he's pretty heated up, and when you come to think of it, nobody was as little likely to get actually heated up as this same Smiling Charlie was.

He meant business, but I wouldn't have him hanged for killing me, just because he'd been man enough to warn me of what he intended to do. I touched a match to that note, and when I'd watched the black cinder of the paper float away into the air, I turned around and walked for the Colonel.

Things was piling up with interest. I had told Charlie that one day I would get him. Now he had turned around and told me the same thing. So, all around, it looked like business.

The Colonel was ready to see me right off. And we sat in the library with the gold of the western sun floating in through the long windows and making everything look shadowy and unreal inside of the house. He says:

"The devil is up, my friend. The devil is actually up and walking the earth, and he seems to have taken a most special interest in Stockton House. What I'm wondering just now is, what do you know of all of his doings?"

"I only know," said I, "that Charlie Lamb seems to have disappeared."

"You should know more than that about him," said the Colonel. "The fact is that he is very hot against you, Jacks."

"I gathered that, too," said I.

"However," said the Colonel, "you needn't worry about him, because I've given orders to have him watched out of the valley. He's being accompanied by six good men to the first pass, and after he's seen through that, I don't think that he'll be able to jump back over the fence into our garden!"

He made a pause, and knocked the ashes off his cigar. There was still a good deal on his mind, so I just waited, saying nothing.

"Very odd," said the Colonel, "how deeply you've become involved in this affair. But I think that there is something more for you to do with it. I am going to open my heart to you, Jacks. The fact is that my daughter gave Master Lamb his marching orders."

"Miss Olivia!" cried I.

"Yes, yes," said he, and his eyes glittered, so that you could see that he was tremendously satisfied. He went on:

"When she heard what had happened at the same time that he was paying such attention to her she was naturally sickened, and she asked me to send for him. I don't think that the scoundrel will wish to see her face again! Not after what she had to say to him. In the meantime, he has done his damage, and poor Baron Wakeness is on the way back to England at the present moment!"

I looked down at the floor. Of course I could see through this pose on the part of the Colonel. And, as a matter of fact, while he talked I was wondering how any man could be so devilish clever as he had turned out to be. In the first place, he had gotten rid of the Baron, and in the second place, he had gotten rid of the tool which he had used to discard the Baron. All down the list, he was the winner, and yet he had done it so neatly that only Charlie Lamb knew what he had really had in mind. And Charlie Lamb was out of the problem now, so it seemed.

Well, there was also me. But what I knew was chiefly by accident of having listened in at the window when the Colonel was talking with Charlie. The Colonel never guessed that I knew the combination as well as Charlie did. Perhaps he wouldn't have been talking so freely, if that had been the case.

"Betty, you'll be glad to know," says the Colonel, "has recovered. She seems to be a girl with a great deal of mental muscle. And the shock was soon digested by her. You'll be pleased to know that."

"Yes, sir," said I. "Of course I'm very glad to know that."

"There remains, however, the problem of my daughter. You see that I talk to you not as an employee, but as a friend whose advice I need, Jacks. Olivia is a girl whose heart is really not often deeply moved. It is moved now. She is badly broken up, and as long as this man is above ground, I'm afraid that she will never fix her mind on the life that lies ahead of her. She may always be looking back to him with regrets. He's such a worthless, romantic devil, you know. The very type to attract the eye of a girl. But you've had the bitter proofs of that, yourself!"

I didn't quite follow that. But what I did follow was that the Colonel was indirectly angling for me to take a hand in this matter and try to remove Charlie Lamb. Remove him how? Why, with a bullet, perhaps. I suppose that the Colonel really didn't care how.

"As a matter of fact, sir," says I, "in due time me and Charlie Lamb has got to meet, and when we meet, one of us will die!"

"If he should kill you, I think I could see to it that he hung for it," said the Colonel.

252

"But as a matter of fact, there is no danger of that. I know him, and I know you, and of the two, you are the more capable fighting man, my lad, simply because you are the less confident."

Very neat, but there was something else revealed. It hardly mattered to the Colonel. Let me kill Charlie—and there's an end of Charlie Lamb. Or let Charlie kill me and be hanged for it. In either case, an end to Charlie Lamb. You see how it worked out? Like one of those problems in the newspapers. You can't see how it fits together until the last piece is in place!

I admired the Colonel a lot. His brains, I mean. But more than ever I felt that he was a tiger.

"I am glad to see," went on the Colonel, "that you are leaving it to time to bring you and Charlie together. Certainly I should hate to see you fight it out. But at the same time, some men are so hasty when they have been injured as he has injured you——"

"Injured me?" says I, bewildered.

"Why, man—is it possible that you don't know? I thought that you understood and were being a philosopher about it!"

I stood up, my brain reeling.

"Will you tell me in little short words?" says I.

"Tell you? I don't like the responsibility, because, if you're ready to kill him without knowing this—what will you be afterwards?"

I set my teeth.

"Sir," says I, "you're driving in the spur pretty deep!"

"Poor lad," says the Colonel, "God knows that I don't wish to torment you. But I don't know that the knowledge would be wise to place in your hands."

He got up and walked the room. I followed him with my eyes, still weak with the thing that I was guessing.

Suddenly he stopped on the far side of the room and pointed. It was a big room that went straight through the house, and the windows on the other side looked into the garden where the willows were.

"There she is now," said the Colonel, "and looking cheerful and strong enough. Why don't you go and ask her yourself?"

I looked out the window, and there was Betty and Miss Olivia.

"Miss Olivia?" I said.

"My daughter? No, no, poor fellow. I mean Betty, of course. Your Betty."

Well, that was enough to strike me blind and the light didn't come back across my eyes until I was out there in the garden and seen the dresses of the two girls flashing between the leaves of the trees ahead of me. Then I stopped a minute and I tried to pull myself together. It didn't seem possible! I couldn't believe what the Colonel had made me guess.

And I looked up to the windows of the library above me, and seen the figure of the Colonel, glimmering and dim, as he stood well back from behind the glass. He didn't look like a fine man to me no more. He looked like a devil, because of the misery that he had poured into my life all at once.

Then I went stumbling ahead, and I come out into the open and the last rays of the sun fell blinding in my eyes, and I seen Betty and Miss Olivia like two black shapes before me. There was a scream from Betty.

"Miss Olivia! Help! He's come to kill me!"

"Hush, Betty! Hush!" said Miss Olivia. "He'll not touch you nor offer to. Don't be afraid! Don't be afraid, Betty!"

Well my eyes cleared a little after that and first of all I could see Miss Olivia, and it seemed to me that she was very pale and set in her expression, but it wasn't on account of me that she looked older and so sick.

And, after that, I could see Betty, as she clung to Miss Olivia and trembled and looked as though I was a hawk and she a chicken getting under the wing of its mother.

What had she done?

Well, I only knew beforehand that there was a curse over Stockton House.

I took off my hat, not out of politeness, but to rub the sweat off of my forehead. And I blinked at the pair of them.

"I've come to find out," says I. "Betty, talk up!"

CHAPTER 31

Now, WHEN I had a good look at Betty, I could see that there was something pretty bad wrong with her. She didn't look at me, but she looked straight back at Miss Olivia as if to say, "Help me! Keep him away from me!"

And Miss Olivia put an arm half way round her and said:

"Billy Jacks, you know so much already that you can know more, and I think it's your right to know this——"

256

"No, no!" says Betty, in a half scream. "He'll kill me if he knows!"

"He must know, and he must know now," said Miss Olivia. "I think that I understand Billy Jacks better than you do, and I know that there is nothing vicious about him. The truth is——"

She got that far, when Betty, with a wail, scooted away and headed for the house.

Miss Olivia looked after her, and I was half of a mind to run after that girl and bring her back by force, but I didn't. I just waited for the bad news to happen. And Miss Olivia says pretty soon:

"This isn't pleasant to tell you. I know that you'll forgive me for having to tell you such unlucky tidings. But it seems that Charles Lamb was simply a lying and hypocritical scoundrel. You know that he was pretending to be greatly—interested—in me!"

She brought out the words with a little effort, but she didn't wince in spite of the pain that the speech gave her. She went right on, and I admired her a lot for it.

"Yes," says I, "I know."

"But all the while that he was making that pretence, he was making outright and violent love to another person, Billy Jacks. I suppose that you can guess who?"

Well, I looked at her for a moment, hardly daring to believe that I had heard straight. It never had entered my head, you understand, that while a hound was pretending to be in love with Miss Olivia he would dare to keep half an eye for any other woman. Because I ask you who else was there in the world that could be compared to her for a minute?

But then it come crash in my mind: that voice that I had heard from the girl that had been sitting with her head on the shoulder of Smiling Charlie the other evening—that familiar voice of her that I hadn't been able to place—why it come thudding home like a bullet into me. It was Betty!

"Betty!" says I. "It was Betty!"

And Miss Olivia nodded.

"It was Betty!" says I, feeling the world turn black in front of me.

I begun to turn away from her but all at once she run after me and touched my shoulder.

"Don't imagine too much that——"

I brushed her hand away. There was nothing that mattered to me, then. Not even the hand of Miss Olivia touching me. I just brushed her away, and I headed straight away out of the garden. I thought that she called once behind me. But I didn't turn back to make sure.

Because—well, I was walking through a queer sort of a darkness, and there wasn't much that I was able to take in.

I went up to my room and there I got together my blankct roll and I went on out to the stable and got hold of my bay and put the saddle on him. Then, from the gun room, I picked out my rifle and I had two pairs of Colts—one for the holsters of the saddle, and one for the hips. I had chose those guns with a lot of care. I had used them a lot. And I knew that they were perfect. But now, as I sat my hands on them, the black cloud lifted off of me, and everything it become as clear as day to me.

I should like to say something right here about that new sort of clearness that I had in my mind, because it's hard to explain. I don't mean to say that I was right, and I suppose that, in a way, I was a crazy man. That's the way I like to explain myself and some of the things that I done. But while the mood was on me, it was just as though I had telescope eyes that seen everything at a great distance as clear as could be—the hearts of men as well as distant mountains.

I looked over those four guns—no, one of them was *not* perfect, after all. And then I turned over the rest of the stock and found what I wanted. I hardly had to touch a weapon before I saw what was right or wrong in it. My head was just wonderful clear— like a frosty morning.

And I felt that my strength was doubled and trebled in me, so that I could undertake about anything in the world.

I looked around me, as I put the guns into their places, at the gents that I had knowed. I thought of the Baron, and his damned supercilious content with himself, and I thought of the Colonel's hypocrisy and underhandedness, getting things by indirection that he was ashamed of going out and trying to take frankly. He seemed to me like a fox more than a man. I thought of Betty, too, and how she had lied to me, and how she had strung me along, and with a lie in her heart, how she had used my love for her in order to pry the Baron's secret out of me. And then I laughed, and the laughter it didn't open my heart but just closed it all the more. And my lips, they felt like iron. I thought, last of all, of Smiling Charlie Lamb, and as I was thinking of him, Dick Wace, he come into the gun room.

He was wearing a hawk's feather stuck in his hat and sticking up high above the crown—long, gray feather. And I whipped up a Colt and blew that feather straight in two.

"Christ!" says Dick, and jumped backwards, bringing out a gun.

I dropped my own gun to full arm's length.

There had never been a man that I ever liked or respected better than I respected and liked Dick Wace, in the old days, but now it seemed to me, or to the devil in me, that he was the most cocksure, contemptible gent that ever lived. I says to him:

"What's the matter? Afraid that I was going to spoil your pretty face?"

Dick glared at me, his gun twitching in his hand.

"What in hell has taken a grip on you?" he asked me finally.

"The power to see through the lot of you!" says I. "That's what's taken possession of me. Y'understand? Why, by God, it makes me sick now as I stand here facing you. I tell you what you are—you're a sneak, Wace. I'm standing here and telling you that, and you got a gun in your hand. What're you doing about it?"

261

He didn't do a thing. But he looked scared. Not as you would look scared of a man, but of a mad dog.

I seen that look, and it sort of pleased me. It was a lot of fun, I thought, to crush poor Dick. I says:

"Keep the feathers out of your hats, after this. Or real men may happen along and take them out for you—and they might shoot a mite lower than I done."

I walked past Dick, and still he stared at me as though he'd been turned into stone—or as though I was a walking devil. Which perhaps I was, just then!

Outside, I mounted the bay and just then old Albemarle walked up.

"You ought not to ride the bay for a week," says he. "You've been working him down too much. He needs to flesh up a little."

"Listen to me," says I, riding the bay right up to him and sitting the saddle with my shadow in his face. "Listen to me, because I'm gunna give you some good advice. You got a lot of low hounds on this place that'll listen to your yapping. But don't you ever open your mouth to me again and give me advice. Because I'm a growed up man, Albemarle, and if you was twenty years younger,

I'd fix you so's you'd remember my words a good deal better!"

Well, Albemarle, he was a sort of a mean old beggar, in a good many ways, and he wasn't exactly easy in his speech, sometimes, but still, there was no call for talking to him that way, y'understand? No excuse at all! He'd always been partial to me and done a lot for me and my ponies. But here I was ripping into him without no mercy. And the same sort of a dazed stare come into his eyes that I had seen in the eyes of Dick Wace.

I enjoyed it a lot, too, and it made me laugh, and I turned away still laughing, with a tremor like metal in my lips, because I knew that that look in their faces meant fear, and that I had scared the two of those men out of about ten years of their life. It seemed a fine thing to me, with that present meanness in me.

Well, I turned around and I walked the bay out into the open and jogged him down the road.

I sort of hated to leave the place, though. Because there was a lot more gents around there that I would of liked to meet up with and tell them what I thought of them. There was a lot of nasty things that I had on the tip of my tongue all ready to fire at them, but there was something that I wanted more than to talk to other men, and that was just to get Smiling Charlie within the range of my rifle, or pointblank with my revolver. The revolver would be better, I decided, because, at a distance, I wouldn't be able to see his face and watch it when death hit it. And that was what I wanted. I wanted to see death catch hold on him and choke him, and me to stand over him and let him see me laughing as he died.

You might ask how come that I was so willing to step up to Smiling Charlie, now, me that had always felt that he was a far better man than me at any sort of a weapon? Well, I'll tell you. The fact is that I didn't have any fear of God or man left in me. I would of walked up to ten fighters and talked to them like I was invisible, or their guns was loaded with wooden bullets. That was how sure I was. My nerves, they was like steel. It hadn't even surprised me when I cut the feather in two that was on the hat of Dick Wace.

I could see the truth about all the men I had ever known, it seemed to me, and also, it seemed as though there was a line drawn straight from the muzzle of my gun to anything that I wanted to shoot at.

As I jogged my horse down the lane, I pulled out a Colt and let loose three shots, and three strands of the wire fence snapped with a ping!

As I went on, the horses in that field come out through the gap that I had made and wandered off down the lane at a gallop. And that pleased me a good deal, too. Yes, anything that would make trouble for other men would please me a whole lot. The more pain and misery that I could bring into the world, the better I was satisfied, because, no matter what I did to other folks, there was nothing that I could do to Betty.

No, she sat back there in Stockton House and grieved about nothing, except maybe that Smiling Charlie had been run out of the valley and that he couldn't sit beside her no more in the evenings and sing her his lying songs!

CHAPTER 32

I WENT ALONG into town, at last. There I stepped in the livery stable, and I ordered the boss to have the bay rubbed down and walked to cool him off, and then throw a feed of good clean oats into him.

He was a fat old chap, that boss. He was always sitting alone beside the front door of the stable, with his chair all comfortable tilted back against the wall. Most usually he was slicing away at a stick with a sharp knife and chewing a quid of tobacco.

He pushed the hat back from his forehead.

"Matter of fact, Billy," says he, "there ain't a soul here to walk your horse and cool him off."

I turned around and I looked at him, and it seemed to me that clearer than the three days' whiskers on his face, I could see the greasy, lazy soul of him. I pointed a finger at him.

"I'm gunna be back here inside of an hour," says I, "and you see that all of those things is done, and done right!"

Well, he jumped as though I'd pointed a gun at him instead of a finger. His hat tumbled off, but he didn't pay any attention to that, he just threw me a scared look as though I'd sent a bullet through him, or was about to, and he grabbed the reins and he led the bay inside. And all the way, he was walling his eyes back at me as though he expected me to open fire on him.

It made me laugh again, with my lips stiff

266

as iron, and I went on down the street with my nerves on edge, and my jaws set.

I went to the Sheriff's office, and there Steve Ross, he jumped up and come to meet me.

"Why, Billy," says he, "you've got to be a stranger in here. I been missing you a lot!"

"Why?" says I. "Have you had some sort of use for me? Something that you wanted to get out of me?"

He give me a weird look. Him and me had always gotten along fine. And he knew that when the Colonel had asked me my opinion of him, I had given him a fine send-off. That was worth a couple of more terms of office to him—the report that I had made to the Colonel about him.

"Now, Billy," he said, "what's happened? What's wrong? Has somebody been telling you lies about me?"

"You know what's wrong!" says I. "I'm thinking, maybe, about the dog's work that I used to do for you. What kept you in office but the rides I made for you and the fighting that I did for you? How many criminals did you ever bring in yourself? And yet you kept me down on pay that a dog would of starved on!"

"My God, Billy," said Steve, "you never once raised a kick!"

"I wouldn't help myself," said I. "I was too proud. I waited to see what generosity would get out of you, but it didn't get a thing. No, sir, I waited, and I got nothing. But I dropped in here today to tell you that I seen through you then and I seen through you clear and clean."

He was silent, a sick-looking man. I could see that he didn't want to quarrel, and the same dull, dazed look that I had seen in other men's faces that day and that had given me so much pleasure, it came now in his.

"Now," I told him, "you can clear off all old scores!"

"I'd like to," said he, very sober, "because there was never a man that I thought more of than I've thought of you, old fellow. But tell me what I can do?"

"You don't have to be scared," I sneered at him. "It ain't your money that I want out of you. It's just some information that you happen to have and that'll be useful to me."

"Name the thing," said he. "You can have anything that I know!"

And he leaned forward a little, very eager to please.

I said:

"Where is Smiling Charlie?"

"We seen him through the Crocker Pass," said the Sheriff. "That's all I know."

"You sent him through the Crocker Pass?"

"Yes."

"Was you along with him?"

"Sure, there was orders from the Colonel himself. And I took him along in person."

It was deep dusk, now. I looked out the window at the stars, where they hung low in the sky, and I wondered whether I should better stay in the town overnight, or maybe I had better get along on my way. And then I remembered, suddenly, that I hadn't brought any money down with me!

Well, that rode me a good deal and bothered me a lot. And suddenly I snapped back my shoulder, and let the worry of it slide down off my back.

What was money to me? Because there was never a time when good guns wouldn't get a man all that he needed in the West!

Well, now as I write this down, it gives me a shiver. But at that time, it didn't bother me at all, and it seemed the most nacheral thing that you could imagine.

After a while, I decided that I would go

269

on through the town and not stop there. I said:

"Have you no idea where Smiling Charlie would of headed after getting through the pass?"

"I got no idea," said the Sheriff. "He didn't act as though he was worried much about where he should head; but I should like to know, old fellow, what happened that put the Colonel down on Charlie, so quick."

"You'll never find out from me," I snapped at him, and I walked out of the office and into the street.

I turned in the street and I called back to him:

"If you got any way of letting the news sift out, you might send the word beyond the Sierra Blanca and everywhere you can, that I'm looking for Charlie Lamb, and that I would like powerful well to meet up with him, night or day. A thousand miles ain't too far for me to travel to have the pleasure of a little talk with him!"

"I'll do that," said the Sheriff in an anxious voice, he having followed me out onto the veranda. "Only, Billy, old fellow, you don't aim to fight with Charlie, do you?"

There was a lot of real concern in his voice, because there was only one opinion about

Smiling Charlie, and that was that he couldn't be downed by any man in the world.

I knew what they thought, and in the old days, when I had looked forward to the fight with Charlie that I had promised to myself, it had used to scare me a good deal, but now it was all different, and as I was saying before, there wasn't a nerve in my body that jumped or quivered once!

I walked back through town, taking it easy, and, at the end of about an hour, I got to the stable and there I found that everything had been done, just as I commanded. And the boss himself was now polishing the bay off with a wisp of hay.

I took him without a word of thanks, and as I was swinging into the saddle, he says:

"That'll be about fifty cents, Billy, if you please!"

"I don't please!" says I.

And I rode off down the street, hoping and praying that he would have the nerve to call some sort of an argument after me. But he was too wise to do that. He'd seen the danger signal.

I got clear of the town and headed for Crocker Pass and never once did I let up until I'd got through the pass. Then I seen the lights of a house winking down the slope.

I headed for that house, put up the bay in the stable and went to knock at the kitchen door. There wasn't any answer. I just didn't wait but put my shoulder to the door, sprung the bolt, and walked in.

I was rattling at the stove and waking the fire up when a gent come down into the doorway, half in a nightgown and half in trousers, and a rifle in his hand. I pointed a finger at him.

"Put down that gun!" says I.

He had jerked the rifle up to cover me the moment that I spoke. But then he yelped, "Billy Jacks!" And he dropped the gun as though it was red-hot.

I smiled at him. I was pleased again.

"I didn't know that it was you, Billy," he whined at me.

"Get some supper started for me," I directed.

He let out a holler for his wife, and pretty soon she and a half-grown girl and the father of the family was working away getting together a feed for me. Says the man:

"I hear that the Colonel has fired Smiling Charlie Lamb?"

"He fired Charlie, and I fired myself," says I.

"You fired yourself!" gasped he.

He turned around, a frying pan hanging from one hand and the eggs in it threatening to slip out onto the floor.

"Yes," said I, "what about it?"

"Nothing!" says he, and put the pan back on the stove, quick.

But now and then he would turn his head enough to steal a look at me, and every time that he done that, he found me watching him and smiling a little, and my smile, it seemed to chase the shivers up and down his spine, and he would turn back to the stove with a jerk.

That whole family, it begun to get nervous, and when I would speak, the whole gang would jump as though I had fired a shot.

And that contented me a pile!

Yes, sir, it was plain that the devil was up in me. I knew it, blind with hate for the world as I was. I knew that it was the devil, and I didn't care, for I felt that the devil was making me strong, and strength was what I needed to kill Charlie Lamb.

After that was done, why it didn't matter a rap what come to me. That was my great job, and until it was finished, I could never draw a peaceful breath.

I ate my supper, finished my coffee, and

turned into their best bed. And as I went to sleep, I could hear them whispering like scared rabbits together in the room below me. And that give me pleasant dreams for the evening.

It was well after midnight when I had my dinner. It was only the gray of the dawn, however, when I was in the saddle again. I says to the scared woman in the door:

"Did Charlie Lamb stop here yesterday?"

"In the evening, yes," said she.

"Which way did he head after he left here?"

"He took the left hand road, where the two fork, just yonder!"

So I headed down in that direction.

CHAPTER 33

ABOUT NOON OF that day, I seen the smoke of a town curling up like thin clouds beyond a nest of hills, and I rode into the place an hour later. I had never been down that way before, but it was plain that they had heard about me, because the Colonel's men, they was all well known, not only in the Sierra Blanca, but in all the countryside around about.

They stared at me as I went by, and I heard my name a couple of times spoke out behind me. But they didn't smile, and I begun to guess that queer reports had been drifting down the valley about me. I didn't mind that. The queerer the reports, the better! Since the devil was in me, folks might as well learn about it soon as late.

I had the bay rode down to a stagger, by this time, and his flanks marked and bleeding from the spur, though I'd hardly ever had to urge him before that day. But, no matter how well he traveled on that trail, he always seemed to me to be just crawling!

So I put him up in the hotel stable and saw a boy rubbing him down and taking care of him. I saw, from the look of him, that I wouldn't be able to get on the road again until late in the afternoon, because already I had done a day's ride, you understand? And done it in damn short time.

So I went idling into the hotel, and I sat down and asked for lunch.

There was a little palaver, because it seemed that the lunch hour was over with and that the cook was away from the hotel, but I made them go and rustle me a plate of ham and eggs. And while I was eating it, a gent come in—a tall gent with a long pair of

275

sandy whiskers and he flapped open the vest that he was wearing and let me have a look at a big, nickle platcd badge. He said:

"You're Billy Jacks, partner?"

"What of that?" I asked him.

"Don't be ugly, Jacks," says he. "I represent the law in this here town."

"I guessed that it was a rotten town before I ever seen you," I told him.

He jerked up his head with fire in his eyes.

"What in hell has gotten into you, man?" says he. "We've had reports from all along the line that you've been taking what you wanted, everywhere, and never paying. That would go very well if you were in the Colonel's service, but we also have heard over the telephone that you're no longer working for him."

"What you've heard don't interest me," says I. "What I want to know from you, Mr. Deputy Sheriff, or whatever you are, is this: Have you seen Charlie Lamb going through this here town?"

"Never mind Charlie Lamb," said he, "unless I know why you want him!"

"Unless you know? And what is it to me whether you know or don't know?" I asked him.

He banged his fist on the table.

"I won't stand for talk like that!" said he.

"You can sit for it, then," I sneered at him. "And now get out of here. I'm a busy man. I got things on my mind that are worth thinking about, and I got no time for a long, loose-couple hound like you!"

His lips twitched and his eyes rolled. He was half choking, he was so crazy mad.

"I'll sit here and see you pay for this meal," says he.

"You'll sit a long time, then," said I. "Girl, get me my hat, yonder!"

A freckled faced waitress, she brought me my Stetson. I slammed it on my head, and then I sat tilted back in my chair—it's a plumb good position to shoot from—I mean, when you're lying far back in a chair!

"Now," says I, "I've finished eating, and I'm going out to the stable and get my horse and what in hell have you got to say about it?"

"You refuse to pay?" he said, grinding his teeth.

"Yes," said I, and smiled at him, with my lips having that same numb, metal feeling.

"You're actually going to make a fight of this, Billy Jacks?" he asked me.

I stood up.

"I'm tired of yapping to you about it," says I, and I started straight past him.

Of course, that was easy for him, and he made a flash for a gun, but all the time I was watching him like a cat. With my left hand I caught his gun wrist. With my right I jammed the muzzle of a Colt against his temple.

I never was any giant, but under the tips of my fingers, that wrist of his, it felt like a rotten pulp. And the speed of drawing those guns was nothing, because they was just like feathers in my hand.

This fellow walled up his eyes at me.

"By God," said he, "you'd like to murder me!"

And I would—that's a fact. There was so much hell in me, that I was fair aching to have a go at him, and touch the trigger of that gun. I wanted to yank a curtain down over his eyes, and leave him spilling out of the chair, a dead hulk of a man!

"You're through, are you?" I snarled at him.

"Yes," he admitted. "I'm through. I got nothing against you, nothing worth a killing, Jacks!"

"Then tell me about Lamb."

"Will you let me know why you ask?"

"No, damn you, but I've asked you the question."

"All right," said he. "You've got the winning hand, here, and I don't mind telling you that Charlie Lamb is right here in town now, unless I'm terrible mistaken."

"In town now!" I gasped.

"Yes, he was putting up at the other hotel across the street just half an hour before you come drifting in."

I jumped back from him with a half stifled shout. It was almost too good to be true.

"Where's that other hotel?"

"Right down the street, hardly fifty yards. But you ain't aiming to make any trouble——"

I jumped through the door without waiting to listen to him. And then out into the street, and I started down the way, running. I remembered, then, that running would be no way to give me steady nerves in the hands, and sure fingers. So I slowed up, and I walked along, conscious of the weight of the guns in my holsters, as they dragged against my legs.

Then, behind me from the first hotel, I heard a yell. I turned and saw the Deputy Sheriff. He was shouting at the top of his lungs:

279

"Warn Charlie Lamb. Jacks is coming to murder him. Jacks has gone mad!"

That was it, was it?

I spun around and tried a snap shot at the Sheriff, a hip shot, but a straight one, and I would of nailed him clean, except that as I fired he was leaping back through the doorway. I heard a clash of glass as the bullet smashed its way through a window, and then I faced about, and laughed again, and ran up the front steps of the second hotel.

I gave the lobby a glance, and there was nothing like big Charlie Lamb in it. I stepped to the door of the dining room, but he was not there. Yet over in a corner I seen a pretty waitress collecting some dishes from one place that had been laid, and something about her prettiness made me as sure as a prophet that Charlie Lamb had actually been sitting in that chair.

Then I seen that there was no use going in the front way, if Charlie had made up his mind to dodge me and go out the back way. It might be hard to realize that Charlie would run away from me, but that seemed to be the case. And I whirled around and made for the front door, through it on the jump, and just then I seen Charlie Lamb racing old Cringle past the side of the hotel.

"Protect yourself, you cur!" I yipped at him, and got out both guns fast as lightning.

Maybe it was the speed of his horse moving, but anyway, I knew the instant that I pulled the triggers that I had missed him clean with the first try. I wouldn't miss him with the second—but before I could put in a second shot, lightning flashed from the hip of Smiling Charlie and I was knocked flat on the veranda.

I got up with the blood pouring down over my face and clothes. Somewhere a woman was screaming something terrible, and men was running towards me.

Charlie Lamb was gone, and I couldn't hear even the beating of the hoofs of his horse. He was gone, and the only token of him was just a thin cloud of dust that was rapidly dissolving down the middle of the street.

The men came up.

"You're shot through the head, Jacks," they called to me. "You're a dead man!"

"You lie!" I told 'em. "No cur in the world can kill me like this before I've got my job done, and that job is the killing of Charlie Lamb. Stop that damned woman from yapping, will you? And then give me some hot water."

281

I got what I wanted. The woman stopped screeching, and I swabbed off my head and seen that there was a furrow down the center of it. I had to admire the skill of Charlie Lamb, to plant a dead-center shot like that from a horse that was galloping at full speed. There was a good deal of pain and I had lost a little blood, but I plastered over that wound, and pretty soon I felt that I was ready for the trail again.

I had met Charlie Lamb, almost too soon to have it more than a dream. And my failure to shoot him down, that was like a dream to me, too. It never occurred to me for a minute to turn back. It never occurred to me for a minute to doubt that I would be able to kill him, finally.

So, when I was patched up a little, I got out into the open, fetched my horse, and I rode on through the town again. And the Deputy Sheriff never so much as winked at me. Perhaps he thought that I was due to get my share of trouble from Smiling Charlie and there was no need in him dirtying his hands with me, or perhaps having one brush with me that day had been enough for him.

What mattered to me was that I was free to leave that town. And the only thing that worried me, was that I had a mighty tired horse under me, and that Cringle had been running like a deer when I last seen him.

CHAPTER 34

CRINGLE HAD BEEN running like a deer!

I remember once when I was a boy to of seen a Newfoundland dog running down the street full tilt with a little mongrel after him. I dunno what had scared the big dog, but the little dog didn't have any doubt about the matter and figured out that it was *him*.

Same way with me after Cringle and big Charlie Lamb. I knew that there was nothing I could do that could actually scare Lamb. But still, he was running, and I had to try to make out what, besides myself, was after him. Something after him so hard and so fast, for instance, that he couldn't even afford to turn aside for one minute and make sure that I was really dead, when I dropped on the veranda of the hotel.

No, when I looked back to that, I was reassured. There was nothing so mysterious about that. For having seen me fall with blood spurting all over my face, he had naturally taken it for granted that he had shot me through the head. And a man don't usually bother to take more than one look, in a case like that.

Well, anyway, that was how I had figured things out. In this particular case, it was simply clear that Charlie had wanted to avoid me. But why had he kept on racing away, then, after he thought that I was dead and down?

Not that I bothered my head too much over what I felt to be very foolish details. No, I just let them rest, for I couldn't be troubled with the side issues. What was really important to me was only to get to grips with Charlie, and close my grip on him like a bull terrier, and so kill or be killed!

It wasn't particular comfortable traveling that day. I had a horse that was completely wore out by the terrible traveling that I had given it. And my head was full of buzzings and songs. But I pushed along until, in the evening late, I got to a river bottom with an old deserted shack in it. There I turned in and slept like a dead man.

I was up and out in the early morning, before there was even so much as a line of light along the horizon. The bay was still lying down, and he cocked his ears at me as I came up as much as to ask me if I was a man or just a bad dream that was riding him so to death!

I called him, and he lurched up with a groan, such as only a tired horse could give. He was getting badly spent. His coat was staring, his ribs was standing out, and his eye was dull. However, that didn't really touch my heart. If I rode a horse to death, it made no difference—so long as, at the end of the trail, I could kill Charlie, or Charlie could kill me!

I saddled him, therefore, give him a swaller of water at the river, and barged on down the stream, where I come into a mite of a village just in the rose of the dawn. A pretty thing to see the light glistening on the dew-wet roofs and the windows of that village, and farther away the same sun sweeping the snowy mountains with flashes and waves of rose.

I mean, looking backwards, I can see that it was pretty enough, but at that time it was nothing but a place to get a feed for myself and oats for my horse.

I found the hotel, and the minute that I got myself settled down, a big rough gent come in with a double-barreled, sawed-off shotgun under his arm. He put himself down in a corner chair, and he pretended to read a newspaper that was sprawled across his lap, but all the time the gun was ready under the newspaper, and both of the two big muzzles was pointed steady at me.

I admired the quiet way of that fellow, and I could tell that he didn't mean a thing but business. Blowing me to hell and back would be nothing in his life. He looked as though he had a heart in him no bigger than a dried up bean.

Well, I finished my breakfast, and as I finished it, along comes the proprietor of the place and walks up to me.

"You're Billy Jacks, ain't you?" says he.

I admitted that that was my name and asked him why he wanted to know. He said that he had a message for me, and he put down a little envelope in front of me with my name wrote in a big, strong hand. I knew that writing in a flash, because it was Smiling Charlie that had slashed down those letters. He wrote the same way that he rode—wild and wide and slanting.

I tore it open, and I saw on the inside this:

Hello, old timer!
I suppose that you'll have this in the morning, and that you'll be hot to get on after me, but I can't help leaving you this

286

note to warn you that you'll be killing your horse for nothing.

Because you can't catch me, Billy. You've made a good chase of it and a game ride which people will remember a long time. But you can never catch me. Not with Cringle under me. Ask the people of this town what shape they saw Cringle in when I went through this evening. He's not worn out, and I don't intend that he shall be. But I mean to float away from you, old man, and never come back into your life again. Give up this trail.

In the meantime, I have to admit that I acted to you like a hound. However, I gave you or tried to give you a warning, and I also tried to make friends with you. If you had taken my offer then, there would never have been any of this trouble. Because I've never broken with a real friend, Billy.

No matter for these things. They're finished. You want my heart's blood, and you won't be happy until you've had it, I suppose. Though I can't see what has been my particular sin in flirting a bit with Betty. God knows I'm not the first man that has made love to her. But I suppose that I'm the first since she promised to marry you.

287

And yet, old fellow, you might remember that a girl like that can be perfectly good, and perfectly true to one man, while she flirts with half a dozen. It's rather her nature. And I know perfectly well that all the time she was letting me pay attention to her, she was entirely devoted to you. I didn't matter. I was a surface affair.

Will you try to believe that I'm talking to you honestly?

I don't suppose that you will.

Then simply believe this: That I'm riding away in an airline for the nearest pass, and that I'll never turn back nor hesitate, so that you can see that your good bay horse can never catch Cringle.

Good-by for the last time, Billy. And I'm honestly sorry that I can't see you again—and infernally glad that I didn't put a bullet through your brains earlier this afternoon!

Yours,
Charles Lamb.

"How far to the nearest pass?" says I to the proprietor, who was standing by and watching me.

"About thirty-five miles," says he.

I took a look at the mountains to the north-west. Of course that clear Western air is a sure deceiver, but I know how to make allowances for that, as near as any man can, and it seemed to me to be nearer to fifteen miles than it did to thirty-five to that pass. I says to him:

"Ain't that split in the face of the mountains a pass?"

"Sure," says he, "that's El Paso Grande."

"All right," says I, "and d'you mean to tell me that that pass is more'n twenty miles from here, at the furthest?"

"Partner," says he, with a grin, "it ain't more'n eleven, but nothing but a flying bird could get there in a straight line."

"I ain't a bird," says I, "except in a manner of speaking, but let me know why I got to spend thirty-five miles for a thing that ain't more'n eleven miles away. I got a tired horse, you see?"

He didn't have to look twice in order to see that I was right. The bay was done, and he was done so bad, that he sure looked the part.

"I'll tell you how it is," says this gent, "you can't see nothing from here, but the river, it lies between you and the pass, and that damn river is about three miles of marsh and quicksands. It's better right now than at any other season of the year, but it's too bad for anybody to cross it. A horse would sink inside of ten steps in that muck. And if the mud didn't get a man, why, the mosquitoes would!"

I looked at those mountains, so near and yet so damned far away. And then I looked down to the sagged head of the bay and I thought of old Charlie Lamb sashaying away towards El Paso Grande and never thinking of me, except to laugh a little.

"Partner," says I, "I been in a good many parts of the world, and I never yet have been in a place where there ain't some sort of a secret way of doing things that seem hard. Now tell me for a fact, ain't it true that there's some way of possibly crossing that marsh?"

"You're in a powerful hurry, I reckon?" says he. And he squinted at me.

Well, I winked back. There was no harm in letting this feller figure that he had something on me. It would make him seem wise and in the know, and there ain't nothing that some people like better than to be on the inside.

"All right," says he, "if it's as bad as that, for you, I'll tell you what I know. Are they close behind you?"

I seen that he thought that I was on the run, perhaps for sinking a slug into somebody. I just turned around and squinted over my shoulder.

"Well," says I, "they ain't in sight yet, thank God!"

"Did you kill your man?" says he, more and more curious.

"I hope to God that he'll die!" says I with a good deal of feeling.

Well, that was enough to convince this gent that I *did* have to get away. And he grinned at me, all on one side of his face.

"I been on the run myself," says he. "I'll tell you what I don't know, but what I've heard from them that *ought* to know. They say that if a gent tries to cross that marsh in the narrowest places, he's sure to get beat. But if he tackles it in the widest section, where the willows come bellying away out from the banks of the river, then I understand that you got a bare chance of getting across—if the season is right! Mind you, this here ain't a promise, but it's what I've heard. You can take your chances if you want to!"

I looked at the bay and laughed.

"I'd rather take a chance with any marsh than with this horse," I says, climbing into

291

the saddle. "So long, partner. And thanks a lot."

"Don't mention it, old timer," says he. "Best of luck to you. But if you get cornered—*don't shoot to kill!* That's where I showed some good bean-work in the old days!"

CHAPTER 35

I COULD OF laughed in his face, but I swallered the laugh, and as I went up the line, jogging the bay, I says to myself that the best way to get on in this world is to let folks think that they're running the game and handling things, and that they got the inside dope on everything. It ain't flattering to yourself, but it extracts the things you want from the other fellows.

When I got over the next hill, I headed down the long slope for the green stretch of the bottom lands along the river. And after a while, I could see the place where the willows bulged away out, and that was where I headed.

When I got closer still, I could see the steam rising up from the marsh like from a washboiler on Monday. It was a bad looking marsh as ever I seen, and I've been in Louisiana. However, when I squinted ahead, I could see the mountains and El Paso Grande looking so almighty close that it seemed to me that Smiling Charlie was already inside of my grip.

And that thought gave me enough courage to tackle anything. I waded into the marsh. Before I'd gone a hundred yards, the bay went down up to the knees. I jumped off and he worked himself out and jumped back onto firm ground, snorting as though he'd seen a snake.

I let him stay there. I wouldn't tie him to a tree to starve to death in case that Charlie killed me. And I wouldn't take him on with me, seeing that he couldn't possibly get through.

Well, as I was saying, I hit along ahead. And things was pretty miserable all around me. The trees was covered with slimy moss higher than I could reach, in most places, and some of the trees had give up the work of trying to hold their heads up to the light and the fresh air. They'd bowed down, plumb spent, and the leaves was gone from them, and they was drenched in greenness and slime, and they was twisted and naked looking, most horrible to see.

All their roots was mostly lost in the bog, and when you stepped on a root, the rotten bark of it would peel off under your heel and let you drive down into the slushy filth of that marsh.

Sometimes I was up to my chest and sometimes I was up to my hips. But those was only patches, and in between them I would come to stretches of pretty good going, so that I could see that there was sense in the saying that the best place to cross the marsh was where it was the widest. Perhaps the reason was that here the ground was spread out at one level, and so the water never stood as deep as it would in the narrower channels, and it would drain off quicker after the floods. But I kept on, making pretty good time, and working hard.

Even in the best places, though, there was drawbacks, because I had to manage my rifle and hoist it out of the danger of water, and with the other hand I was usually hanging onto something to steady my footwork, and that left the mosquitoes a free chance.

They was an intelligent lot, too, and they didn't miss no openings. They come in hosts that looked like a black smudge of heavy oil smoke, at a distance. And when they found me, they poised themselves and then took a wallop at me with all their might. But pretty soon there was no longer any space left for the pickers and choosers, and so the new armies, they lit wherever they could and helped themselves. When they had used up the skin on my face and neck, then they lit on my shirt and bit me clean through the shirt free and liberal. Once in a while I had a chance to take a pass at them, and I wiped off a handful of blood and mosquitoes at every lick.

I knew that they wasn't apt to have time to kill me, but being ate alive slowly ain't any pleasant thing. Particularly when every bite has a sting of poison in it!

I remember, once when I was towards the center of the swamp, that I put my hand on what I thought was a dead green limb, and the limb curled around with a nasty hiss and showed me a flash of eyes, and then two fangs sank into my arm.

Before I could so much as curse, the snake had slithered away through the scum of the marsh, and I didn't even roll up my sleeve to look at the bite. If it was poison, I would die. If it wasn't poison I would live. And taking the chances that I was, for the pleasure of shooting at Charlie Lamb, you can imagine that a little thing like a snake would never bother me none.

And then, when the sweat was running down into my eyes, and my head was swirling hot and dizzy with a pressure of blood, I seen a bit of clean brown earth through a gap in the trees, made for it at a stumbling run, and come out all at once into the good honest sunshine, and the honest, brown earth was under my feet once more.

Well, I was so done that though there was still a cloud of mosquitoes trailing after me like a veil back of a woman's head, I just flopped on the ground and threw out my arms and closed my eyes, and lay there wondering if my heart wasn't going to crack open with the next beat.

But it didn't, and pretty soon I could get up and wave off the mosquitoes, and get along.

Well, I was fagged, and I still had a hard climb into the pass, but I felt that I had saved so many miles that I might have a pretty good chance of heading off Charlie Lamb. And even if I had got there in plenty of time, it might well of been that he hadn't headed for this pass at all, but had gone out of the valley in some other way.

However, he was so perfectly confident in

his horse—and he was so apt to think that nothing in the world could possibly beat Cringle, that I was fairly sure that he would come this way. And, of course, he wouldn't of gone across that marsh!

At any rate, when I got up into the pass, there wasn't any sight of Smiling Charlie above me in the throat of the pass, or below me, where the trail bobbed among the hills, and there wasn't any living things near me except a flock of dirty-brown sheep a ways up on a hillside, and a shepherd taking care of them and leaning on a rifle, like he knew how to take care of himself, too.

It always give me a shudder to look at a bunch of animals like that under the care of a real living man that had to live all in loneliness, like the brutes that he was caring for, and never nothing to interest him, and never nothing to talk to, or to talk about. I spared time even now to look up there and pity that shepherd, and wonder how God had come to put such men on earth. Maybe just so as some folks could have mutton. Well, let them eat mutton that like it. I stick to beef.

Anyway, I took a look up the slope, and then I turned around and began to watch the lower valley, and before I had been watching for five minutes, I seen a rider coming in his own little cloud of dust. I was so terrible excited that I didn't dare to look again, for a while, so I spent some time in cleaning my guns.

There was marsh water in all of them. I realized, then, that I should of tried both Colts and the rifle after leaving the swamp, to make sure that they was free and fine. But I didn't. And now it was a lot too late. However, it seemed to me that the gats was all in pretty fair shape.

So then I looked down the trail again, and this time, sure enough, it seemed to me that by the size of the rider it must be Smiling Charlie Lamb. I looked down for another spell, holding my breath. The next glance made me dead sure. Yes, sir, it was Charlie himself!

Now, when I look back on that time, I often wish that I could give folks a picture of Smiling Charlie, as he was on that day, and how he come careening up the valley on old Cringle, the best horse in the world. And him the best man in the world, as far as that goes.

By best man, I mean the finest looking, and the strongest, and the most out-fighting-est devil that ever stepped. Which I've see some, but none to equal Smiling Charlie at all.

He come up the pass letting Cringle take it easy, and as he rode, Charlie was strumming away at his guitar and making music that was pretty good to listen to, I can tell you. Well, it done me good to see him. If I was to kill him, I would never have to ask for a chance to kill a finer man. That much was certain. And I would never have a bigger or a fairer target.

I got my rifle ready, I slid it out in front, lay on my belly, and let Charlie ride right into the sights.

He was a dead man. I could feel the soul of him twitching in the nerves of my right forefinger. But somehow I couldn't pull the trigger. Killing was what he needed, for my sake, and the sake of the world, and for the sake of Charlie's own soul, before he done no more harm to folks. But you see, he was meant to die fighting in the daylight, with hundreds against him. Somehow, I couldn't shoot him down like a dog.

Besides, as I had thought before, what was the pleasure of killing him by surprise, when he couldn't see death walking up on him?

CHAPTER 36

WELL, SIR, I have had gents say to me: "Did you really have ideas as low and as mean as shooting a man from ambush?"

Yes, I got to admit that I have. And maybe more than once. There ain't anything fine and high-faluting about me. Whenever I been fighting, I been what you might be free to call a practical fighter. That is, my idea was like the idea of the Indians: All killing was good, but safe killing was far and away the best kind of all!

Yet, when the grand chance come to me, I couldn't take it!

I realized, too, that Charlie was a better man than me. But there was that much terrible hate in me, that I sort of depended on it to make me as strong and steady and fast and sure as the muscles and the nerves which God had give to Smiling Charlie.

I saw him dip out of sight, and then I went down and took my stand on the near side of a rock, which had a steep shadow falling down from it. There I would wait until I seen the head of Charlie's horse bobbing around the corner of the stone, and the instant that Charlie was full in sight of me, I would make my draw. Even that would give him hardly more than a dog's chance—him being taken by surprise, like that. But still, it was the sort of a chance that men have got to take when they go making love to women that belong to others.

I remember that there was an ache at the corners of my mouth. I suppose that it was because my lips was strained back so hard with a grin of hate and joy. For I was shaking with hunger to get at him.

And then, whang! There was the head of old, ugly Cringle. And the next instant, there was Smiling Charlie.

I dunno exactly what come into my mind. I shoot a gun from the hip, always fanning it at my target the instant that it has its nose clear of the leather. The first shot will often hit the dust, but the second hits flesh. But that is probably the best way, because if you want to land your target, you better use the six shots in a revolver like they was the six drops in a spray of water, throwed in the general direction of what you want to hit, aimed by feeling and not by the eye.

But this time I was so worked up that I made that draw exactly as I had used to make it when I first learned to shoot with a revolver, when I was a boy. For twenty years I had never drawed a revolver in that fashion, but this time maybe I was so excited that all of the new instinct was rubbed out and only the old instinct was left to handle me. I threw that gun high and sighted down the barrel. And in that tenth part of a second that I wasted, Smiling Charlie had time to throw his gat and fire from the hip.

His slug hit my gun fair and square, turned it in my hand, and dashed the muzzle into my face. What it done to me would be hard to describe. Lucky for me that there was no front sight, me always filing them off, because they only hamper you in the draw, and what good is a sight when you shoot from the hip?

But that gun tore the flesh across my eyes and blinded me in my own blood. And before I could wipe the gun away, there was a roar of hoofs, and when I could look through the blood again, Smiling Charlie was out of sight around a bend in the trail! I leaned up against the face of that rock and let my blood drip.

Now, the first time that I had shot at him, the day before, and when he had dropped me, I could of said that he had *thought* his bullet killed me. But this time, he had simply seen me stagger, and he must of heard the ring of his bullet against my gun. No, there was no doubt that he didn't want to kill me either time.

And that was a fair staggerer for me. I couldn't conceive how it come that any man would have another shoot at him and not kill. Particular, when it was clear self-defense, with at least one witness, each time. No, I couldn't understand.

I found a little thin trickle of water near. There I washed my wound and tied it up, though the jagged scar of it still stares at me every time I look into a mirror, these days.

And by this time, I was a fair mess, with two bloodstained bandages over my head and face, and what was left of me torn and ragged from the passage through the swamp.

But when I says to myself that the reason that Smiling Charlie had not fired into me with a second bullet and finished me off was because he didn't know that I was free of the Colonel. He thought that the Colonel was still behind me, and with the Colonel free to press a murder charge, what chance would an ordinary gent have?

That was the way that I worked it out for myself. And, on the other hand, I wondered if God hadn't had a hand in it—meaning that with the third try I should kill Charlie, and no mistake.

That third try was what I wanted. But, in the meantime, I couldn't follow Cringle on foot.

Most likely you won't think it possible, but the fact is that I turned right around and, in spite of what I'd been through, I went through that swamp again to the bay, where it was waiting for me on the farther side!

Yes, sir, there was a strength in me that passed what I can't even think about, these days. I just write down the actual facts and the things that I did, in the order that I did 'em. And though those of you that know the marsh in front of El Paso Grande ain't going to believe that I even got through it once, the cold facts are that I went through it twice in one day.

I got the bay I was too weak, then, to climb into the saddle until we come to a stone. I got onto the stone and from that I sort of fell into the saddle, and started that honest horse on the long march around the marsh to pick up the trail of Smiling Charlie once more.

Half way around, the night come back and overtook me. And as there was a house close by, I went there and put up my horse and went into the farmhouse feeling like a dead man, and looking even worse than what I felt, I suppose. I'll never forget how the woman in the kitchen screamed and threw up her hands when I walked in on her. She didn't get over it, either, but had to go to bed, in hysterics. But the farmer and his son, they took care of me pretty good.

It was a queer thing that they knew how I had met Charlie for the second time. The news of my doings on the trail of Lamb, somehow they got abroad as fast as though a newspaper reporter was behind me every step of the way. And there was even a good deal of betting around, mostly at odds on Charlie Lamb. Because you didn't have to know the facts about what Charlie had done. You only had to take one look at him to tell what a ripping, cracking man he was.

The farmer, he was a mild sort of gent what had worked too hard all of his life, and everything that he said, he put "Well, sir," in front of it. "Well, sir, it's kind of cold tonight," he would say. Or: "Well, sir, you look like a herd of wild horses had stamped in your face."

Which I sure looked that way, and no mistake. I took a mirror and admired myself, for a time. And I wondered what man had ever looked so bad in the history of the world!

But I got a meal into me and got to bed, and then how I slept! I lay there for a while just letting the waves of sleep start at my feet and rise and swell and bust in my head while I was gradual paralyzed. And, finally, I was all ironed out, and smoothed, and the pain stopped shooting across my eyes, and I was asleep as sound as any child that you ever heard about.

I remember that that night I had fine dreams about how I met Charlie Lamb, and I took both his hands with my left hand, and I held him so that he couldn't move, and then I pulled a gun and shot it into his face, and shot again, and laughed as he died. I was laughing out loud when I woke myself up and seen myself staring into the face of Sheriff Steve Ross. He was leaning over my bed.

"D'you know me, partner?" says he, very concerned.

I seen that I must of been raving some in my sleep. But now I sat up, waited until my head stopped spinning, and I said:

"I was never feeling more fit than I am right here and now. What in hell has brought you here, anyway?"

He didn't seem at all peeved by my rough way of talking. He just says:

"That's all right, old man. I'll do all of the explaining that you might want."

He looked a bit scared.

I says:

"I ain't crazy, Steve. And you don't have to humor me. Have you come to try to arrest me?"

He looked down at my hand, that was on my Colt, because I'd been too tired to even take my gun belt off when I went to sleep the night before.

"No," says Steve, "I ain't come to arrest you. I've only come to show you that I'm your friend, Billy. It don't make no difference what you've said to me that last time that you met me. I'll swaller that. I've knowed you too long and too well to let such things bother me."

I had a little flash. Like a rift through a cloud. I seen the fine truth of Steve, and what a gentle, strong, manly gent he was. I dropped a hand on his shoulder and I says:

"God bless you, Steve. I'm sick in the head. But when I get better, I'll tell you what a friend I know you are!"

It touched him up a good deal to have me

speak to him like that, and finally he says to me:

"Billy, if you got the least trust in me, take my word and get off of the trail of Smiling Charlie Lamb, because the third time that you meet up with him, he's gunna kill you, sure!"

"Is he?" says I, turning cold and hard again.

"He is!"

"And how do you know?" I sneered.

"I'll tell you how. I was sent out by the Colonel to find the two of you. And I managed to get in touch with Charlie by telephone and I told him that I wanted him to come back—because the Colonel said that it would be all right——"

"The Colonel said that?" I shouted.

"Yes, he said that. And Charlie answered that he *would* come back. But for me to head you off of his trail, because he had passed you up twice. But the third time he would shoot to kill, so help him God! And he meant what he said!"

CHAPTER 37

WELL, WHAT CHARLIE had said he would do to me didn't matter at all. I was too busy thinking over the first part of the news that had been given to me by Steve.

"He goes back—with a clean slate!" says I.

"Yes."

"It's a lie! It's a damned lie!" I yelled at Steve Ross. "I know about the whole thing. The Colonel he wishes that Charlie was dead and in hell!"

"Sure he does," admitted Ross quick as a wink, "but he don't particular wish to see his daughter dead, too."

"Hold on. What're you driving at?"

"Why, Billy," says Steve, "it's like this. That girl has taken to carrying on. She cries in her sleep. She don't take kindly to her food, none at all. They say that you wouldn't recognize her, if you was to see her. And I've seen with my own eyes that the Colonel is ten years older."

"Rot!" I barked at him.

He shook his head.

"We both know the Colonel," he said.

"He ain't any baby. But I'll tell you that the Colonel's voice shook and he looked pretty weak when he told me for God's sake to go find Charlie and get him back."

"And that's the wind up!" I said through my teeth.

"It ain't one that pleases you, but I'm telling you the truth of exactly the way that things are. If it was only that you had Smiling Charlie against you, why that would be bad enough, but with the Colonel in the deal to back up Charlie—why, man, I would say that I have always knowed you to be a damned brave man, but I would hope that you ain't so brave that you're foolish!"

I listened to Steve, and while I listened, I was seeing pictures with those eyes that look inside of you and make something out of nothing. They showed me a lot of things that I didn't want to see. They showed me beautiful Olivia, very glad to be shut of that light-of-love philanderer, Smiling Charlie, until she learned that I was on Charlie's trail and dead set on getting his scalp. I could see that news sink in on her. I could see her weakening, and all at once throwing up her hands and asking her father to save the man that she loved, and I could see the Colonel fighting a terrible battle with his pride.

Hadn't he planned it all? Hadn't he done the cleverest work that ever any man ever did, and the most far-sighted, in getting Charlie to undermine the Baron, and getting me to play off against Charlie with guns? His ideal picture, as I could see it now, would of been the Baron sent back to England, and me and Charlie killing each other in a grand fight.

I thought of this, and began to feel helpless, but then I had another unlucky thought, and that was of another person in the Sierra Blanca that would be pretty happy when she heard that Charlie was coming back—and that was my girl—Betty. And all at once I says slowly to Steve:

"You get in touch with Charlie. You tell him that he has fought fair and square twice and that both times he could have killed me, and that I know it. But you tell him that now I'm coming after him for the third time, and that this time I'll get him, and the luck will turn my way. But as for talking any more, Steve, why, you've said all that you can say, and it ain't any good. I'm set and I can't be bent out of shape!"

Well, I was in a mean mood, and I was ready to see bad in every man, but I couldn't quite find any outside reason why Steve should of looked so broken up unless he had really cared a little for me. He got up from his chair and stood a minute at the window.

"Is that final, old timer?" he says with his back to me.

"That's final," I told him.

"Well, then," says he, "you'll bear me witness, old man, that I've done what I could to settle this game peaceable?"

"I'll bear you witness," says I, getting up in turn and stretching.

He went to the door. It seemed as though he was going to leave me without another word, he was that cut up, but when the door swung open, I had a slant out of the corner of my eyes at McGinnis and Dick Wace standing there in the entrance, with guns in their hands.

I made a pass at my own Colt and stopped my hand with the gat half out of the leather. I stopped, in fact, with my soul already about half way to heaven or hell, but both of those boys had fast eyes, and they seen that I didn't complete the draw.

It was no use, and I didn't attempt any funny passes, but let the Sheriff turn back and take my guns away from me. I knew McGinnis and I knew Wace, and I knew that there wasn't any man in the world, not hardly Smiling Charlie himself, that could of stood up to the pair of them in a fair fight.

"I hate this job, old man," said Dick Wace to me. "I hate it like hell, and partly because after the way you parted from me, you may think that this is spite on my part. But there's no spite, no spite in it at all. Nothing but the Colonel's orders, Billy!"

I didn't say anything, because talk was no use, but hell was up and riding high in me, I can tell you! Some of that hell couldn't help showing in me, of course, and the Sheriff snapped out:

"I hate to hurt Billy's feelings more than any of the rest of you, but now that we've had to take him, watch him, I tell you, or some of us will be dead men!"

I turned my back on them and stood at the window.

"Keep back from that window!" commanded Steve.

I didn't budge. But the blood jumped into my head and made it fair ache.

Outside, there was nothing much to see except Dick Wace's blooded chestnut, one of the finest horses that was ever raised on Colonel Stockton's place, as I'd heard tell. And beyond the chestnut I could see the road

313

driving past and then thrown into sight here and there as it crossed the hills.

It was a hard thing to see that fine horse all fresh and full of go, and taking his spirits out in biting his bit and throwing his head and begging somebody to jump into the saddle and give him a ride.

"Billy's going to play white with us," said Dick, just then. "You'll give us your word not to try to bolt, Billy?" he went on.

"I'll see you all damned!" I broke out at them, and I was shaking with fury.

"Damned we may be," said the Sheriff, very quiet and grave, "but not by you on this day, if I can help it. Give me that rope."

"Not a rope on him, Steve!"

"Yes. It's got to be. He won't promise us to go straight, and I'm not taking any chances!"

"But there isn't a sign of a weapon on him! What can he do?"

Said Steve:

"Nothing's too hard for a desperate man, and that's what Billy Jacks is today."

With that, he tied the rope around my wrists and gave it an extra pull to make it snug. Then he stepped back with a grunt.

"You drove me to it, Billy," says he, plumb regretful.

Still, I wouldn't answer. I was too choked with meanness to talk to any of them. And after a while I heard Steve say:

"Well, boys, we'd better be starting on. Ready, Dick?"

"I'm ready. But I hate to ride Billy out into the open day with that rope on him and his hands tied behind his back!"

"I hate it worse than you do," said the Sheriff, "but he's had his choice, and this is the pick he's made. I'm waiting for his promise, and the minute that I have it, his hands are free. Until then, I watch him like a man-killer. You understand, Billy? Hello! Get back from that window!"

"What in hell can I do at this window?" I snarled at the Sheriff. "Jump down and break my neck?"

And I looked down to the ground and laughed, and sneered as I laughed, because it was really a long fall. But then, somehow, I remembered what the Sheriff had said: Anything is possible to a desperate man!

And I was desperate. God alone could tell you how I was feeling at the thought of big Smiling Charlie sashaying up into the valley and there taking charge and marrying beautiful Olivia and finally having the whole Sierra Blanca for his own to keep forever!

Yes, and just under that window there was a bush, tall, and broad and growing very thick and wiry in the branches. There was nine chances out of ten that I would go through that bush and smash my head on the ground. Or maybe, bust my back and die plumb miserable. But the tenth chance was sure worth taking.

"Are you ready Billy?"

"I'm ready."

I turned around and made a couple of steps towards the door—enough to set all of them in motion in the same direction. And then I whirled and sprinted for the window and dived out of it head first as though I was diving for deep water beneath me.

I heard the screech of the Sheriff, and somebody sent a bullet after me—afterwards I never could tell who it was, because none of them would blab.

But as I shot through that window, I seen that the bush was not as close to the wall of the house as I had thought. No, there was only a hard stretch of ground, close in.

I thought it was the finish. I twisted over in the air—and I came down sitting straight up, with a crash, in that very bush that I hoped for!

What it done to me I would hate to say,

because that was a thorn brush. It cut my clothes to pieces in long, straight edged slices, as though a scissors had been at work on them. And as for the flesh under the clothes, it treated me like a thousand wild cats had all taken a pass at me with their claws.

I jumped out of that brush a mass of blood—and covered with shallow cuts that seemed to have red pepper sprinkled in them. I've had bullets through me before and since, and I've had cold steel run into me. And both is a pretty sickening sensation, but I never was up against anything half as mean and low and miserable and painful as that briar bush.

It helped me to get to Dick's chestnut in one bound. He turned, and I thought that he would bolt in spite of the fact that his reins was throwed, but he didn't hardly have time to bolt.

Did you ever try to mount a horse with your hands tied?

I dived high into the air. I hit the pommel of that saddle and nearly broke my breast-bone, and then I managed to swing a leg into the saddle just as the voice of Dick Wace yelled from the window, and a gun opened fire on me.

But I was in the saddle, now, and the chestnut was under way.

CHAPTER 38

DICK WITH HIS fine marksmanship riddled me with lead, you say. No, but he didn't. Fact was, that chestnut, as I hit the saddle, had begun to run. The reins flew behind him, and he made the ground slide away beneath him faster than anything that you ever seen in your life. He fair tore, and the direction that he headed in was not down the road, but straight across the face of the house.

That was straight across the field of Dick's vision, too, and a finer shot than Dick might of missed in a case like that. Even Smiling Charlie couldn't of been absolutely sure.

In half a second the pair of us were around the corner of the house and as the chestnut swung back towards the stables, which would have been the finish of me, I sank both spurs in his sides. It hurt him so bad that he let out a squeal of pain and rage, but it straightened him out again, and he buck-jumped the fence into the field beyond.

They say that all the fine riders, they scorn

to use their hands, but doggone me if they don't need their arms to wave around and help balance them when a horse is pitching!

I never was a bad rider, having lived in the saddle, and taken my share of the bad ones, but I never had a worse time than the next mile that the chestnut gave me.

He was running all out, and every tenth leap, he went up into the air and come down stiff-legged, and every time he came down I was clinging with my legs with all my might and praying with all my might, too.

After the first mile, though, he settled down to plain running, as though he was pretty sure that he could work up such speed that the wind of his gallop would blow me right off his back, and every now and then he would rise at a fence and wing his way across it. And I would rise in the saddle, and nearly go out of it.

But still I stuck. For a whole half hour— it seemed a half day—I had that chestnut running like a fool. And then it was done, and come to a halt, head down, and legs braced.

But behind me, there was never a sign of any pursuit. And a good reason, too! Because nothing in that company could keep the pace of Dick's horse, even with him in the saddle.

And with my light weight, the race was in my own hands.

Well, I managed to kick the chestnut over beside a tall barbed wire fence, and then I leaned out from the saddle and began to saw my hands backwards and forwards.

It was awfully mean work. Sometimes I missed the rope and got the flesh of my arms. And twice I got tired of the crazy position in which I had to hold myself by the grip of my legs, as I leaned out from the saddle, backwards. But after all, I worked fairly fast.

By the time the chestnut got his second wind and began to lift his head, I straightened up in the saddle and swung my freed hands above my head with a yell of joy. I was my own man again!

Such a man I guess there never was before and there never will be again, because I was one mass of cuts and slashes from head to foot, and blood was oozing out all over me, and my head was pretty near covered with two big, bloody bandages, and altogether, I was one grand mess.

But I tell you man to man that I didn't feel sting or ache out of any one of my wounds after I had my hands free again. I just looked down to my bleeding wrists and I laughed, and then I hauled out the pair of

Dick's saddle Colts and looked at them, and seen that they was perfect, as any guns that Dick had would be sure to be. And then I eased the long Winchester out of the holster that passed under my right knee, and that was perfect, too!

So what more could any head hunter in the world want better than that? All I had to do now was to say to myself:

"How am I going to lay a course that will cross the course of Smiling Charlie?"

I figured it hard and I figured it fast.

By this time, the Sheriff and his men, they was making the telegraph wires buzz with the news that I was loose again and that I was dead bent on killing myself before I would give up my third chance at Charlie. And if that news got to Charlie—well, what would he do?

No, he wouldn't turn back. He was pretty near too proud to pay any attention to the things that other folks had to say about him, but he couldn't help being too proud to turn back from his way because another gent was riding out to fight him.

At least, something told me that he would never turn back from the trail that led him to Olivia!

But the next question was, would they be

able to get the news to him before I could meet him?

Somewhere yonder in that ragged sea of mountains old Cringle was drifting his boss along, and floating him every day nearer and nearer to the Sierra Blanca. If Charlie should know where I was apt to go to head him off, he would be able to dodge me easy, because I knew that no man and no horse in the world could out travel that pair. But if they couldn't get the information to him in time, then maybe there was a chance in ten of heading him off by surprise.

One chance in ten had given me freedom, by the taking of it. Now I figured on trying the same long shot again.

I dunno that I can tell you just how I was feeling about everything, but I might write it down that all the while it seemed to me that God was telling me what to do, and that I could put my luck and my trust in Him, because he would teach me how to find Smiling Charlie.

God—or the Devil. It didn't matter much to me, so that I could see Charlie lying on the ground and dying with my bullets in him, and the knowledge that it was me that turned the trick on him. But, anyways, I should never be alive to worry about the way that Betty would smile and laugh and carry on when she heard that Smiling Charlie, he had come back to Sierra Blanca. Well, this was the way that I sat in the saddle and thought things over, and then I says to myself:

"Yonder lies the Great Jingo Pass, and yonder is the Santa Croce Pass, and both of them, they lie in the straight way back to the Sierra Blanca, for Charlie. But away off there with white Mount Chandler marking it, is the Chandler Pass, and all the time that he was running, the chestnut was pointing his nose straight that way. Well, if the Devil is really in it, and wants to give me to Charlie, or Charlie to me, he put the sense into the head of this horse, and through the Chandler Pass, Charlie Lamb will surely come."

Now, when I had thought the thing over to myself in this fashion, all at once, I was able to stop worrying. Something like a foreknowledge filled me full, to the throat. And I says to myself that surely now I am close to the end of the long trail that had brought me up to my man twice already and that had twice let me down with bullets.

That was the way of it. Then I figured out, cold and steady, all of the landmarks that I was to follow, and the shortest cut,

323

and how fast I could keep the chestnut going, and how far he could make his marches,
and where I would reach water with him,
and let him rest, and where I would have to
go a bit out of my way to let him have good
grass.

When I had mapped out all of these things
in my head, I knew that I could finish the
march to Chandler Pass sometime between
the dawn and the midmorning of the next
day. So I started traveling right away.

I say that I was mighty sure, at the start,
but I got to admit that before the white, hot
afternoon of that day's ride was over, the
surety was out of me, and I was almost ready
to curl up and quit. But when the evening
came, and the friendly coolness was everywhere, and the mountains was soft and big
and distant, why, it seemed easy to go on.

Along about midnight, the chestnut was
going fine, and I'd saved his strength for the
last hard climb upgrade to get into the hollow
throat of Chandler Pass. But just when I was
getting sure of myself, the fool horse put his
foot in a hole and broke his left foreleg. He
went down with a crash, and threw me
twenty feet over his head.

When my senses came back, the chestnut
was sitting up like a dog, one leg hanging

crooked and limp, and he had stopped fighting to stand up, and he was watching me with his ears pricked, like he hoped that I would help him.

I did, too, because I spared a bullet to put him out of his misery, and then I closed his eyes and went on up the grade, my legs spraddling and wobbling, because I was still dizzy with that fall I had had.

But the Devil—or God—wouldn't let go of me, and still I hammered myself along. Wonderful time I made, too. I strode up the grades, and I jogged down the inclines, and I think that even a horse could hardly of beat my time for that last march, because when the pink was just beginning in the east, I come right over Chandler Pass, and I looked twenty miles east along the bottom of it, and there was no sign of a rider. And I looked twenty miles west, and there was no sign. Either I had missed him by a whole lot, if he was coming this way, or else, he hadn't come yet at all.

So I jogged down into the heart of the pass, and curled myself up in the shadow of a stone. I needed a little rest to steady my hand, and always I've had the gift to sleep for five minutes and then wake right up, if I wanted to.

But this time I'd underestimated what fatigue would do to a man. When I woke up, the sun was burning the backs of my hands and down the valley there was the sound of a singing voice that had mixed into a nightmare I was having, and so startled me out of a sound sleep.

I sat there for a moment, calling back my wits to the spot and realizing who I was and what I was doing there, and then my wits was gathered for me—because the voice, it begun to sing again, and I knew in advance who it was, because nobody else in the world could of had such a fine singing voice as that. It was Smiling Charlie Lamb!

I got down on my knees, though not a praying man.

"God or the Devil," says I, "whichever of you has hold on me, though I know I'm a low hound, maybe you could use me for some job that you got on hand. Anyways, all I ask is to kill Smiling Charlie with me, or kill me with Smiling Charlie, because I don't want the sun to go down again on the pair of us. Or if I can't kill Charlie without dying myself, then I'll die ready and willing. Amen."

CHAPTER 39

THERE IS A good many that I have heard run down the power of prayer, but I would like to say to them disbelievers that after I had prayed that way it was the same as though I had had a ten hour sleep and put a big plate of ham and eggs and a couple of cups of strong black coffee under my belt.

I felt strong, I mean, and steady, and connected with the way that things was, and even the strongness and the sweetness of the voice of Smiling Charlie, as he come up the pass, it didn't dishearten me none.

You understand what I mean, maybe—I was in the hands of God. If He wanted me to win, I'd win. If he wanted me to lose, why, I was past all hoping for. But I couldn't help thinking that He wouldn't of put Charlie into my hand for the third time without meaning to finish off Charlie Lamb by my hand.

That was the way that I worked it out to myself, and then I peeked around the corner of the rock and took in the picture that was in front of me. Why, it almost made me laugh, except that my teeth was set so hard that my jaws ached.

I mean, there was a girl along, of course. You could hardly expect that Charlie would be alone very long in any part of the world, but still, somehow you wouldn't expect him to be riding the high Chandler Pass with a girl!

What a girl, too! She was the finest thing that you ever laid your eyes on. I don't mean that she was as beautiful as Olivia. I mean, she was almost too big to be called beautiful, but she was mighty handsome, and she rode a horse as straight up as any man.

"This is the gent that's to marry Olivia!" says I to myself.

And I sneaked a hundred yards up the pass, keeping in the cover of the rocks so that I couldn't be seen. In that way, I come alongside of a little brook that gouged across the pass, and the pair of riders would have to ford it close to where I was hiding, because the rest of the way it was rushing fast through sharp-toothed rocks.

Now, when I seen these things, I was pretty satisfied. I was sorry that there had to be a woman on hand for the fight, but after all, I was glad that there was to be a witness to show that I fought Smiling Charlie like a man, and that I lived or died fighting with clean hands, and not like no damned Indian.

In the meantime, I could sit easy and watch the pair of them come. Smiling Charlie, he whanged his guitar and finished his song and then he chucked the guitar to the girl and she caught it with one hand and that minute she began to hit up a tune on it just as good as Charlie's, and she cut loose with a song in a mighty powerful voice that rang something wonderful down the valley.

Well, as I listened to her, I says to myself that maybe after all Charlie won't marry Olivia, because this is a girl that is sure cut out to be his mate. Big like him, and fine looking, and strong, and gay, and cheerful, and all of that.

What could he expect half as good as her, from his point of view? All that she didn't have was the loads of money that Miss Olivia would come into when the Colonel died.

Right by the edge of the brook, where it pooled out into shallows with a firm sand bottom for a ford, they stopped, and I heard the girl say that this was a good place for breakfast. So down they got and in a minute they had built up a fire and had a pot on the fire, and the steam of coffee beginning, and the sizzling of bacon, very good to smell.

Charlie was handy, but the girl was, too. She wasn't no helpless beauty, I'll tell a man!

They got that breakfast started and cooked quicker than a wink, and then they sat back to enjoy it, while I had to pull up my belt three notches to keep my head from spinning with hunger.

They ate as fast as they had cooked, and then Charlie jumped up and cinched up Cringle once more.

"Hold on, Jerry," says the girl. "Why are you rushing, so?"

"You know, Lou," says he, "that I told you that I'd take you on this trip if you'd promise not to ask questions."

"I'm only human," says she. "And besides, that fellow Jacks that you've spoken about so much is safe in the Sheriff's hands, by this time."

"Jacks is never safe in any hands," says Charlie, "and I'll never be sure of him, as a matter of fact, till I've had to put a bullet through him."

"You never did explain why he hates you so bitterly," says she. "Is he just a plain bad lot?"

"No," says Charlie. "He's rough, but he's not a bad sort. As a matter of fact, the thing that makes him hate me is the same thing that has made other men hate me."

"You mean a girl, of course?"

"Yes."

"I do hope that the day will come when you can leave the pretty little fools alone!" says she.

It was a queer thing to hear her talk like that. She was pretty enough herself, but she wasn't little, and it was pretty clear that she wasn't a fool, either.

"Some day I shall! Some day I shall!" says Charlie.

"But," says the girl, "why did you have to pick on the girl of Billy Jacks, if he's such a dangerous person?"

"That's the very reason," says Charlie. "You understand how it is, Lou? The very fact that Billy is a known gunfighter and mankiller made his girl a shade more attractive than she would be otherwise. But at that, she's the prettiest girl in Sierra Blanca, bar one."

"Bar one?"

"Yes. But what harm is there in holding the hand of a pretty girl and telling her how fond you are of her? And I *am* fond of 'em, Lou. I tell you, I love all the pretty girls in the world. Got room in my heart to love 'em, Lou."

He leaned back against Cringle and laughed. It was a fine thing to see him

331

laugh, with the yellow morning sun on his face.

"It's disgusting," says the girl called Lou. "I really think that it's disgusting, Jerry."

Why did she call him Jerry?

Then she went on:

"And what about this girl of Billy's? Did you take her away from him?"

"No," says Charlie. "As a matter of fact, I was able to turn her head a little, but after all, she remained pretty true to Jacks. I think that she was afraid, actually, to leave him! And if you ever knew him, you would understand why. He isn't a pretty man, my dear. I've shot him down twice, and he's still on my trail, tied up in bandages, but just as formidable as ever!"

"B-r-r!" says the girl. "The horrible brute!"

"He's not horrible," says Charlie. "Are you ready to start?"

"Why do you have to hurry so? Is it to get back to the Sierra Blanca and see that other girl who's even prettier than Betty?"

Charlie closed his eyes a moment.

"If I tell you something, Lou," says he, "will you promise not to make a protest or say a word?"

"Of course I'll promise! What's the secret?"

"No, I can't tell you."

"Jerry, I've traveled across the entire country to see you, and now don't I deserve to know one little secret?"

"You don't really deserve it, but I have to tell you something. The prettiest girl, Lou. is the one that I'm headed for now."

"You say that seriously."

"I mean it seriously."

"Jerry!"

"Well?"

"As seriously as all that?"

"Why—as a matter of fact, it is serious."

"You've compromised yourself!"

"I've asked a girl to marry me."

"You've asked a thousand girls to marry you—and run away before that could happen."

"This is really different."

"Jerry Chisholm," she snapped, "what do you mean? How long has this lasted?"

"More than a month," says he.

"Heavens," says she. "I didn't dream—Jerry, Jerry, Jerry!"

Kind of queer, you would say, to hear a gent like that fellow telling such things to any girl?

Now he answered up and said:

"Don't worry, honey. She's a lady!"

"In calico?" says the girl.

"She's Colonel Stockton's daughter," says Mr. Jerry Chisholm, alias Smiling Charlie Lamb.

"Colonel Which?" asks the girl called Lou.

"Haven't you ever heard of him?"

"No," says she. "There's a Major Stockton in Connecticut—but——"

"You're a thousand miles away. Did you ever hear of the Sierra Blanca?"

"I've heard you speak of it."

"Do you know where or what it is?"

"Mountains, I think."

"Wonderful!"

"In Colorado—or some Western state."

"You're not a thousand miles away from the truth, Lou," says he.

"Don't sneer. This is frightfully serious."

"Honey," says he, "we're ridiculously wealthy, aren't we?"

"Yes. And it isn't your marriage with a pauper that bothers me, but the knowledge that some brown-faced little adventuress has been able to——"

"Hush! Hush!" says he. "If even these rocks should hear you, they'd break out laughing. I tell you, my dear, that Colonel Stockton could take the Chisholm fortunes even at their palmiest height, and drop them into a pocket, and forget that they were there!"

"Now you're laughing at me, of course!"

"I'm in dead earnest."

"Because I'm your sister—is that a reason you should mock me?"

Sister? I couldn't wait any longer. I could sort of feel my hate for this gent melting away. And in another minute I would of rode that long trail all for nothing, without the pleasure of winding it up with a good, hard fight. I stepped out from behind the rock.

CHAPTER 40

THE GIRL, SHE seen me first. Her eyes popped out, and she gripped her hands together. Then she grabbed for a rifle. She says to her brother in a gasp:

"Look out! Danger!"

And she pitched the rifle up to her shoulder with a good, steady, swift hand, the same way that a man would of throwed it there.

But I didn't pay any attention to her. It was Smiling Charlie Lamb that I wanted, and Charlie I intended to have. I yapped at him:

"Charlie, I've come for you. Me—Billy Jacks!"

I say that I yapped at him, and I mean just that, because my voice, it sharpened up and got as thin as the edge of a razor blade, and I barked the same way as a bull terrier barks, high and small.

But what was strangest to me was to see how Smiling Charlie reacted. I mean to say that usually when Charlie moved in an emergency, it was like a spring uncoiling when pressure is taken off of it—a steel spring snapping into place. But it wasn't like a steel spring that he moved this day.

Or maybe it was that I was now so heated up and excited and everything taut in me that I was seeing and feeling and moving about ten times as fast as usual. And that was why Charlie seemed to be going so slow as he stood up and whirled around on me.

I was crouched over a little and both my hands hanging low down, and the tips of my fingers filled with electric sparks, I was so dead set on yanking out my guns that I had strapped to my belt. But I wouldn't make the first move. I waited for Smiling Charlie. And yet he didn't shoot!

No, sir, he even winced a little as he looked at me! And that was like a taste of blood to me. Not that I could actually say that such a man was afraid of me, him never having ever been afraid in his life, most likely, but still, he was scared of something, and he had to control his fear—him that had laughed at a dozen fighting men at a time!

Well, I eased up and I stood a mite straighter.

Charlie hadn't said a word, and the girl broke in at me:

"If you try to touch a gun, Billy Jacks, I'll send a bullet through you!"

Oh, she meant it, too! I didn't have to throw a glance her way. I couldn't take my eyes off of Charlie, where they were fastened in a death-hold on him. But by the very tone of her voice I knew that her fingers was steady as they held the rifle in place.

"She's a beauty!" says I to Smiling Charlie. "But it ain't gunna be my luck to be downed by a girl. Get her out of this, will you?"

"Hold on," says Charlie, and I thought that his voice was just a mite uncertain. "Hold on, old fellow, and tell me what there is that I've ever done to you to heat you up like this?"

"Hell!" says I. "D'you want reasons? First, you sapped me on the jaw and got

337

away from me when I had the drop cold on you. You made a fool of me that day and took away all the reputation that I'd been fighting for years to build up!"

"Come, come!" says Charlie. "Open your ears, man, and ask about yourself through the mountains in any direction. You'll never find a person who speaks as lightly of you as you speak of yourself!"

"And after that," I told him, "you took a special pleasure in makin' love to my girl. Not because she interested you none, but just because you wanted to do a meanness to me!"

"It's true, Billy," says he. "It's true that it was a devilish low, mean thing that I did, there. But I've repented for it, Billy. And I've given you proofs of the repentance!"

"What proofs? What proofs?" says I.

"I've had you helpless under my gun twice during the past few days, and each time, I've let you get away. That's something, isn't it? That's a proof, isn't it?"

It made me growl. I was being filled up with savageness, and the more that he drew back, the more meaner I got.

"You should of sunk a second bullet in me each time," I told him. "And because you was a fool twice over, does it make up for the other times when you was a hound? It don't make up to me, Charlie, for the day that you shamed me, or the day that you busted my heart!"

"No," says he, sort of thinking out loud, "it's true that there's still a balance on your side. I'm sorry for that!"

"Maybe you'll apologize?" says I.

"Yes," says he, quick as a wink, "I'll gladly apologize! I've been in the wrong, and I'm glad to admit it!"

"Oh!" gasped the girl, lowering her rifle.

For though, being a woman, she didn't want to see her brother face a gun, still I suppose that it took a good deal of wind out of her sails to hear Smiling Charlie actually make an apology, no matter for what good reason.

"You'll apologize," says I, "not because you think that you're wrong, but because you know that today I'm a faster and a stronger and surer hand with a gun than you are!"

That was like a cut with a whip across his face.

"My dear," says he to his sister, "will you go back there among the rocks?"

"Not an inch!" says she. "I won't budge an inch!"

He turned his back on me and faced her.

"You're talking like an ordinary woman now, but if you'll think the matter over, Lou, you'll see that my honor is engaged. And I don't want you to be in touching distance of this. One of us is going to be a dead man, and if I should fall, if you were standing too close, you might be tempted to turn your rifle on Billy Jacks!"

She hesitated, her eyes flaring at me like a tigress, and he went on, as quiet as could be:

"According to Billy's code, he would be a shamed man if he didn't try to trail me down and kill me. He's tried twice, and now he's on my path for the third time. How he did it—on foot—God alone can tell. But the vital matter is that he's here! And I have to fight him. I've lived in the West according to Western ways. I can't shift them now. If I'd followed the Eastern ways, I would have been hanged long ago for the crimes that I've committed out here against society and decent good fellowship. So now I intend to take my medicine—if this is my day to receive it. And if you'll think the matter over, you'll see, like a brave, wise girl, that there's nothing else for your brother to do!"

Why, it was a wonderful thing to see

the fear and anger go out of her eyes and the understanding come back into them! She made a step into his arms, and she kissed him good-by, and the next moment her back was turned on us, and she was walking for the rocks with a fine long swinging step, like the stride of a boy.

"That's that!" said Charlie, and he turned back on me.

"Are ye ready?" I breathed at him.

"Man, man!" he said, wincing as he looked at me. "You look as if every devil in hell had had his claws in you! You're sick and shaking, Billy! I can't fight you when you're like this!"

"Damn your heart," I told him, "if I shake it's because of the hate for you that's in me."

"Hold on, Billy," says he, "whether you think so or not, you're not in the condition to stand up to me."

"Man," I snarled at him, "ain't I been through hell? And ain't all the hell that I've been through cheap for the pleasure of standing here and having another crack at you with a gun? Will you draw?"

He hesitated still, and then I added:

"Or are you plain scared of me and ready to crawl and quit?"

He bit his lip.

"I hate to fight three times in a bad cause, Billy," says he. "I've let you go twice. And the third time, I hate to shoot you down— sick man as you are!"

"You lie!" I yelled at him.

And in the distance I could see the girl turn around and look back at us.

"You lie," I told him again. "Because the fact is that you're scared almost to death! You know that your time has come!"

Well, it would of done you good to see him swell up and straighten to his full height, and what a grand looking man he was standing there! And he made a little half step towards me, and he smiled down at me.

"Billy," says he, "I've taken enough of your lip. Start your draw, and I'll polish you off!"

"Start my draw?" I shouted. "You fool, I could give you the ace from the pack and still beat you, today. You know it, too. Look at me, Charlie, and you'll see in my eyes that I'm already tasting the death of you!"

Why, he looked at me, and his color changed a little, and it seemed to me that a ghost of a tremor went through him.

"Start for your gun, then, Jacks!" he said

sternly. "Because I've wasted my last words on you!"

And he whipped out his Colt.

Nobody ever could move a gun faster than Smiling Charlie—except that on this day there was a difference, because the devil that was in me and that had taken complete control of me had made my eyes faster than human, as you might say. And while I pulled my own gun, it seemed to me that the hand of Charlie wasn't lightning no more, but just plain, slow lead.

And as his revolver come clear I put a bullet straight through his body—and missed him with a second shot—while Charlie froze his revolver on me—and then tossed it aside where it fell with a rattle on the rocks.

"Because I'm a dead man," says Charlie, "there's no reason why I should take you to hell along with me!"

And he opened his coat and looked down quietly, and I seen the blood pouring down in a stream along his breast.

Well, sir, the Colt fell out of my own hands. And the strength, it seemed to leave me, and I hunched up a little, like an old, hunchbacked man, because it didn't seem no ways possible that I had actually finished the great Charlie Lamb!

"Tell the girl that it's only a scratch," says he, as cool as could be. "Get some water out of the brook, there, and make a pretence of bandaging the wound.—I won't last long!"

But still it didn't seem possible to me that he was actually badly hurt until he started to sit down, lost control of his weight, and slumped down very heavy, and lay on one elbow, gasping out bloody foam. I heard the scream of the girl from the distance. The mountains rocked before my eyes. And the roar of the creek crashed suddenly right against my ear and seemed to say:

"You've killed Charlie Lamb."

CHAPTER 41

I FAINTED DEAD away, which was a fool thing to do, as I would most freely admit. But the Devil, who had kept me going for so long, deserted me the minute that I had done his work. My knees buckled under me.

"I'll get you water—Charlie—old boy!" says I, and I only took one stumbling step, and then I dropped on my face.

When I come to, which could only of been two seconds later, I could hear the voice of Charlie saying quietly:

"It's nothing, Lou. You might tear up a bit of cloth for a bandage—and bring me a drink of water from the brook—I'm—rather—thirsty!"

His voice came husky and thick, through the last few words, and as I heaved myself to my knees, I saw the girl running to the creek.

She came back in a moment and he drank off the whole canteen and then sighed and nodded his content to her.

She had a rather stiff look about the mouth, and her eyes were big, but she went right ahead with the bandaging of the wound. Then I heard a moan from her.

"Charlie! Charlie!"

"Tush," says he, "the bullet slipped; simply glanced off the ribs and around my body——"

She went on with the bandaging, in spite of her cry.

"Turn a little, dear!"

He turned on his elbow, and as she passed the bandage around to his back, I heard her scream again, and this time I knew what for. She had seen the place where the bullet had tore its way out of his back, a place three or four times as big and terrible as the place where it entered his breast.

And I staggered up to him and tried to help, but I could only fumble towards him, and then drop on my knees, clean done up. It was a most amazing thing the way I was spent. Like a horse that has been rode till he drops, and then he can't get up. Everything in the way of energy that was in me had been used up and exploded like a great electric spark when I faced and fought Charlie, and now I was wrung out and limp and useless.

I says to myself that I would clear my head and find a way to fight back to senses and strength and help to save the life of Charlie, now that it had once been in the hollow of my hand. But I was dizzy and groggy and my head reeling, and then I could hear Charlie saying, very steady, but quite faintly:

"I'm all right, Lou. Really, nothing but a flesh wound. Steady, old girl. If you have any doubt, ask Billy Jacks and he'll tell you the truth!"

She gave me a white-faced look, and all at once the need of saying something pulled me up, and I managed to tell her:

"It's only a glance, and it'll barely keep him in bed for a couple of weeks."

"Tush! Not that long!" says Charlie.

And I tell you, that while I saw a shadow

of the pain burning in his eyes, he made himself smile up at her.

Well, I've seen and heard a lot about heroes, but there was nothing that I ever seen or heard of that compared with that smile which Charlie give to his sister.

It seemed to ease her mind. Then, since the bandage was complete and there was nothing to do for the minute, she threw a wild look around the valley, and a still wilder look at me!

I says to her:

"Don't you worry. I'll stay on and do what I can. I'll promise you that! We'll build a lean-to right here against the rock. Bed Charlie down in fir and pine boughs. And there's plenty of game in the hills for us to shoot! We'll keep going fine!"

She let her eyes steady a bit on me.

"I think you mean what you promise!" says she.

"May I be damned blacker than a dog if I don't!" says I.

And then, as she turned back to Charlie, I could not let my eyes rest on him. She could hardly tell, because he was always smiling at her and keeping her attention employed steady, but me, I could easily see the white spreading across his face and the shadow darkening under his eyes.

And every beat of my heart, it was like a terrible voice bellowing inside of me:

"You've killed Charlie Lamb! You've killed Smiling Charlie! You've killed the grandest man that ever rode a horse! You've killed him that spared you twice, when he had you in the grip of his hand like a rotten egg-shell!"

Oh, it was a damned and miserable time for me.

I seen his eyes roll towards the creek. I knew that he was raging for water, but that he didn't dare to ask so soon again, for fear that the girl would guess that something terrible bad was wrong.

I fetched him another filled canteen, and set it down beside him. My hand was shaking so that even out of the mouth of the bottle I splashed some of the water. He took it and poured it down.

"Thanks a lot, old man," says he. "I'm feeling more as you'd hope."

"Ay, Charlie," says I, "I pray to God that you—I mean, I thank God that it ain't serious!"

He stared up at me, very wide-eyed.

"Why, Billy," says he, "I think that you mean it!"

"I do mean it," says I, "because, all at once, I see what the facts are—and they mean that Betty ain't much to me. I can get on without her. I shall get on without her."

"Ay," nodded Smiling Charlie, "that's a better idea. She's not worthy of you!"

He would have said more, but just then a spasm hit him and he set his teeth and looked down to the ground, and his face turned the color of chalk.

And all at once the girl dropped on her knees beside him and caught his hands.

"You've lied to me—you're dying!" says she.

He could just roll his eyes up at her, and give her another smile, and then he collapsed.

I sat dumb and sick, not able to move, but the girl, she didn't let up for a moment. She brought water and bathed his face in it. She pressed her head against his heart and listened, and then she asked me for brandy and took my flask and poured some between his teeth.

After that, she sat back, holding one of his hands; and leaning over him, and keeping her face so close to his that you would think that she was transferring strength into him out of her body and her soul—and maybe she was, for all that I know. But all of the time, he lay there white as chalk, and his breast never stirred with a breath, and his smile never changed on his lips.

I thought it was a death-smile, and that the girl was whispering to a dead man. And even in the brightness of the morning sun, that was a terrible idea to me, like a ghost at midday.

Presently, she gave a little cry. I looked back at her and saw that her head was pressed to his breast again.

"He may win through!" she gasped at me. And then she pointed up at the blazing of the sun and shook her head and made a shadow with her body to shelter the face of Charlie.

I took that hint and went to work. I was best pleased not to stay there and watch the agony and the silence of that girl, because it seemed to me that she was a sort of an index that pointed out the truth about Charlie. He had been a smiler, too, and a cheerful, happy-go-lucky sort of a fellow. But there was a lot more in his heart than there was in the heart of an ordinary man. There was a lot more in him, and most of us had never guessed at it. We had figured that he was a hound, except as a fighting man, but I had had a chance to see that there was decency and kindness in him. And somehow, watching his sister made me realize that he was still better than I had guessed, because the same blood that was in her was in him, also.

Now, when I thought over this, I took the hatchet from Charlie's own pack and I headed into a group of pines that stood near the edge of the creek. My hands was wonderful weak, and when I looked up and raised my arms above my head, a spinning blackness shot across my eyes. But after I had made a few strokes and barely dented the bark of the young branches, I got stronger again, and pretty soon I was hammering away and getting results.

I brought back long, straight, supple saplings and branches. I leaned them across Charlie and against the face of the rock that lay just north of him. In that way, we made a shelter that kept off the sun from him. And in between trips, I would stagger down to the river and bring up water for the girl.

Twice, she made me stop everything else and help her rub Charlie, to bring the circulation back into his body. And still he lay there like a dead man, and never stirred, and never seemed to breathe!

Have you ever had too much red-eye, so's you wake up the next morning with your head all in a daze, and not remembering much of what happened the night before, but with a vague feeling that you must of done terrible disgraceful and mean and horrible things?

Well, sir, I'll tell you that that was the way with me. I felt that I had smashed one of the finest men in the world. And I wanted to creep off among the mountains and there hide my head and never let anybody ever hear about me again.

That was my main idea, but I didn't dwell on it none, because I was too busy in fetching and carrying, and working like a Trojan, while the weakness kept growing on me. I was so feeble after the work I had done on that long trail that the least little thing would bring out a flood of perspiration on my body and make me tremble. And all the wounds which the Devil in me had made me forget, they now began to pain and burn and ache and send hell-fire through me. I'd been hysterical; the hysteria it was passing off; and I was as shaky as a baby, now!

Well, the noon of that day came, and I

heard the voice of the girl calling me. I come staggering back with an armful of pine boughs with which I was making the bed for Charlie.

"You must lie down and rest, now," says she. "Look!"

She was pretty triumphant about it, and she had reason to be, because when I looked at Charlie I seen that there was the least mite of color in his face, and instead of that terrible weak, relaxed smile, he was frowning a bit. And that meant a sort of a strength.

Altogether, I was satisfied. I started to lower myself to the ground, lost control, and slumped down on my face. I didn't bother to move my head. I just lay where I fell. And my last thought was something of thankfulness to God, before I went to sleep.

No, there was one thought after that—of the girl putting something over me to shut away the heat of the sun.

CHAPTER 42

AFTER THAT, WHAT I passed through was a series of sort of shadows and flickering shapes. I couldn't tell whether I was a shadow among dancing flames, or a flame

353

among dancing shadows. Cold froze me one minute and heat burned me up the next. And sometimes I remembered that I called out that it was because I had killed Charlie Lamb, and therefore I deserved what had come to me.

But, after a time, I waked up and I raised a hand that looked too thin to be mine, and I touched a face that was covered with weeks of beard. And I says:

"It's true, and I'm in hell!"

A deep voice says close to me:

"Steady, old fellow!"

"Ay," says I, "in hell along with Smiling Charlie!"

But here a girl's laughter come fluting in, wonderful sweet and clear.

I turned my head, and there I seen Smiling Charlie leaning against the side of the rock, looking sort of thin and pale, of course, but a long, long ways from a dead man.

"Charlie, Charlie," says I, "it ain't hell after all. It's heaven!"

"Of course it is," says he. "But we thought that you'd never wake up, old fellow!"

"I never would wake up? There's a long blank, right enough."

"There is," says he. "You've had a little

touch of brain fever, I guess. But, at any rate, that's passed over." He added: "Do you want to sit up a little?"

"Hush, silly!" says Lou. "Don't you move an inch! Don't you dare!"

"Look here," says I to her. "Did I turn in and get sick on you just at the time when you needed all your attention for Charlie?"

"You were nothing," she grinned at me. "Just company, and talk—lots of talk!"

She laughed again. She was a game one, I can tell you.

"I been out cold for weeks!" says I, fingering my beard.

"Yes," nodded Charlie. "You've been a great deal sicker than I."

"Why, Charlie," says I, "maybe I'll be well enough to ride down into the Sierra Blanca with you, then!"

"Would you do that?" says he.

"Ay, would I!"

"You've laid aside malice, then?" says he.

"Of course I have! I never had a right to go gunning for you, Charlie."

"Old man," says he, "I've got to go back to my own name, which is Chisholm, and I've got to leave the new name behind me."

"Chisholm," says I, "may be a grand name, but Smiling Charlie is your name for the Sierra Blanca, and in the Sierra Blanca you belong!"

"Hush, dear," says the girl to her brother. "Don't excite Billy!"

"It ain't doing me any harm, ma'am," says I, "only it makes me damned mad to hear how a gent like him would throw himself away on any other part of the world!"

"And what could he do in Sierra Blanca that he couldn't do elsewhere, wearing his rightful name?" says she.

"I'll tell you what," says I. "Lead him back to his old name and life, and you give him a good chance to go wrong again. But keep him in the new life, and no matter what else he may be, he'll be a man!"

The girl frowned and looked hard at me.

"Besides," said I, "under what name would Olivia Stockton be marrying him?"

"Marry me?" says Charlie sadly. "Old timer, that's the main reason that I'll never enter the Sierra Blanca. Because I know that I'm not worthy of her."

I jerked myself bolt upright. I says to him:

"You know which? Man, man, if you ain't worthy of her, she'll make you worthy. You had ought to know that. Take her and thank God for her. A girl like that don't make mistakes!"

He started to answer, and then he turned his head slowly to his sister, and she looked back at him.

"Maybe he's right, after all," says Lou Chisholm.

Well, the story of what that girl had done was a marvel. How she had managed to nurse the pair of us was told to me by Smiling Charlie, and how she had taken time off to slip into the hills and shoot game, and how she had worked night and day, harder over me than over him.

There was another long ten days before, finally, we walked into the railroad station at the head of the pass and there we put Lou Chisholm on a train, and there we sent on a telegram to Colonel Stockton to say that we was coming as fast as horses would bring us.

After that, we headed through the pass as hard as we could go, him on Cringle, of course, and me on the girl's horse.

The sun burned us brown again. A razor had lifted the whiskers from my face. We looked nacheral as could be when we come to the entrance to the Sierra Blanca, except that our clothes was wonderful tattered, and especially mine.

We passed the outpost, where a gent that was riding the guard throwed up his hands and yelled and then turned his horse and scooted for a campfire, yelling:

"The ghosts of Charlie and Billy Jacks is riding the mountains!"

Ghosts?

That told us what people must be thinking. The Colonel hadn't had time to send his news through all the valley, and folks thought that Charlie and me had met and fought and killed each other and our bones was picked white by the buzzards in some lonely mountain valley, waiting for the snows to come and cover them over.

But we felt considerable different from ghosts as you might guess. And I think that the grandest moment of my life, bar one, was when we rode in the early morning into the town and the first soul that we seen was Sheriff Steve.

He come for us with a yell and a whoop. And there he was, wringing our hands and making us welcome, and when we started on up the valley, there was about half of the men in the town on their horses to follow us. Says Charlie to me:

"I think I'm going to settle down, Billy. I think that you let the bad blood out of me for keeps!"

And, perhaps, I had. Leastwise, I had done my best!

We seen the tall walls of Stockton House in the distance, then, and pretty soon, we was riding in sight of the house close up, when a cluster of gents come tearing towards us. News had been wired out from town, and here was Dick Wace and the rest of the Colonel's men plunging for us.

They fair swallowed us up. There was no need for me to apologize for the things that I had done, because everything seemed to be forgiven, and everybody had a strong hand and a kind word for us, until we came up to the big house itself, and there we dismounted and come into the garden.

I wondered why it was that the Colonel hadn't appeared, but it was explained as soon as we showed ourselves here, because, in the middle of the garden, we seen an old man with white hair, seated in an invalid's chair, wrapped in a rug. And we had to look twice before we knew that that was Colonel Stockton.

He was finished, burned out, done for. And he would never plan and scheme again so long as he lived. And beside his chair there was standing Olivia looking mighty pale and thin and trembling like a poplar in a spring wind.

Well, the rest of us turned our backs and went off and left Charlie and Olivia and the Colonel to talk things over.

I went back with the rest of the boys to the dining room, and there we had a feast that would of done your heart good to look at. And, after that, I went up to my room, and found everything just as I had left it. It was good to be back, but sad—terrible sad. It was like returning after twenty years had flowed under the bridge. And all of that time had not changed the old place, but it had changed me and Charlie, you can bet.

However, there was one thing more that troubled me and saddened me more than all of the rest, but I had decided that I would never let it enter my mind so long as I could rule it out.

A tap come at my door.

"Come in!" says I.

There was a little silence, and then another tap.

I bellowed out loud:

"Come in, will you? Are you deaf?"

There was another silence, and then another tap.

I jumped to the door and yanked it open, yelling:

"Is this some damned joke?"

And there was Betty standing on the farther side of the hall, looking like she wanted to shrink into the stones.

"Betty!" says I.

She managed to get her eyes up from the floor and send a pale smile at me.

"You haven't forgotten me, then?" says she.

"Lord, Lord," says I, "how could me and the devil ever forget you? Come in here!"

I took her into the room. She was wonderful changed, I thought, standing very quiet by the window.

"What has brought you here?" says I.

"To see you, Billy," says she.

"Well," says I, "I ain't changed."

"Do you mean that?" she asked sharply, and she looked up at me with a sort of brightness in her eyes.

"I ain't changed a bit," says I, "I ain't even learned how to play a guitar while I was away—I ain't even tried to learn!"

That made her wince.

"I suppose that I'd better go again," says she.

I waited, and said nothing, staring hard at

her, and she moved over to the door, but when I thought she was about to go out, she whirled about at me and stamped her foot.

"You might tell me in so many words, you great lump!" says she. "Do you still want me, or don't you?"

Well, sir, it scattered my good resolutions to the winds. I got to her in one step and took her into my arms.

"You little hell-cat," says I, "you've scratched the soul nearly out of my body, but what there is left of it still loves you, I suppose!"

"Oh, Billy, you idiot," says she, "to ever of thought that I really cared about him!"

"Prove that," says I, "before you go another step ahead!"

"Prove that? Dead easy," says she. "I can prove it by marrying you, Billy darling!"

Why, who could possibly hold out against that sort of proof? Not me, for one! I listened to her, and I laughed at her, I couldn't help it. Laugh I could, but answer her I couldn't.

And it was about two weeks later that we got married.

Charlie and Olivia, they stepped off a few days later, and they started on a trip to England, where maybe they met up with the Baron.

The heart of the Baron had been fractured, maybe, but not clean broke, because he had already recovered enough to get himself married to a rich American girl. And so, I suppose, there was nothing but happiness received by all of the chief members that have had a part in this history.

And yet, after so much trouble, you would say that somewhere there would be left a big legacy of pain? Well, you're right, and sitting here at my window, I can look down into the garden and see the old Colonel lying in the sun with his eyes closed, but never a smile on his lips. He has a face of iron—white iron. Black iron he was in the old days. Old, brittle, white iron, now.

He was beaten but he never surrendered, as you might say, while there was a man left to fight the ship for him.

To this day I know that he's never forgiven his daughter for marrying Smiling Charlie, but he can't talk about what he thinks, and the bitterness which he locks up inside of him is gradually choking and killing him, poor devil.

But that's often the final way with them that are wiser than God meant a man to be.